His Lordship's Folly

Book Five of His Lordship's Mysteries

Samantha SoRelle

Balcarres Books LLC

For all my readers.
Thank you.

Contents

Chapter I

Fife, Scotland

August 1819

"What did I say about putting your boots on my side of the carriage?"

Fixing his gaze on the Scottish countryside beyond the carriage window, Dominick gave Alfie's question no more attention than the man himself deserved.

Then he felt Alfie's boot tap against his own. A hard tap. Coming from anyone other than an earl, it might have even been called a kick. Clearly, Alfie was exactly the sort of nobleman who believed rules only applied to others but not himself. And that included rules about where people's feet belonged and how much of a carriage counted as "his half".

A shared childhood of squabbling and roughhousing had Dominick kicking back instinctively. Alfie clutched his leg and let out a pained hiss.

"Stop it," Dominick said to the man he loved more than his own life, but could happily throttle. "That's not your bad leg and you know it. And keep your boots to yourself. I *am* on my side."

Between Alfie's need to keep his wounded leg stretched out and Dominick's large frame, any carriage ride of more than a few minutes was bound to grow uncomfortable, but poor weather, a washed-out bridge, a broken axle, and not one but *three* thrown horseshoes had turned the journey from Bath to Balcarres House into an unending nightmare. They'd at first thought a more meandering journey to see some of the sights along the way would add some charm to the trip. But the added weeks in a hot, stuffy carriage had worn on them both. That they were usually forced to stay in crowded inns with thin walls meant they hadn't even had a chance to work out their daily frustrations by their usual methods.

Dominick wasn't ashamed to admit that under the strain, they'd regressed.

"Oh? Certain of that, are you?" Alfie sneered. "Just like you were certain you didn't take my last slice of roast at the inn and I must have forgotten I ate it?"

When Alfie kicked him again, Dominick barely had time to throw out a few choice words about where he could stick his damned boots before Alfie was hurling himself across the carriage. Years of training at how to be refined, gentlemanly, and, most importantly, *noble* were shed as easily as his fine silk coat and he was the workhouse scrapper once more.

Alfie didn't let the tight confines of the carriage slow him, coming at Dominick hard, aiming for a kidney, a stomach, anything soft and easily damaged. However, he was forgetting that Dominick had years of experience facing far more terrifying opponents in the ring than the one person he knew would never truly hurt him. If Alfie wanted to pretend the cramped space was the reason his blows barely landed, he could, but Dominick had been the one to teach him to fight and he'd done a far better job than this.

That didn't mean it wasn't incredibly annoying.

He shoved Alfie back into his seat. His love had grown up being knocked down into Spitalfields mud, so the padded seat of his personal carriage was nothing. Alfie sprang back as quickly as he could given the lack of space and his injured leg—*not* the one Dominick had kicked. However, this time Dominick was ready for him.

In fairness, even if Alfie was a damned backbiting liar, Dominick might be able to admit he'd assumed Alfie had finished his meal and possibly helped himself to a slice of roast without asking. Then perhaps he'd lied when confronted. And there was a chance he had been encroaching on Alfie's side of the carriage, just a little. He liked being near Alfie, even when they were both irritating and irritated by each other.

As Alfie lunged, so did Dominick, meeting him halfway. While they were of a similar height, Dominick had the advantage in weight, easily knocking Alfie back into his seat, being sure to still mind his bloody leg. Alfie might only choose to remember he'd been shot when it suited him, but Dominick never forgot.

"Nick, you great brute, get off me!" Alfie railed, his voice muffled by Dominick's shoulder. He threw a flurry of quick punches, but Dominick could tell his heart wasn't in it.

The way they were entwined now with his arms wrapped around Alfie's head and shoulders, there was hardly room enough between them for Alfie to move his arms at all, never mind put enough force behind a blow to do any damage. And the way their legs were slotted together, if Alfie really wanted to hurt him, he'd have kneed him in the bollocks already. Instead, Alfie's thigh sliding between his own was a much more welcome sensation.

Perhaps they'd gone about this journey entirely the wrong way. The carriage was theirs alone after all, and while there were certain positions Dominick wouldn't want to be caught in when a wheel hit a rut, in the cities at least, the noise of the road could cover a multitude of sins.

Too late now. Graham had met them in Edinburgh with Alfie's personal carriage to replace the one they'd hired in Bath so long ago, and the road since leaving the city had been nearly as quiet as their driver. Still, with any luck they'd be back to Balcarres House by nightfall and could make up for lost time in a proper bed. After a bath though, with as much hot water as Janie and Jarrett could carry.

The thought was enough to make him smile, even as Alfie punched him again in the ribs.

"I taught you better than that," Dominick said, squeezing Alfie's head tighter. "Don't strike at the rib bones, cut up under them."

Alfie chose that moment to remember their childhood squabblings, twisting his face into Dominick's elbow, which gave him just enough space to pull his head free from Dominick's grip. The simultaneous shoulder to the gut was unexpected, knocking Dominick back just long enough for Alfie to get the upper hand.

The air was knocked from him a second time at the look on Alfie's face, a scowl that was desperately trying not to be a grin. His cheeks were flushed and the fading twilight lit his auburn curls, still not quite regrown to their former glory, but thoroughly mussed from the scuffle.

He was just about the most glorious thing Dominick had ever seen. Then Alfie raised his fists in a mock pugilist's stance and the last of the daylight glinted off the ring on his left ring finger. Dominick's ring.

"I say, sir," Alfie said in his most lordly voice. "My honour in the matter of the boots has not thoroughly been satisfied. Shall we settle this like gentlemen? Broughton Rules?"

Dominick snorted. From the gleam in Alfie's eye, it seemed Dominick wasn't the only one looking forward to post-bath activities. Still, he'd been driving Dominick mad all day and kicked him *twice*. That couldn't be allowed to stand.

He batted Alfie's hands out of the way, tapping him lightly on the side of the head before Alfie could block, and then they were tussling like puppies, fighting because they could, not because either of their lives depended on it. It was a welcome change.

But just because it was all in play didn't mean Dominick's head didn't get knocked against the seat back more than once. When his head struck the door, however, it was hard enough to make the carriage sway around him. It stopped after a moment, so he grabbed a fistful of Alfie's coat, ready to return the attack.

But Alfie had frozen, the heel of his palm pushing against Dominick's chin. It took a moment to realise what was wrong.

The carriage had stopped swaying. *The carriage had stopped swaying.*

Oh Christ. They'd arrived.

Alfie was the first to come to his senses, sliding out of Dominick's grip and smoothing down his coat. His hair was a lost cause, but hopefully that could be put down to the long journey rather than the Earl of Crawford and his male companion wrestling more intimately than was proper—or likely, legal.

There was a quick knock on the carriage door and Dominick threw himself onto the opposite bench just as it was flung open.

"Good evening, Your Lordship and um, Mr. Trent, sir," said Graham's son, Davey. The stable lad gave them a gap-toothed grin and held up a lantern. "I was told to keep watch for you and bring a lantern if it got too dark. Been out here for hours, even though I told them Pa weren't going to be back before night. I think it was to keep me out of the house. I'm not supposed to know what's going on. But I do! I'm not a child!"

Davey proved this by wiping his nose with the sleeve of the arm holding the door open. Dominick caught the door before it could fall back and hurt him.

"Thank you, Davey," Alfie replied. "It was most kind of you to wait for us. I think we can find our own way in if you want to help your father with the horses."

Davey beamed, barely remembering to drop two quick bows before darting off, clambering onto the driver's box to pepper his father with questions about the horses and the journey and the city and the horses' journey to the city without leaving time for Graham to answer.

"He could have at least left the lantern," grumbled Dominick. Still, the cover of darkness let him offer his hand to help Alfie down, something Alfie's pride would never allow otherwise, preferring for his leg to give out from under him than be seen needing help. As if sprawling flat out on the pavers would somehow make him look less weak.

Ridiculous man.

Alfie took advantage of the darkness too, linking his arm with Dominick's as they climbed the stone steps to Balcarres House.

By day, it was an imposing building, the grey stone of the turrets stretching up to the sky, only to be dragged back down by the darker grey of the slate roof which cut at strange angles. The walls of the house twisted at even stranger angles, a hodgepodge of additions built over the centuries to create a maze of winding corridors that he never seemed to be able to follow.

By night, however, little could be seen of the manor other than the glow of light peeking out from between the front doors, promising a warm fire and an even warmer welcome.

"Do you think Mrs. Finley will have ordered supper prepared for us tonight?" asked Alfie. "I could do with a hot meal, but I'm not sure I'm ready to face Janie's cooking again."

Dominick's stomach turned at the thought. "Perhaps a soup? How hard is it to ruin soup?"

He didn't need to be able to see Alfie to know the look he was giving him. If anyone could manage it, it was Janie.

"Now that I think of it, I'm not that hungry."

Alfie bumped his shoulder against Dominick's. "Of course you're not. You stole the last slice of roast. But I'm willing to forgive you in exchange for the first turn in the bath. And you come to my room tonight, rather than me make the journey to yours. Agreed?"

A journey of a whole eight feet through the secret passage between their rooms, but Alfie had the slightly larger bed so Dominick was willing to be generous.

"Agreed."

Christ, he was glad to be home, where he could be with Alfie anytime they wanted without having to worry about suspicious innkeepers peeping through keyholes or listening with a glass pressed to the wall.

As they reached the front door, Alfie sighed. "I hope they don't make too much of a to-do about our return. After that whole rotten trip I'm just glad to be somewhere with a bit of peace and quiet. God, I've missed the quiet. I don't think I can face any fawning right now and I certainly can't face whatever ways Jarrett is going to offer to 'soothe you after the long trip' or 'remind you of the rewards of returning to Scotland' or however he's going to phrase it.

Dominick grinned. Jarrett was as brazen a trollop as he was a terrible valet, but it would be good to see him again. All of the servants, in fact.

"Don't worry about Jarrett. I can handle him."

"Yes, that's exactly what he wants."

Dominick snorted and pushed open the door. The first time they'd arrived at Balcarres House, all the servants had lined up for inspection. Hopefully, the sound of the carriage coming up the drive hadn't given them time to mobilise, but it was going to be nice to hand off his coat to Mr. Howe in exchange for a glass of local spirits before putting his feet up by his own—or Alfie's—fire.

The door creaked open, revealing an empty hall.

"Well," said Alfie after a long moment. "That teaches me to be careful what I wish for. I didn't want a parade, but *some* welcome would've been nice."

They stepped into the hall. A fire burned low in the grate, still giving off light, but clearly not having been tended in some time. The rooms on either side were dark and cold.

Dominick's skin prickled at the eerie silence. Perhaps Janie's fear of Balcarres being haunted wasn't so unreasonable.

Suddenly, a pale figure appeared from nowhere, its ghastly pallor too white to be anything living. It floated several feet off the floor, wavering from side to side. Dominick couldn't hold back a gasp as it rushed towards them out of the darkness. As he raised his fists, he heard the click of Alfie unlatching the clasp on his sword cane, both of them ready to fend off the attacker, be it man or ghost.

The apparition never slowed, but as it stepped over the carpet, it seemed to stumble, some of its white body falling off the top and fluttering to the floor.

"Bollocks," said the ghost.

Dominick tried to slow the beating of his heart. "Jarrett?"

The ghost jumped, causing several more of its top layers to fall to the floor. Over the remainder, Dominick could just make out the narrow nose and high cheekbones of their valet.

"Oh, good, you're back," Jarrett said. Ignoring Alfie completely, he strode determinedly towards Dominick.

Even he can't be that brazen, was all Dominick had time to think before a load of towels was dropped into his arms.

"Take those up for me. I'll fetch more." Jarrett turned away, then said to himself in a nasal, high-pitched voice like a witch in a puppet show, *"Must be clean. Must be clean."*

With a sigh, Jarrett gathered up the towels that had fallen to the floor. "Oh, welcome back to you as well, Your Lordship." He cut as passable a bow as was possible over a load of laundry, then disappeared back into the darkness.

After a moment of shocked silence, Alfie said, "It seems we have taken them somewhat unawares. Perhaps they haven't finished preparing our bedchambers yet?"

"Perhaps," said Dominick slowly. "And Jarrett's being..."

"Efficient? I did tell Davey we could find our own way. I suppose that means to our chambers and not just the front door. Lead on."

As they climbed the many stairs, something occurred to Dominick. "How could we have caught them unawares? Davey said he'd been sent out to watch for us hours ago."

Before Alfie could answer, another figure emerged from the gloom. It was just as well Dominick's arms were otherwise engaged or he might have given their butler a strong right hook to the temple on instinct alone.

"Your Lordship, Mr. Trent," Mr. Howe said, his thin build looking especially skeletal in the darkness, "my sincerest apologies for not greeting you at the door. As you can see, we were all caught by surprise. I'm off to fetch more hot water now."

"That's quite all right," Alfie said, but it was in the same tone he'd used when the older boys had gotten some special treat at the workhouse but not the younger ones like himself. If Dominick could see him better, he'd bet Alfie was even making the same petulant face too. "Our baths can wait, but why—"

His question was cut off by a woman's scream.

At the sound, Mr. Howe took off, not in the direction of the scream but away from it, dashing down the stairs as quickly as his long legs could carry him, an empty water bucket thumping against his bony knees.

The scream came again, a wail of utter agony from somewhere in the darkness ahead of them. Ahead and upwards.

Cursing the butler for a coward, Dominick dashed forward into the dark, hearing the slightly uneven tattoo of Alfie's steps following closely behind him.

He stumbled at the top of the landing, casting about in the darkness until he saw a glow at the far end of the hall. With nothing else to guide him, he ran towards it and up the bare wooden staircase there. It wasn't the smartest thing he'd ever done, charging into the dark towards unknown danger, but it wasn't the stupidest either.

Heartbeat thudding in his ears, he could barely hear Alfie shouting at him to slow down. A lamp was lit at the top of the stairs, and he stopped there, raising his fists only to find he was still holding the damned laundry. A door closed further down the corridor and he whirled around, finding himself face-to-face with the intimidating figure of Mrs. Hirkins, her hands on her hips.

"Don't you dare drop those towels or I'll drop *you* right down those stairs and kick you all the way to the laundry to get fresh. See if I don't."

He opened and closed his mouth several times. Whatever demon he'd been prepared to fight, he clearly wasn't needed. She was more than a match for it.

"Mrs. Hirkins?" Alfie panted as he climbed the last few steps. Dominick could tell the moment they laid eyes on each other because the retired housekeeper softened. Just a bit. After all, iron was softer than steel.

"We weren't sure you'd made it here," Alfie said, taking Mrs. Hirkins' hands in his own. "Not that you would've known how to reach us. Things went terribly awry in Bath and then this awful journey. Are you well?"

"Well as can be expected, Master Alfie, given the circumstances. And far better than you, by the looks of things. You've not been taking as much care with yourself as you should."

She let out a harrumph in Dominick's direction as if Dominick didn't tell the pigheaded man the same thing every day.

Seeing the two of them together made the knot of fear in his throat loosen. Not that either of them could admit it, but Mrs. Hirkins was the closest thing to a mother Alfie had, and Alfie her favourite son. It was clear in the way she spoke to him, never "Your Lordship" or even "The Right Honourable Alfred Pennington the Earl of Crawford" as he fully deserved, but always "Master Alfie", as if he was still the same small boy who'd walked into her life the day he'd first walked out of Dominick's.

A door just beyond Mrs. Hirkins flew open, emitting a small, hunched, elderly woman Dominick didn't recognise.

"Give me those, if you're just going to stand about tratling," she said, snatching the towels from Dominick's arms. "Are they clean? They must be clean, you know. Must be clean."

Whoever she was, she was clearly the inspiration for Jarrett's impression. The voice was uncannily similar.

Before Dominick could respond, another scream came from the room behind her, even more heartrending than the last.

Dominick stepped forward, catching a glimpse inside the room. In the centre, a young woman lay on a bed, her brow sweating and hands clenched in the sheets. Her knees were drawn up under the sheets but that wasn't enough to hide her damningly large belly.

"Agnes' baby has come sooner than we'd expected," said Mrs. Hirkins, both worry and pride clear in her voice.

"Oh? Oh!" Alfie said, turning his back so quickly he nearly fell off the landing in his rush to avert his eyes. "In that case, we must send for the doctor at once. Graham likely hasn't had time to unhitch the horses, he can—"

"Doctors! Bah!" the hunched woman said, looking as if she was about to spit on the floor and only grudgingly decided against it. "What do men doctors know of birth?"

"I must insist," Alfie said, sounding less like the lord he was and more like a man who would pay any sum to be elsewhere at that moment. "At my expense, course."

"Oh, I'll already be paying Mrs. Randall here out of your pockets," Mrs. Hirkins interrupted. "Fetch me and my poor granddaughter all the way up to bloody Scotland, us worrying the whole way how things would be when we get here, only to find a right proper cunning woman one town over. You should have said!"

That wasn't quite how Dominick remembered the Hirkins' departure from London, but he knew when to keep his mouth shut.

She then gave Alfie a gentle smile. "Still, it's good you're here."

With that, she went into the room with Agnes, taking the towels with her. The closing door behind her didn't quite muffle her soothing words to her granddaughter.

The three of them, lord, fighter, and cunning woman, were left standing awkwardly in the hall.

"*Is* there anything I can do?" Alfie asked.

"No, my lord," the cunning woman, Mrs. Randall, replied. Surprisingly, her tone was more respectful than anyone else's had been tonight. "But you could find out when we'll be getting that hot water. It's not long now."

"Ask and ye shall receive," a cheery voice called up the stairs, before the beaming grin and golden spectacles of Gil Charleton came into view.

He carried with him a covered bucket from which rose tendrils of steam. He set it on the landing beside Mrs. Randall, who watched him through narrowed eyes. "I thought I'd give Ol' Howe's knees a rest. He's down in the kitchen with Janie. I think this has all been rather much for him. Hello to you both."

Dominick shook Gil's offered hand. He'd once been suspicious of Gil's easy charm, but the property overseer had been there when Dominick needed him before and he was thankful to see him again now.

Mrs. Randall didn't seem quite as thankful. "Kitchen's the place for you then, or anywhere not hereabouts. Not a time nor place for menfolk."

Gil nodded, giving the old woman the most charming of grins at his clear dismissal, which only caused her to narrow her eyes further.

"Gentlemen, I say we take the dear woman's advice and remove ourselves from where we do not belong. Perhaps a room with a suitable collection of spirits? I'm sure you're tired from your travels and I think we could all use a drink."

Gil stopped with one foot on the stair. "I nearly forgot. Janie burned herself pouring the water. Mrs. Finley says it's nothing you need to trouble yourself with, Mrs. Randall. Certainly not now of all times, but she needs to see to the poor lass."

At this, Mrs. Randall spit on the floor and let out a string of curses, some of which even Dominick had never heard before and certainly not in that order. She then grabbed Gil's hands before he could protest, squinting at his palms in the lamp light before tossing them aside. At her look, Alfie offered his for inspection. She turned them over, tracing one of the lines on his palm.

"Is that so?" She chuckled, then tossed his hands aside as well. "Fair for fortune but far too fine."

She took Dominick's hands then, inspecting them and gripping his wrists before giving a decisive nod. "You'll do. Grab the bucket and go on in."

"What!"

"Go on. You've strong hands and a touch of luck. Not as good as a woman, but we may need your strength by the end. Night bairns rarely come easy."

Dominick looked to Alfie for help, but there was none to be had.

As Agnes let out another scream, he lifted the bucket. He'd faced Bill "The Bodysnatcher" Nunn in the ring and lived to tell the tale. He could handle this.

Several horrifying, bloody, educational hours later, Dominick stumbled into the library to find a fire blazing and Gil in *his* chair.

"Well?" asked Alfie. Gil rose so Dominick could collapse down and poured him a glass of what looked like whisky.

Dominick tossed the drink back in one. Without waiting to be asked, Gil poured him another.

"Boy," said Dominick, only downing half of it this time. He didn't want to drink himself into oblivion, but *Christ*. "Healthy too, both mother and child. She's named him James."

Alfie's smile was soft.

"Well done," he whispered, and the warmth in his voice made Dominick feel like he'd done something grand and not just followed the older women's orders, terrified all the while.

"I think that deserves a toast," said Gil. He raised his glass in the direction of the servants' quarters upstairs. "A cup of kindness then, to new acquaintances and to those returning."

Alfie touched his glass to Dominick's. "Welcome home."

Chapter 2

Alfie rolled his shoulders, trying to ease the stiffness from his muscles. A single night's rest in a decent bed wasn't nearly enough to undo the weeks of strain.

By the time he'd realised Dominick had forgotten his promise to come to Alfie's room and gone in search of his wayward lover, Alfie had found him passed out face down on the bed, one boot still dangling from his foot. It'd taken a good deal of pushing and pulling to get him undressed and under the covers, but it was worth it to awaken in the morning and see the sunlight that peeked through the curtains falling across Dominick's bare shoulders as he slept. Alfie left him to it, the morning light lifting his spirits as he made his way back to his own room to dress.

He'd been away from Scotland too long, because he'd forgotten that just because it was sunny now, didn't mean there wouldn't be rain later. In his case, the rain was purely metaphorical, which made it worse. It was one thing to be miserable when it rained, at least that had some sort of poetic feeling to it. It was far worse to be miserable when the sun was shining and birds were chirping merrily outside the window.

The first metaphorical raindrop had been the raw egg he'd gotten for breakfast, Janie apparently afraid of burning herself again. Then the deluge followed when Gil set a stack of papers on his desk. A sizable stack. Several months' worth, in fact.

"Only correspondences, some investment opportunities you might consider, and an interesting paper on increasing the yield of wool per animal that I thought you might find edifying," Gil had said. "There are, of course, the rents, taxes, property standings, and various local matters to attend to, but there's no need for you to get into business your first day back. Enjoy the respite."

Now it was well past noon and if Alfie had to read one more word about the superiority of the Border Cheviot over the Scottish Dunface for both meat and wool production he might start bleating himself.

He pushed away from the desk to go look for a distraction. Fortunately, his greatest distraction chose that moment to walk in.

"Here you are," said Dominick. He looked down at the stack of papers that had only slightly dwindled. "Why are you wasting such a fine day on paperwork?"

"I was just asking myself the same question. Care for a walk?"

"If you're up for it."

Alfie rapped his cane gently against Dominick's chest. "I might be gripping this a bit tighter than usual, but I should be fine."

Dominick grinned, placing a hand over the end of the cane. "The cane, you mean, or me?" With his other hand he closed the office door behind him.

It was certainly a tempting thought. By God, it was a tempting thought. But as much as the idea of Dominick bending him over the desk and thoroughly making a mess of the paperwork appealed, doing so in the middle of the day with the windows open and house full of servants wasn't worth the risk.

Alfie held onto the image a moment longer, then released it with a sigh. "Later. You said yourself, it's too fine a day to spend indoors. Shall we detour through the kitchen and see if there's anything we can eat?"

Dominick looked more pleased than he should at Alfie countering his offer of sex with a bit of cheese and apple, but as long as he was happy, that was what counted.

When they reached the kitchen, they found Janie with a bandage wound around her hand being tutted over by Mrs. Finley.

"Is your hand still troubling you, Janie?" Alfie asked. "I heard you'd burned yourself last night."

"Sir!" The word came out of Janie in a squeak. "You ought not be down here! That is, this is your house and your kitchen, of course. What I meant was, I wasn't expecting you, your sort, to come down here. Am I late for luncheon? I apologise, sir. It's been some time since I've done it. I'll make something up right away."

Alfie held up his hands at the barrage. "No need, in fact we just came down to scrounge up a picnic. Your hand though, it's all right?"

Janie blushed fiercely, the bright red of her face clashing with the even brighter red of her hair.

"Yes, sir. Thank you. Mrs. Hirkins gave me a salve the last time I burned myself that I've been putting on it."

Mrs. Finley muttered something under her breath. Alfie raised an eyebrow. His housekeeper was usually a model of her species: proper, professional, and pleasant to a fault.

"My apologies, sir," she said at his look. "Only it doesn't smell like the salve *I* would have made."

And that was just what Alfie needed, some sort of feud developing between his current housekeeper and his former one. As his eccentric parents had never had more than a handful of staff, he wasn't entirely sure how an earl was supposed to handle squabbles amongst his workforce, so before that could go any further, he changed the subject. "Speaking of the Hirkins family, how is the newest arrival?"

Mrs. Finley's face lit up at the question. Whatever animosity she might or might not have with the eldest of the Hirkins clan, it obviously did not apply to the most recent addition to the set.

"Oh, James is just the most beautiful thing. He was sleeping when I went in to see him. Bairns do quite a bit, the first few months. They use up all their strength being brought new into the world. He looked like a perfect angel from Heaven. Agnes as well, like the Madonna and Christ Child, bless them."

"I'm glad to hear it." Dominick said. "If he grows up half as strong as his mother, he'll be a man to watch out for. She gripped my hand so tight she nearly broke it."

From anyone else, the words might have been meant as a joke, but from Dominick they were the highest praise. He'd been gathering up some odds and ends around the kitchen as Alfie chatted, and gestured towards the kitchen door with a nod of his head.

"I look forward to seeing them both when they're ready for it," said Alfie, then followed Dominick out into the glorious sunshine.

⬥○⬥

For once, the weather seemed inclined to remain sunny, at least for the foreseeable future. Likely it was just biding its time, waiting for them to grow overconfident and stray far afield before the heavens opened.

But for now at least, Alfie could enjoy walking through the overgrown gardens so long neglected by the previous earl, the distant views of the sea ahead of him and Dominick by his side. Dominick was content to walk in silence, the hum of the bees in thickets that had once been neatly landscaped flower beds only punctuated by a crunch of his apple. Even after all their time together, Alfie couldn't help but steal sideways glances at him, the way Dominick's golden hair glinted in the sun, the way his shoulders eased here in a way they never had in London. The country air suited him.

Alfie grew so caught up with his glances that he missed a root that had broken free from a rose bed and now snaked across the path. He stumbled, Dominick's sudden grip on his arm the only thing keeping him from a faceful of thorns.

"All right?" Dominick asked. He'd dropped his apple to grab Alfie and it rolled to a stop against the treacherous root.

"I'm fine." Alfie knocked the half-eaten fruit into a hedge with his cane. "Perhaps that's enough being a jungle explorer for the day, however. Shall we take the road into town? I'm not sure I'll make it that far, but the exercise will do me good."

He recognised the pinched look on Dominick's face as one that meant, "I'll agree, but I'll be watching you like a mother hen to make sure you don't overdo it."

Although Dominick might have preferred the word "hawk" to "mother hen". He'd gotten better about his hovering, but there were some things about Dominick that were just, well, *Dominick*. It shouldn't please Alfie quite so much that looking after him was one of them.

They exited the gardens through a rusted gate that required their combined strength to force open and strolled along the oak-lined drive towards the main road to Kilconquer.

Along the way, one of the barn cats emerged to inspect the trespassers to its kingdom. It was a tiny thing, but its objections to their presence were loud. Dominick paid for their passage with a bit of hard cheese he'd packed away for lunch. Alfie then spent some minutes dangling his pocket watch for the cat to bat at before it finally tired of its clockwork prey.

He smiled as it trotted back towards the stables, tail held high and more certain of its position of master of Balcarres than Alfie had ever been.

From there, the drive curved gently and the trees became thicker, the woods fully surrounding them by the time they finally met the road to town. When they reached the front gate, it seemed like a good chance to rest his leg and have whatever cheese the cat had left them.

The gates themselves had long been removed, but on either side of the drive stood tall stone pillars announcing the entrance to the manor, despite the distance still required to reach it. At the base of one of the pillars lay a large log perfectly suited to both a rest and a picnic. Alfie sat, his upturned face warmed by the sunlight that filtered through the trees and his whole body warmed by Dominick's thigh pressed against his own.

Eventually, he heard the rattling of wheels coming down the road. A farm wagon heavy with hay turned the corner, the nag at its head trundling along at an even but slow pace, the farmer at the reins clicking his tongue at her occasionally in some sort of man-to-animal communication Alfie would never understand.

It was quite the bucolic picture, something his adoptive mother might have bought on a whim to be hung on a wall somewhere and promptly forgotten about. He raised a hand in greeting as the farmer approached.

"Good afternoon. Beautiful day, isn't it?"

The farmer didn't respond, merely continued on his steady way. Perhaps he hadn't heard him.

"I say," Alfie tried again, casting about for any topic of discussion less banal than the weather. "That's a lovely beast, does she have a name?"

At that, the farmer glanced over at him sharply before quickly looking away again. Without a word, he shook the reins, urging the horse faster. She complied, increasing her plodding to a brisk stroll and within a few moments they were past, disappearing around the next bend.

Dominick snorted. "I may not have figured out all your fancy toff manners yet, but I know an insult when I see one."

"Yes," Alfie said, shaken by the unexpected disrespect. "A near perfect *cut direct*, in fact. At the wrong soiree, a look like that could mean a duel."

"I doubt he'll be attending any soirees any time soon. Just as well; the wagon wouldn't fit through the doors."

"No," said Alfie, but he wasn't really listening. It wasn't his first time being disliked or even hated, but those had all been by people he knew. Such clear dislike from a complete stranger bothered him more for some reason. "Do you think he realised who I was? Perhaps we thought we were vagrants."

That made Dominick laugh out loud. Alfie looked over and all right, perhaps Dominick had a point. While their clothes were simple by his standards, their shirts were still of the finest linen, their trousers expertly tailored, and there was gold thread embroidering the buttonholes of Dominick's coat. The ebony sword cane that rested against Alfie's knee with its silver trim was probably worth more than the farmer's house.

"Besides," Dominick said, laughing again, "after we came rattling through last night with the earl's carriage, the earl's horses, and the earl's driver, likely every household within fifty miles knows the Earl of Crawford has returned."

Even though the sun still shone, the day didn't feel quite as warm as before. Something in the farmer's look made Alfie feel the way he had the first day of university, small and somehow guilty at the same time.

"Let's head back," he said stiffly, swiping up his cane and heading back towards Balcarres House without waiting for Dominick's reply.

Dominick caught up to him quickly.

"We were sitting a bit close," Dominick murmured, his voice a heavy rumble.

"That's my concern," replied Alfie. "We've been away for months, and if there's been talk in the meantime about the strange new earl and his handsome companion..."

"You are very strange and I am quite handsome."

"Nick."

"I know, I know. What should we do about it?"

Alfie took a moment to think. The wind had picked up and the rustle of leaves sounded like hushed whispers behind their backs.

"I'm not sure there is anything to be done," he said at last. "At least not right now. If there are rumours, enquiring about them would only make things worse. Still, a bit of discretion wouldn't go amiss."

"I'm discreet."

Despite the seriousness of their conversation, Alfie barked out a laugh. "Nick, you're about half an inch from holding my hand."

Dominick looked honestly shocked at their proximity before he stepped over, putting a few feet of space between them.

"All right, all right, I see your point. No strolling arm-in-arm. Anything else?"

Alfie shrugged. "Spend more time apart? I don't mean I'm going to pack you off on the next mail coach, but you go riding more without me and I'll do more of whatever it is earls do. Paperwork, apparently."

"I'll happily leave you to that," Dominick said. "This is all a lot of bollocks, but then you've always been a hassle."

Halfway up the drive Dominick snapped his fingers. "I know what it was! It wasn't me at all. It was you asking about his horse!"

Alfie furrowed his brow. "What was wrong with that?"

"It wasn't what you said. It was how you said it." Dominick waggled his eyebrows. "Longingly, I would say. Lustfully, even."

Alfie let out a squawk at the absolute obscenity of Dominick's suggestion, but that only spurred the man on.

"Like the way a bull looks at a cow. Or a blacksmith at a milkmaid," offered Dominick with glee. "Downright obscene, it was."

Alfie couldn't help but laugh, his mood lightening just a fraction. "And what would you know about any of those things? Lots of milkmaids wandering around Spitalfields, were there?"

Dominick had drifted back towards him without either of them noticing. He bumped their shoulders together and leaned in, his lips brushing Alfie's ear as he spoke.

"I know obscene," he whispered. "And I know the way I look at you. The way you look at me."

With that he pulled away and the look in his eyes... Yes, that was a look Alfie knew too. Perhaps he could be tempted to spend such a fine day indoors after all. Discretion be damned.

Chapter 3

Unfortunately, temptation would have to wait.

Alfie had rather suspected it would. If Dominick had been some giggling countess fresh off the marriage market, no one would've said anything about them disappearing into Alfie's bedchamber for a few hours in the middle of the afternoon. They might have *thought* things, yes, but they wouldn't have said any of them. As it was however, men like them had to be irritatingly careful, even in their own homes.

But the need for discretion didn't make what they had any less meaningful than any other marriage. From his experience, what he and Dominick shared put most of the marriages in England to shame. Certainly all those amongst the peerage.

He'd take Dominick over hundred countesses, giggles or not. He just couldn't take him *now*. Supper first.

He rolled Dominick's ring lazily around his finger, letting the lamplight catch the carving of the bird from every angle.

"...which is, of course, when the dratted beastie decided to show himself. I don't know who shrieked louder, me or the mouse!"

Alfie chuckled at Gil's tale. The man had a way with words and was an entertaining companion. It had been second nature to invite him to stay for supper when they'd run into him after their walk. He'd given a funny sort of smile at that, but graciously agreed. If Alfie was really his friend though, he should've warned the man to go home and spare himself the hardship that was one of Janie's meals.

Before he had the opportunity to offer Gil a last chance to escape, Janie came into the dining room carrying three bowls on a platter. The rest of the long dining table stretched endlessly away, empty and bare as Janie made her cautious way to the end where the three men sat.

It might have been more discreet to sit Dominick halfway down the table, but Gil had dined with them enough that to change things now would only draw more suspicion. Besides, the man hadn't noticed anything between them before, he certainly wouldn't now that they were on their best behaviour.

"Your hand feeling better?" Dominick asked as Janie set a steaming bowl in front of him. He kept his face upturned to hers rather than examine the soup too closely. From past experience, that was probably wise.

"Yes, sir," she said, "I hardly feel it at all. Mrs. Hirkins is a miracle worker."

"I'm glad to hear it," added Gil. "While you earned your injury in noble service, I would hate for you to be in any pain over it. Not that any burn would ever dare to mar such fair skin as yours for too long."

Janie spilled a little of Alfie's soup as she set down his bowl, her focus clearly elsewhere. An elsewhere featuring a certain gentleman with sable hair and golden spectacles and with no Alfie or soup anywhere nearby. At least, he hoped not.

"Oh. That is, thank you. Ifthatwillbeallsir." Janie hurriedly served Gil his soup, flushing scarlet from her collar to her maid's cap. Poor girl. Her infatuation with Gil was obvious, but with Gil's reputation as a shameless charmer of women, Alfie might have to step in before they had a heartbreak on their hands. Or worse, another baby.

He was torn from that worry when Dominick suddenly dropped his spoon and clasped a hand over his mouth.

Alfie was beside him before he'd even realised he'd moved. "What is it? What's wrong?"

An icy fist clenched his heart as he remembered another bowl of poison set in front of Dominick. They'd been fortunate that time, even if others hadn't, but their luck couldn't last forever.

"Bloody hell," swore Dominick between his fingers. Then he grasped up the spoon again and went for another serving of the deadly poison.

"Nick!"

"No, Alfie, try it. It's *good*."

Alfie glanced back at his own bowl. Now that he looked at it, it certainly appeared appetising and Dominick seemed to be enjoying it, but the best he'd come to hope for from Janie's kitchen was "passable". Cautiously, he took a sip.

"Good God."

"I know," replied Dominick between mouthfuls.

A perfect broth, neither too thick nor watery, fragrant herbs, and pieces of vegetable and rabbit cut to just the right size to balance in a spoon.

"Perhaps Janie improved while we were away?" he offered.

"No," said Gil with a wince. "She really didn't. I mistook her last soup for the laundry water. I can't imagine how she came up with this."

By the time the woman of the hour returned, her tray now carrying plates of fish with mushrooms and some sort of wine sauce, their bowls were completely dry.

"Well done, lass," Gil said, rising to unburden some of her load—or to get at his own plate all the faster. Janie looked as if she might faint with pleasure at the attention. "If this course is half as good as the last, then His Lordship here will be forced to never throw a dinner party again, lest the secret get out and you're snatched up by a household with an even grander title."

"My compliments on the soup as well, Janie," Alfie said.

"Oh," she said softly, not quite as radiant as a moment before. "I'm afraid I can't take credit for that, sir."

"Nonsense, it was delicious."

"No, I mean, it wasn't my soup. I was too scared to go near the pot after yesterday and then in comes Mrs. Hirkins, the older one, saying the younger one wanted time alone with the bairn. But I could see she was all nerves and happiness with nowhere to put them, so I asked if she knew how to make soup. I know I oughtn't have, she's not employed here, she retired, but she didn't seem to mind helping. Then I told her what I'd planned for the main, but she made this instead."

God was in His Heaven, Mrs. Hirkins was back in Alfie's kitchen, and all was right with the world.

"It's quite fine, Janie. More than fine. Please allow her to help whenever she wishes."

A more seasoned cook would bristle at allowing an interloper into her domain, but Janie just looked relieved.

"Thank you, I will. She's got some cakes in the oven now, says it will be a bit until they're done, but I'm to bring you them with cream and fresh blackberries."

Alfie salivated at the very thought, but he tried to retain what little lordly poise he had.

"That will do very nicely, thank you."

As soon as the door closed behind her, they descended on their plates like a pack of wolves. Wolves with silver cutlery, granted, but wolves nevertheless. When they were finished, Alfie leaned back in his chair with a pleased hum. Dominick hummed right back in agreement, dabbing the last of the wine sauce from his lips.

"I must thank you, gentlemen," said Gil. "That is by far the best meal I've had in months."

"And more to come," said Dominick happily. "Mrs. Hirkins' cakes. Alfie, why did you ever let that woman retire?"

It was a jest, but at the moment, Alfie was wondering the same thing. "She said she trained her granddaughter just as well. Once Agnes is up and about, we might have meals like this to look forward to every night."

Transporting a pregnant girl and her elderly grandmother to Scotland to spare one of them from ruin and the other from a lonely life in a house where murder had been committed was hardly how Alfie planned on acquiring a cook to replace Janie, who was rightfully not even a kitchen maid but a housemaid. But here they were. It was possibly the second most brilliant idea of his life. The first being to follow that angry boxer into a dark alley.

He looked over at the boxer in question, but Dominick had his eyes fixed on the door, awaiting Janie's return with barely-contained joy.

Gil cleared his throat. "While we're on the subject of the Hirkins women, that is something I need to speak to you about. I was going to wait until tomorrow, but since you mention it now, there has been some confusion about their place in the household. Agnes in particular. You are aware that most maids are fired when they have a child, not hired? It has caused... some upset, shall I say, since her arrival."

"That explains the farmer then," said Dominick with a nod. "Didn't hold with you bringing in some fallen woman. From the sinful pit of London too."

Just as well the farmer didn't know about Dominick being a former fallen man, or the depths of the pit from which he and Alfie had both emerged.

"A man in his cart gave me the cut direct today," Alfie clarified for Gil. "Now we know why."

As much as he didn't want Agnes to be subjected to any further scandal, it was a relief to know word hadn't spread about his relationship with Dominick.

Gil shifted in his seat. "Aye, that's likely *one* reason, but we'll get to that. Are you sure you want to go into it now? It can wait until morning."

"Go ahead," said Alfie. It was better to know the full extent of whatever mess he was in now rather than be up all night worrying about it.

He had other plans for tonight.

"Very well." Gil removed his spectacles and began to polish the lenses with his napkin. "I say this to you not only as your overseer, but also your friend. The previous earl neglected his duties here for decades, left the house and lands to fall from their former glory, and ignored any but the most urgent letters about the estate. Your tenants suffered from his neglect. You have been here less than a year and even including your recent departure of several months, you've already approved more improvements than your father ever did. However, in that same year, there have been two runaway servants and three murders tied to the household."

"Only two," protested Dominick, as if that was significantly better.

"Three. They thought Jarrett committed one while you were gone."

Alfie started. Gil could have mentioned that while they were waiting up the night before, rather than press him for the details of their trip. Apparently, it was yet another thing that could wait until after Alfie had finished catching up on his social correspondence.

He couldn't help but ask. "Did he?"

"Oh no. Completely innocent. Well not—that is to say he had nothing to do with the crime. This crime, at least. But, well, it's a long story. Suffice to say none of the common people still quite trust him, and I'm rather *persona non grata* with my family at the moment, so that's the local gentry out."

Alfie frowned, "If you're not with your family, where are you staying?"

"Here," said Gil plainly. "At least until your return. I should have mentioned it last night, but I didn't care to walk to the inn in the dark. And I may also be *persona non grata* there as well."

Now Alfie understood the funny look Gil had given him when he invited him to their supper table. It seemed he was already quite familiar with it.

He looked over at Dominick. As entailed property, the house was solely Alfie's and nothing could be done to change that, but it was as much Dominick's home as his. His love nodded back immediately, as Alfie knew he would.

"You're welcome to stay as long as you like, Gil," Alfie said sincerely, even as he had to bite back a sigh. After all, it was an enormous manor, one more person wouldn't make it that much harder for Dominick and him to find privacy.

"Thank you," Gil said. He resettled the spectacles on his nose. "Truly, you don't know how much that means to me. But back to the matter at hand. I think to solve your other issues, you should hire some more servants. A dozen should do the trick, but I'm open to more."

"A dozen!" shouted Dominick.

"Surely that's not necessary." A dozen more sets of ears listening at doors and peeking through keyholes. He and Dominick would have to be a dozen times more cautious.

Gil looked between them. As an earl's "cousin", Dominick had no right to any say in Alfie's affairs. Whereas as far as Alfie was concerned, Dominick had given him a ring. What was his was Dominick's and Dominick's was his. Reaching for his spectacles again, Gil stopped, spreading his hands on the table instead and addressing them both.

"I will ask plainly: how many months of the year do you intend to spend at Balcarres?"

"All of them," Alfie replied immediately.

"Save travel," Dominick added. "We'd like to do a bit of that at some point. But if you're asking if either of us plans on haring back to London to set up shop, it'll take more than one farmer's ugly look to drive us off."

Gil looked a bit taken aback. "Ah. Had I realised that, I could have spared myself several night's worry."

He brightened. "I am glad to hear it though. The Earls of Crawford have used Balcarres as the family seat for centuries. It's only right that you're back, but it does make the hiring of additional servants that much more important. Now that you've returned, Jarrett will be doing the work of valet and footman both, and errand boy as well, at least until Davey grows into a little more common sense. I admire you taking Agnes on, but even if she is able to take over her role as cook, someone will have to keep an eye on the bairn while she's handling knives and such."

"Why not just hire a nanny along with the rest?" Dominick asked.

Gil winced. "Hiring a nanny for a servant's child would only fuel further speculation. At best, it might be seen as... eccentric. It is my experience that when a man is eccentric in some ways, it is best he not draw attention to himself by being eccentric in others. If you catch my meaning?"

Dominick nodded solemnly as if he understood what Gil wasn't saying, but Alfie certainly didn't. The way he said it, it almost sounded like he knew about what Alfie and Dominick were to each other. But that couldn't be the case; he'd said "in my experience" and everyone knew Gil's reputation as a notorious womaniser.

Still, Alfie nodded as well and if anything, that made Gil look even happier.

"Excellent! I'm so glad that's all out in the open. Now, as far as hiring, the two men who accompanied the Hirkins women and your carriage from London claimed you'd offered them positions. Naturally, I wanted to wait for your return to confirm this. They're working as ostlers at the inn for now. If you have offered them employment though, I suggest you keep that promise but fill the remainder of the positions with local people or their relatives, if possible, before broadening the net and hiring from the cities.

"For one, that would mean most of them wouldn't be required to live in and could go home at night. No reason to disturb all the bats in eaves by shoving cots under them, eh? For another, it would foster goodwill amongst the community."

Dominick interrupted. "I hate how this sounds, but does he really need their goodwill? He's an earl."

Gil ran his fingers over the tablecloth, visibly collecting himself before he spoke. "Need? No. But again, it is my experience that a place is far easier to live in when people like you than when they don't."

A look of such melancholy washed over him that Alfie was about to reach out, offer some sort of comfort, but Gil shook his head as if banishing the mood and when he looked up, his smile was as charming as ever.

"Will that plan suit you, my lord?"

"Yes, I suppose," Alfie said, a bit taken aback by the abrupt change in Gil's demeanour. "A dozen servants. Very well. It's not like I can't afford them."

"Well, a dozen once we have everything straightened out," replied Gil. "We'll need at least twice that to get things set to rights in the first place. Roofers, cleaners, gardeners, the whole lot. Bless Mrs. Finley and Mr. Howe, but I don't know how they've kept this place together for as long as they have."

Alfie rubbed a hand over his eyes. "Gil, as my overseer, you have access to my various accounts, correct?"

"Aye."

"And Dominick, he's trusting you to manage his not-insubstantial fortune as well, correct?"

"Aye?"

"Then by God, if you're intent on robbing me blind, why don't you find an easier way to do it?"

Both Gil and Dominick laughed at that, and Alfie felt a tap against his shoe from Dominick's side of the table, a sign of his approval Alfie always welcomed, except when confined to a carriage.

"Aye, I suppose you're right. I should've just told you I'd invested in miniature tigers for your zoological garden and give you tabby mogs instead. That'd turn me a profit."

"How about a moat large enough to sail," Dominick added with a grin. "Only never specify what size boat."

From there, the two of them descended into trading increasingly ludicrous ways Gil could pilfer the earldom's funds. Alfie didn't actually mind spending the money on more servants, and Balcarres *had* been allowed to fall into a sorry state. It was just that despite their wealth, his parents rarely had more than the smallest possible staff in London, including the lodestar that was Mrs. Hirkins. It was a lot to take in.

Around him, the hilarity ensued.

Dominick tapped his finger against his lips. "I think this house is lacking in hallways. Add some more secret passages."

"I'll have the mice alerted immediately," Gil laughed. "Very cheap labour, mice. And good at tunnelling. I'll make a fortune. Alas, that species tends to revolt if not properly supervised."

"Which is where the miniature tigers come in!"

Gil was laughing so hard he had to remove his spectacles to wipe his face. "After that, would you prefer me to add an ornamental lake or a folly on the crag?"

Dominick suddenly stilled. "Could you really?"

"What?" Gil hiccupped out a laugh. "A lake that's a puddle or a folly that's a single rock? Aye, easily enough. But I'll need more mice."

Even Alfie had to snicker at that, but then he caught the look on Dominick's face. Dominick had looked at him that same way when Alfie had first told him he loved him. As if the idea was so wonderful that he didn't dare hope it was true.

Alfie's jaw dropped. "You can't seriously want one of those stone monstrosities?"

"The one in Bath was nice. I know *I* thoroughly enjoyed myself there."

Alfie couldn't believe what he was hearing. On a hill overlooking the city of Bath were the ruins of a castle gate, not crumbled from centuries of battle, but sham ruins built only a few decades ago for no other reason than to provide a more picturesque view from the window of some wealthy resident of the town. And yes, Dominick had enjoyed himself in the room built within the folly with the door that locked and stone walls thick enough that they could make as much noise as they wanted. He'd also thoroughly enjoyed Alfie there. At least twice.

The memory was fresh in his mind, not only because of the sheer novelty of it, but because it was the last time they'd had the opportunity to really take their time with each other in their long months of travels, something that weighed on him ever more as the conversation went on. If that many new people were skulking around Balcarres, would they ever truly be safe enough to be together?

They might, if only there was some sort of scenic destination they could claim to be venturing to, where no one would be surprised if they returned later than expected because they were so caught up in the view. A place on his estate where they were unlikely to be bothered. One with thick stone walls and a door that locked.

God damn it. It wasn't a terrible idea. He could even envision a little stairwell running up to the top so they actually *could* take in the view.

"Gil, I don't suppose you know of any architectural firms that could do that?"

The moment Alfie asked, Dominick grinned at him with such force that for a moment, Alfie was certain he was going to pull him over the table and kiss him, Gil be damned. Dominick winked instead, which was somehow worse, because now Alfie knew that kiss was coming eventually, but there was nothing he could do to make it happen *now*.

"I believe I have a few names that might suit," Gil said, sounding amused. "Even some that could tackle the folly and rebuilding the gardens both if you'd like to keep things simple."

As if anything in Alfie's life was ever simple. "Perfect."

On cue, Janie came through the doors, bearing thick slices of cake for each of them, still warm from the oven so the cream melted and slowly slid down each slice, dragging the tart berries along with it. From the smell alone, Alfie recognised it as cake Mrs. Hirkins only made a few times a year, so delicate it peeled away with the fork, but so rich he dreamed about it in the months between her baking it.

In the face of such a treat, it was hard not to be at least a little optimistic. Perhaps all the darkness and death was behind them now. Perhaps Gil was right and the way forward was to air out all the linens and throw open all the shutters. Let Balcarres House once again be the home to an earl it should be.

Perhaps then I'll feel like the earl it should have.

He crushed the thought down. Now was not the time for his insecurities. They'd be making Balcarres *theirs*, leaving a mark that would last long after they were gone. It was a time to celebrate. And celebrate he would, now with cake and soon with Dominick.

He wasn't sure which excited him more.

CHAPTER 4

"Christ, I thought he'd never leave." Dominick said as soon as he heard Alfie bid Jarrett goodnight and click the lock firmly in place behind him.

"I know," said Alfie, already tugging at his cravat. "Come here."

Powerless to resist, Dominick tossed down the book he'd been pretending to read for the last half hour. Jumping up from his chair, he met Alfie halfway across the room and kissed him with the hunger of a starving man.

Given the chance, he'd have taken Alfie to bed the moment they'd walked back through Balcarres' doors or even just taken him up against the front doors if that was on offer.

"Servants are a bloody menace," Dominick said the first time they broke apart.

"I'll have them all fired," panted Alfie.

"Do." Then Dominick kissed him again.

After weeks on the road with little more than a few stolen kisses and the hasty use of hands or mouths in the quietest hours of the night when even the most inquisitive innkeepers would be abed, having to listen to Alfie make polite conversation with their valet after a whole evening of making polite conversation with Gil had been maddening. From what he knew of both men, Dominick likely could have told them to bugger off and why, but apparently, they had to be more discreet.

Well, not any longer. He had Alfie, a locked door, a bed, and no one expecting anything from them until morning. He wasn't going to waste the opportunity.

He licked into Alfie's mouth, revelling in the feel of his lover opening up for him. Alfie's tongue slid against his, pushing back with equal hunger to taste Dominick, because the bloody man couldn't just relent and let himself be kissed.

Just as well. This was far more intoxicating.

There were plenty of men who'd seen Dominick—seen his size, his scars—and wanted nothing more than to roll over and submit to him. He'd happily taken their money and given them what they wanted, but Alfie had never submitted to a damn thing in his life. He was a stubborn, contrary creature and it'd gotten them both in trouble more than once, but it only made Dominick love him all the more.

Although if he'd stop fighting Dominick's attempts to get him naked by trying to undress him first, they'd both be the happier for it.

"Hold still," he said, yanking Alfie's banyan far enough down his arms to trap him so Dominick could start work on his trousers.

"Absolutely not." Alfie shook himself free of the banyan, dislodging Dominick's fingers in the process. "It's been months since I've had you fully naked. I'm not waiting any longer."

"So hold still. The sooner I get your clothes off, the sooner you can have at mine."

Alfie kicked off his slippers. "Then *you* hold still and let me go first."

"Fine!" Dominick threw up his hands in exasperation. Alfie looked absolutely delighted.

He expected to be stripped quickly so they could move on to the next step in the evening, the one involving the bed, the bottle of oil hidden in the dresser, and Alfie writhing beneath him. But instead Alfie closed the distance between them, a soft smile on his face, and placed his hands on Dominick's chest. He ran them over the fabric of the banyan that Dominick had happily exchanged for his constricting coat and waistcoat while Jarrett had been fussing. Alfie took his time, feeling the shape of Dominick's chest through the rich fabric.

Dominick huffed in impatience. Alfie rolled his eyes at him, but undid the three buttons holding the banyan closed before returning his attention to Dominick's chest, now through only the thinner linen of his shirt.

Dominick let the banyan slide off his shoulders to the floor. "I thought you weren't waiting a minute more to get me naked."

"I changed my mind," Alfie said, unwinding Dominick's cravat with deliberate slowness. "Now that I've got you to myself, I want to enjoy you."

"You'll enjoy me more naked."

Alfie laughed and flicked Dominick on the chin. "I will. But I'm enjoying this now. Patience."

Unlike Alfie, Dominick recognised a lost battle when he saw one. If he continued to fight, Alfie would only drag this out even longer.

So he let himself be caressed and fondled, Alfie running his hands over every inch of his body in the name of getting him undressed. It wasn't the worst feeling in the world to have Alfie's clever fingers brush over his nipples as he finally pushed Dominick's shirt over his head or stroke against his wrists as Alfie undid his cuffs. By the time Alfie was wriggling them under his waistband, teasing them back and forth before finally getting to work on the buttons on his fall, Dominick was gritting his teeth to hold back some truly embarrassing noises.

"No need to keep quiet on my account," Alfie said, the devil. Then he pushed Dominick's trousers down, hands dancing over his thighs as he went, intentionally avoiding all the places that Dominick wanted them most.

He whined as his cock sprang free, hard and wanting just from Alfie's teasing. Lifting one foot and then the other to free himself from the trousers, Dominick peeled his socks off at the same time so he was finally, *finally* naked before Alfie.

Dominick shivered, but the chill of the room was nothing compared to the heat in Alfie's eyes. He didn't say anything, but walked around Dominick, occasionally tracing a finger across his back, or down his arm.

"See something you like?" Dominick asked, unable to keep from flexing a bit under Alfie's admiring gaze.

"Shh," replied Alfie as he continued circling.

Dominick fought to stay still as he was looked over. There was a lot to see. Alfie probably knew his body better than he did at this point, knew the placement of every scar, the shift of every muscle.

Certainly Alfie had a better idea of what his buttocks looked like than he did. And he was far more fascinated with Dominick's body hair, running his fingers through the hair on Dominick's chest the nights they were able to fall asleep together. He did the same now, running his hand down the centre of Dominick's chest from breastbone to belly, but pulling his hand away before he reached his cock.

Dominick growled.

"Well," Alfie said, taking a step back and licking his lips. His eyes were very bright. "I suppose it's your turn now."

Unlike *some* people, Dominick didn't waste another moment. He ducked his head down and charged.

Alfie let out a squawk as Dominick lifted him over his shoulder and made for the bed.

"Nick! What are you doing? My God, put me down this instant!"

Dominick did as he was told, heaving Alfie onto the bed. The mattress and Alfie both protested the rough treatment, but at least Alfie stopped when Dominick swung a leg over the top of him, straddling his hips. He sat down heavily, grinding down on Alfie's prick where it remained still trapped in his buckskins.

"Enjoyed that, did we?" He asked, grinning as Alfie hissed and tried to thrust up against him, only to find himself pinned by Dominick's weight. "If only you didn't still have all your clothes on, you might be able to do something about it."

A blush was rising from Alfie's collar, and between that and the very hard cock beneath him, Dominick had no doubt he enjoyed it very much. But as Alfie had said, it was his turn now.

He cursed at Alfie's cravat, the knot only confounding him more as he fought with it.

Naked or not, he was about ready to hunt through the house for scissors when it finally parted. He yanked it off, then followed with Alfie's shirt, forgetting the cuffs in his haste. They caught on Alfie's wrists and Dominick cursed again as he fought to unfasten them from the inside out. Alfie giggled, and Dominick was tempted to just leave him like that. But no, he wanted Alfie naked and by God he was going to have him that way.

Fortunately his buckskins put up no resistance, and Dominick finally, *gloriously* had what he'd been wanting for months: Alfie naked in a bed with no one to disturb them.

Now there was just one more thing he needed.

He leaned down and Alfie strained upwards to meet his kiss. Dominick gave it to him, then whispered. "Stay put."

It was nearly impossible to leave Alfie looking like that. The flush that had peeked out of his collar now stretched up all the way to his ears and ran down his chest. His arms were raised, fingers curled softly on either side of his head as he watched Dominick through heavy-lidded eyes. He was completely on display, the long flat planes of his chest and stomach drawing Dominick's eye down to the hard jut of his cock, the head already dripping onto his hip bone. He shifted his long legs, and Dominick wanted to run his tongue along the entire length of them to see what noises Alfie would make when he did.

Instead he forced himself to turn away, going over the dresser as quickly as he could. It took him a minute to find what he was looking for. It'd been months since they last tucked this particular bottle into its hiding place, and Alfie's linens seemed to have multiplied in his absence. At last he turned around, holding the bottle over his head in triumph, only to find Alfie hadn't stayed put.

He hadn't stayed put at all.

He'd rolled over and was now up on his knees and elbows, his arms folded under his head, back arched, arse high in the air and legs spread.

Dominick fumbled the bottle, barely catching it in time. Dropping it would mean not being able to take advantage of the bounty laid out before him and that would be an absolute disaster.

Uncaring of the catastrophe that had so nearly befallen them, Alfie grinned at him over his shoulder.

"See something you like?"

Dominick couldn't wait any longer. He was on the bed before he even realised he was moving. The bottle had become mysteriously uncorked in his journey and he wasted no time pouring some into his palm, oiling up his fingers.

During the interminable carriage rides, he'd thought about all the things he'd do once he had Alfie in a proper bed. In his mind, it'd been a slow seduction, lasting hours. In truth, he'd be lucky to last minutes, and he had the sneaking suspicion he'd been the one seduced. He slotted into place behind Alfie, putting a hand on his hip to steady him.

Alfie tensed at the touch, the join where his thigh met his hip being one of his many sensitive areas. Then he immediately relaxed, canting his hips even higher. It was a truly breathtaking sight, but there had been one constant in all of Dominick's carriage imaginings, and even if the rest of the night went nothing like he'd planned, he'd have this one thing.

"Roll back over," he said gruffly. "I want to see you."

Alfie furrowed his brow, but then a sweet smile stole over his face. "I always knew you were a romantic at heart."

Dominick shuffled back so Alfie could roll over without kicking him in the face. "If I am, it's your fault. Never understood why anyone would bother with poetry and the like until you came along. Makes more sense now."

He'd meant it as an accusation, expecting his love to have some witty reply, but Alfie just gaped up at him, stunned into silence. Well, Dominick knew one way to get a response out of him.

He bent down to give Alfie a quick peck on the lips, just enough to tide him over until later, then slid one well-oiled finger into him.

That had the desired response. Alfie gasped, tilting his hips to get a better angle.

Dominick began to work him slowly. After all, it'd been some time since they'd done this. A fact he had to keep reminding himself of as his body screamed at him to just sink himself into that silky heat and damn the consequences.

He gritted his teeth and slowed even further, stretching Alfie slowly, only adding a second finger when he was certain he could take it.

"Fuck, Nick." Alfie breathed out in a long sigh that became a moan. "Fuck, I missed you."

Dominick spread his two fingers, earning himself another moan. "I'm right here. Another?"

"Don't need it. Just need you."

Dominick had to look away and focus on something else or he was going to spoil this for them both. He then added another finger, doing his best to ignore Alfie's curses. As much as they both wanted it, it'd be worth the wait to make sure Alfie was fully ready for him.

However, what little patience Dominick had left was rewarded when he twisted his fingers deep and Alfie gave a shout, his body surging up and nearly knocking them both off the bed.

Dominick crooked his fingers and drove in again, harder this time. "There?"

Alfie twisted his hands in the sheets as if he might fall off the world if he didn't. "There! There, there, there, there, there!"

Dominick obliged, striking that spot again and again.

Alfie thrashed his head back and forth, letting out little hiccupping sobs mixed with low moans that sounded suspiciously like, "Niiiiiiick".

Dominick knew how good it felt, that place inside that sent bolts of lightning striking his body everywhere at once, carrying blinding flashes of pleasure in their wake. Alfie looked thoroughly debauched, his auburn curls dishevelled, that sweet pink mouth open and gasping.

Dominick's cock throbbed and he couldn't take it any longer. He poured out more oil, nearly upending the entire bottle over his cock in his haste. He just about bit through his tongue at the first touch of his own hand, but forced himself to focus on how much better it would feel soon. After slicking himself as much as he could stand, he set the bottle on the table by the bed and pulled a pillow down to tuck under Alfie's hips.

"Ready?" he asked.

Alfie gave him a very unimpressed look for a man who'd just been panting his name. Then he wrapped his legs around Dominick's waist and tried to hoist himself onto his cock by willpower alone. The first slide of his prick over Alfie's gleaming entrance made them both gasp. The last thread of Dominick's patience snapped and he gave them both what they wanted. He lined up, feeling Alfie's knees tighten around his ribs, and pushed in.

All his imaginings couldn't compare to the real thing. Alfie was impossibly hot, and tight, and slick and every other wonderful thing. Dominick pulled out, then thrust in again, a little deeper this time.

To distract himself from coming at the sheer bliss of finally fucking Alfie again, he wrapped his hand around Alfie's cock, hoping to give back even just a fraction of the pleasure he was feeling. His hand was still slick, and running it up and down Alfie's length felt nearly as heavenly as rocking in and out of him did.

Alfie kicked him in the back. "N-not. Not going to last. Harder."

Dominick obeyed, snapping his hips forward. Alfie howled and kicked him again, like Dominick was a horse to be spurred onwards. The encouragement wasn't needed. Dominick did his best to match the motions of his hand to his thrusts, but it was impossible to focus when everything felt so damned good.

Too soon, he felt the tell-tale creeping up his spine that meant he was about to climax, and urged himself faster, deeper, needing to bring Alfie over the edge with him.

In the end, he didn't know which of them came first, whether Alfie tightening around him as he came brought Dominick to climax, or whether him crying out Alfie's name as he spent was enough to make Alfie spill as well.

Either way, he couldn't stop his hips from thrusting again and again even as he began to soften, determined to wring every ounce of pleasure from both their bodies until Alfie's legs loosened around his waist and fell limply to either side of him.

At that, Dominick finally collapsed down on the bed, barely avoiding crushing Alfie beneath him. He was thoroughly spent in every way possible. Heaving an arm over Alfie's waist took the last of his strength, so Dominick lay there, basking in the warm glow still seeping into his bones.

He was about to fall into the best sleep he'd had in months when the sweat-damp body under his arm shifted as Alfie rolled onto his side to face him.

Dominick cracked an eye open to look at him. If Alfie had been debauched before, then he looked absolutely lewd now, like the sort of art that got pamphlets written about it. The ones that always made Dominick snicker at their dire warnings about the dangers of libertines, who were tireless in their efforts to corrupt good men.

He went willingly when Alfie pushed him onto his back, gripping Alfie's thighs to steady him as he climbed onto Dominick's lap.

"You got to go first," said Alfie, his grin turning wicked. "Now it's my turn."

Dominick moaned as Alfie began kissing his way down his chest. Perhaps he should have heeded those pamphlets after all.

CHAPTER 5

B y the time the architect arrived weeks later, Alfie had all
but forgotten Dominick's preposterous idea.

If pressed, he could concede that Gil might be right about the
need to hire more servants, but fortunately Gil was still putting
together his highly specific requirements as to who might be
hired locally based not only on ability, but on with which
families could be trusted to work together and weren't locked in
a bitter war because of a dispute between great-great-great-great
grandfathers about the ownership of a pig during the reign
of Charles II. So far, a single maid had been added to the
household, which had only caused Mrs. Finley to assert that
more were absolutely essential.

Fortunately, the two men who'd driven the coach up from
London were settling in nicely. Martin, the younger of the two,
wouldn't have been hired by any noble home in London as a
footman, falling far short of the ton's aesthetic requirements for
the role. He wasn't anywhere near the standard six feet tall and
his clothes probably looked neater hung on their hooks than
from his skinny shoulders, but he was energetic and happy to
go to and fro on whatever task Mr. Howe assigned.

The older man had stayed with the horses, keeping his role
as driver and allowing Graham to focus fully on his role as
stablemaster. The two had taken to each other like long-lost
brothers. When it came to talking about horseflesh Frank had

no trouble understanding Graham's impenetrable brogue, nor Graham any trouble with Frank's London vowels.

Alfie was still a little unsure about the wisdom of hiring the Londoners—they'd been a little too keen to leave the city when offered the chance—but he could at least be glad they were settling in. Indeed, the other day, he'd seen one of the barn cats contentedly curled up on Frank's lap as he worked on a piece of tack. He'd taken that as a good sign, trusting that a cat's assessment of a man was likely better than his own.

He also trusted Gil's assessment of the number of servants eventually needed to run a home of this size, the country baron's nephew having a far better idea of the needs of manor houses. He could even agree that the garden was an absolute jungle, and if it could be set to rights while also putting some wages into local pockets, then all the better.

But really, Dominick? A folly?

He looked over at the absurd man in question. Dominick had gone out either riding or walking every morning of the last few weeks and positively radiated happiness. Despite it still being a good idea to be seen spending time apart, Alfie joined him for many of his walks, although he was sometimes forced to turn back earlier than anticipated if his leg was bothering him. Sometimes Dominick returned with him, other times Alfie would wave him on. It wasn't as if he wouldn't be seeing plenty of him later.

Dominick was thumbing through a book containing prints of castles and other fortifications they'd found in the library.

"We should get one of those," he said, pointing at the page.

Alfie rolled his eyes. "Nick, a folly is a piece of small, ornamental masonry meant to compliment a view. *That* is Stirling Castle."

Dominick squinted at the picture again. "I think it'd fit."

Before Alfie could get into the many ways that no, Stirling Castle wasn't going to fit on their tiny crag, there was a knock at the drawing room door.

"Enter."

The door opened to reveal young Martin, flanked by a man and woman of middle years.

"Your Lordship. Mr. Trent." Martin said, executing a better bow than any Jarrett had attempted in his time as footman. "This is Captain Clyde McConnell, the architect, and his wife."

Alfie rose from his chair. "A pleasure to meet you both. Please, do sit down. Martin, some refreshments for our guests."

"That's very kind. Thank you, my lord," said Captain McConnell. He had a plain, straightforward Scottish accent, neither too city nor too country, which suited the rest of his features.

His dark hair was greying, but only at the temples, where a pencil tucked behind his ear marked him as one of his profession. He was a larger man, but not too large, with a body that looked neither to run too much to fat nor to muscle. His suit was well-cut, but not too well-cut, and of a brown wool that was neither in nor out of fashion. Neither too old nor too young, too prosperous nor too poor, too fit nor too fat, he was so impressive a specimen of mediocrity that Alfie suspected it had to be intentional.

The only thing noteworthy about him at all was the large case he carried, nearly two feet high and three long, that he placed beside the settee with obvious care.

"Thank you also for seeing me, sir. And you as well, sir," McConnell said, shaking both Alfie and Dominick's offered hands in turn. "It's quite an honour that you would consider McConnell & Co. for such a prestigious undertaking. May I introduce you to my lovely wife, Mrs. Olive McConnell."

Mrs. McConnell's attempt at mediocrity was less successful than her husband's. Her hair fit the part, neither too blonde nor too brown and tied back in a bun that was neither too severe nor too loose. Her poplin dress, neither too old nor too new, was equally unremarkable, and of a colour that Alfie forgot the moment he looked away.

But she was a striking woman, with brown eyes that glittered with a fierce intellect that was impossible to disguise. She was petite, barely reaching her husband's shoulder in height, but Alfie would be the last to label her as fragile, as she carried a case the same size as her husband's in one hand and a pair of long leather tubes tucked under her other arm, tightly sealed to protect the rolled papers within from the elements.

"I appreciate you coming out to meet us," said Alfie as they all took their seats. "This is my cousin, Mr. Dominick Trent. This project is his idea, but I back it wholeheartedly. I take it my man of business sent you a rough idea of what we were looking for?"

"Wholeheartedly" might have been a bit strong, but it was worth it for the smile Dominick flashed him.

Captain McConnell nodded. "Yes, I have Mr. Charleton's letter here. Olive, dear, would you—" but Mrs. McConnell had already retrieved the letter from her case and was passing it over.

"I've actually met Mr. Charleton briefly," said Mrs. McConnell, her accent marking her as an Englishwoman.

"Baron Charleton hired my husband's firm to redesign their rose gardens at his wife's insistence some years back. It was very kind of Mr. Charleton to think so highly of Clyde's work as to recommend us to you after all this time."

"As you see, my wife likes to accompany me on longer projects," said the captain fondly. "And she makes a most excellent secretary."

Mrs. McConnell shook her head. "Clyde exaggerates my abilities."

Alfie doubted that very much.

The fact she remembered Gil after all these years was hardly surprising as he was a very handsome man. But it was also slightly worrying—as he was a very handsome man. Surely, Gil wouldn't have used all this as an excuse to bring back his married paramour? Alfie hated to think it, but he did know the man's reputation with women.

Especially since Gil would likely remember an English woman. There were few enough of them in Scotland and those mostly either in the cities or ensconced at various house parties. Alfie couldn't quite place where in England her accent set her from, but he'd only seen a fraction of the country, which was itself a bare sliver of the world. She could have been from just a few miles outside London for all he knew.

"*Captain*, I believe?" asked Alfie. Out of the corner of his eye, he could see Dominick doing his best not to huff. Yes, he'd rather get down to business as well, but there was an etiquette to these things. "You're a military man?"

"Formerly, yes. Of the Corps of Royal Engineers. That's where I had my training. Mostly surveying work, although I can claim the Georges Head Battery as one of mine. My wife has illustrations of some of the bridges I designed from that time as well. I'm afraid they're rather far away to inspect in person. I was attached to the New South Wales Corps for many years, so much of my work is in Australia.

"When we were recalled in 1810 following that unpleasantness with the rebellion, I decided to make a clean break of it and began my own firm focused purely on the ornamental. I hadn't seen a proper garden in all my time away. Now, it seems that's all I want to do. So, if you're expecting to be able to repel invaders with the folly, I'm sorry to disappoint you."

Australia. Alfie vaguely remembered hearing his father talk about some rebellion there a decade or so back. The place was so remote he might as well have been discussing a war on the moon. So remote, in fact, that even his adoptive parents, known for their travels, had never set foot there and Alfie wasn't sure he'd even met anyone who had.

Dominick might though. Those poor wretched souls who made their way back from penal transportation for their crimes were more likely to end up in Spitalfields than Mayfair, after all.

Not that either of the McConnells seemed like wretched souls. Instead, they seemed quite genial and positively devoted to one another. When Janie came in with tea, Captain McConnell poured his wife's cup before his own. Alfie usually did that for Dominick too, but only when they were alone. Now they each had to fend for themselves.

"Shall we discuss the gardens first, or the folly?" asked Captain McConnell.

"Let's work from the ground up," replied Alfie.

The captain nodded. "An excellent place to start."

They waited while Mrs. McConnell opened one of the tubes and removed a thick roll of papers. Dominick lifted the serving tray and set it on the floor, clearing the low table between the McConnells' settee and his and Alfie's chairs.

"Mr. Charleton sent along a most detailed description of what I might be facing," said the captain. "But I'll need to get a look myself before making any final plans for the garden. I hear it's been neglected for quite some time. Are you more inclined towards the picturesque or gardenesque style?"

Alfie was inclined to let the bloody plants do whatever they wanted and leave him out of it, but apparently that wasn't an option. "I'm afraid that's not an area in which I have enough expertise to judge. You'll have to decide for yourselves."

He waved a hand towards the gardens in question. They were sat in the drawing room, and with the curtains open wide to let in the light, the gardens were only footsteps away. Several large windows ran along the wall, ending in a set of French windows that opened out onto the overgrown mess. If the McConnells wished, they could be in the thicket in moments and see what kind of "esque" it struck them as.

"Very wise indeed, sir. Since your home does have such lovely views of the sea, my inclination is towards picturesque."

As the drawing room was attached to an odd angle of the manor that faced more of the woods that ran up to the chapel than it did the sea, it was clear the McConnells had done their research before meeting. Alfie wasn't sure which idea was more amusing: them skulking around before the appointed meeting hour, taking measurements and hoping they weren't spotted, or Gil sending them detailed sketches, no doubt accurate down to the inch.

"Although many chose to combine the styles," added Mrs. McConnell.

"True, true," her husband replied. "Now that I think of it, a small gardenesque pleasure garden with terracing directly behind the home, then picturesque beyond. Something like this."

He took a clean sheet of paper from his wife's already-outstretched hand and drew the pencil from behind his ear. After a few minutes of furious scribbling, he handed the paper over to Alfie for examination. Seeing Dominick leaning over on the arm of his chair, Alfie tilted the drawing so he could have a better view. He couldn't make much of it himself, lots of circles and intersecting straight lines, but he hummed approvingly.

"Naturally, we'd be able to provide you with a more accurate plan after measuring the existing gardens ourselves," added Mrs. McConnell, which answered that question.

"Naturally," said Alfie.

The next few minutes were filled by an interrogation of botanical preferences neither Alfie nor Dominick had any idea how to answer. That didn't seem to frustrate the McConnells, however. While outwardly, Captain McConnell didn't act overly eager to have free reign over such a prestigious project as the complete redesign of a peer's acreage, Mrs. McConnell was perched on the edge of her seat, furiously scribbling down what few answers they had and adding quite a bit more besides.

"Of course, we will be submitting the final plans for all of this for your authorization and correction before we begin," said Captain McConnell when his wife stopped to get a new pencil, having worn hers dull. "Shall we move on to the star of the piece?"

With that, he unlatched his case. A single rectangular object wrapped in muslin filled the interior from corner to corner. Pulling the cloth back with a flourish, Captain McConnell revealed a painting of a tower on a hill.

But not just any tower, a ruined one. A folly.

All that stood was a single turret, crenelated at the top as if it had once been the corner of a mighty castle dating back to the age of legend, still capable of defending archers in battle or, more likely, saving drunken visitors from falling off the top while admiring the view. There were slits for more archers or sightseers along the tower itself, one large vertical slit near the base for those afraid of heights, followed by a higher one with an additional horizontal slit for whatever crossbow work might need to be done against rampaging sheep, and a final star-shaped opening than had no clear purpose other than decoration.

Jutting out from the tower's base like wings were two ruined sections of walls, one with an arched gap for a window, the other with an equally arched doorway that beckoned the viewer to walk through and perhaps find himself in another realm altogether. The artist had drawn the hillock the folly stood on in bloom, little blue and white flowers making it all look like a place from one of the fairy stories Dominick had told him as children. All in all, it was as fantastical as it was ridiculous and far too much of both for what they were looking for.

Alfie was nearly about to say as much, but then he glanced over at Dominick. He was staring at the painting with a look of wonder. Suddenly, Alfie felt dizzy and for a brief moment it wasn't his strong, brave lover he saw in the chair next to him, but the boy he'd been once. The boy whose blonde hair was perpetually dirty and whose gap-toothed grin was always a little more pinched with worry than a child's should ever have to be.

Then the vision faded, leaving only the grown man once more. For the first time, Alfie wondered if those fairy stories had been for him alone or if those tales of escaping to magical lands had meant just as much to Dominick—perhaps even more.

He looked back at the tower. *Bloody hell.* They had to have it.

Captain McConnell pointed to some of the finer details in the painting. "This is only a depiction of what the folly should look like upon construction, as it is an entirely original idea of my own and not yet in existence. I have blueprints as well if you're interested in the more technical specifics. Normally, I wouldn't have this much to show you so early in the process, but we'd already been commissioned by a gentleman of note, who shall remain nameless, to build this on his property in Yorkshire. Alas, he did not have the means he initially claimed, although we did not find this out until a great deal of draughtsmanship had already been done."

Mrs. McConnell opened the other leather tube, laying out a stack of neat, mathematical drawings depicting the construction of the tower.

"We have figures on the material and labour costs from the original design as well," she said, removing a lower sheet of paper from the stack. The amount was eye-watering, but not as much as he'd feared. "It will need to be adjusted for County Fife expenses as opposed to those in Yorkshire. And this is all pending my husband's thorough inspection of the site, but I've never met a problem he couldn't solve. Without bias, I can say that this design is Clyde's finest work. I believe it is fate that such a triumph should end up here instead of its originally intended, yet far less scenic, location."

Alfie didn't even need to look at Dominick again to know what his expression would be. He did anyway, because he enjoyed looking at him.

Dominick's eyes were wide, like those of a child who was being offered some marvellous treat, but wasn't entirely certain he'd be allowed to take it. His eyes kept flickering over different details of the painting and his fingers twitched as if to touch. It was a side to him Alfie didn't get to see very often, the part that hadn't been calloused over by harsher and harsher years to the point where he ignored the things he wanted because he'd never be allowed to have them. He'd almost driven Alfie away before they'd even begun because of this and he still fought tooth and nail every time he was introduced to some new luxury. He'd learned to hide his wants, so at least the wanting itself could never be taken away.

But now, Alfie could see he *wanted*.

And apparently what he wanted was a castle. His lover certainly didn't do things by half-measures.

Alfie turned back to the McConnells. "When can you begin?"

CHAPTER 6

The McConnells began work immediately. Within days, there were men with plumb lines, folding rulers, and brass instruments whose purpose Dominick couldn't even begin to guess climbing all over the crag, the captain leading the charge. The gardens were similarly overrun, albeit at a slower pace. Apparently, there were good times and bad times to cut back plants, and late summer was good for some but not others. It made about as much sense to Dominick as the brass instruments, but he left that to the experts.

Each morning when the men arrived to begin their work, he felt a stab of guilt that he wasn't among them. After a life of scrounging for any penny he could get, sitting back while others laboured was a strange feeling, but it wasn't as if he knew how to tell if a rock was solid, or if the wild brambles in the garden were weeds that should be burned or the rarest blooms in all the world. Perhaps when the real work began, he could lend a hand. He might not know what he was doing, but he had a strong back and could dig where pointed.

And so the summer rolled on, the heat of August at last giving way to the cool of September. More men began to trickle in then as they finished their own harvests and sought other work. By the time the first lashings of autumn wind came tearing through, bearing the scent of storms at sea, the garden had been transformed from a thicket into a patch of near-bare earth, the few plants deemed worthy of remaining spotted amongst the stacks of their fallen comrades. So much had been cut back that he couldn't walk from the back of the house to the forest without encountering stacks of brush taller than a man and twice as wide waiting to be burned. As soon as they were, new piles would be built upon the same spot, even larger than before.

Judging by the greater circle of ash surrounding it, the nearest one wasn't quite at the burning stage yet, but was more solid than some of the earlier stacks, containing off-cuts from trees felled at the top of the crag and now stacked neatly in piles of logs ready to be trimmed down to firewood. Captain McConnell's men had stripped the forest from the crag's peak and in its place, the tower was beginning to take shape. Dominick could see it from his bedroom window and every morning it delighted him anew.

It was a silly, frivolous thing, something he would've sneered at back when he was Dominick Trickner. But he was Mr. Dominick Trent now, and what was the point of having an earl for a lover if you didn't indulge in the occasional bit of fancy?

Someone certainly needed to teach Alfie how to indulge like an earl. His adoptive parents might have gotten him the education and clothes he needed for the title, but when he'd found Dominick, he'd still been living in their dusty townhouse with only a single servant. Back then, it had seemed like a disgusting amount of luxury for one man, but after spending time in Bath and seeing how toffs lower on the social scale than Alfie lived with their wild fashions, glittering parties, and foods so fancy as to be nearly unrecognisable, Dominick had to wonder if by society's standards, Alfie had been living like a pauper this entire time.

Well, that was one thing Dominick could fix. If Alfie wouldn't spoil himself, then Dominick would have to do it for him. Because the folly was a silly, frivolous thing, but it was one he could tell Alfie enjoyed as much as he did, despite his protests. If he truly thought it a terrible idea, he wouldn't stand with his arms wrapped around Dominick in the mornings, chin tucked over his shoulder, pointing out the progress that had been made the day before and placing wagers on how much would be completed by day's end.

By now, it looked like progress had about reached the point where it went from work that needed minds to work that needed manpower. Perhaps tomorrow he'd see if a free hand was needed. He'd have bet on it this morning with Alfie, but the lazy sod had still been abed when Dominick got up for his morning walk, still wrung out from claiming the prize of their daily wager the night before.

Dominick slowed as the dirt path beneath his feet turned to gravel. If someone had told him a few years ago to envision himself as a country squire, he'd have told them that sort of thing cost extra. But now here he was, returning from his daily morning stroll like a proper little parson. Today he'd explored several of the forest paths and couldn't hold back his smile when this one let out on the road just before the manor's gateposts, exactly as he'd thought it might. A few more minutes and he'd be back at Balcarres with a real, Hirkins-cooked breakfast waiting for him, then a full day of riding or exploring or simply annoying Alfie to look forward to. He was the luckiest man alive.

His smile faded as he approached the pillars marking the manor's gate.

Even from a distance, he could tell there was something wrong. The pillars were made of grey stone, but today each of them was topped with something white.

Something white and also red.

At first, he couldn't believe what he was seeing, but the droning hum of flies that grew louder with every step convinced him.

He stopped in front of one pillar and stared up into the dark, dull, dead eyes of the sheep's head. Just the head. The other pillar held the same, although the mouth of that head yawned grotesquely, jaw hanging open in one last silent bleat as flies landed on its lolling tongue. Blood still oozed from the stumps of the necks, the red obscenely bright against the dull stone. In some places it had begun to thicken and darken, but not before running down the pillars in ghastly rivulets.

"Christ," he whispered, the full horror of the scene striking him at once.

Then another, even more horrifying thought struck him. *Someone did this intentionally.*

Suddenly, the woods at his back didn't seem quite so peaceful and inviting. Someone did this. At best, it was a sick joke, but who would behead two sheep just for a joke? And why?

He remembered the farmer's pointed avoidance of Alfie at this very gate just months ago, but surely no one here could hate him so much that they'd kill precious livestock just to make a point. Still, two mollies in the manor, two dead beasts at the gate. If someone had left the heads after hearing rumours about him and Alfie, the message was a clear one.

A crawling sensation came over him and he couldn't help glancing over his shoulders, looking each way down the empty road. Perhaps the animals were being butchered anyway and some of the village youths had decided it would be fun to frighten those toffs up at the manor. Or to impress one of their mates hired to work on the folly.

"Christ," he whispered again.

It was a Sunday, so there weren't any workers today, but by tomorrow the heads would be an even more gruesome sight. At least he'd come across them first, before anyone else saw them. But he couldn't just leave them there. The few members of the manor household who attended church would be leaving any minute.

Message or not, the idea of poor Janie being subjected to something so terrible steeled his resolve. Biting back bile, he reached up and gripped the sheep's head by an ear before flinging it into the bushes beside the road. Then he did the same to the other head, gagging when a fly crawled out of the ear and across the back of his hand.

He shook his hand reflexively and stared at the pillars—now head-free but still bloody. There wasn't anything he could do about that, however. He'd have a quiet word with Martin when he got back, see if he couldn't run down with a bucket and rag as quickly as possible. He'd speak to Gil too. If the sheep had been stolen before being killed, he'd know best how to handle it.

With that, he slowly made his way up the drive, resisting the urge to look back with every step. By the time he made it to the manor, he'd almost stopped listening for the sound of footsteps following him. Almost.

As he handed his coat off to Mr. Howe, he quickly told the man what he'd found, trying to make it sound less sinister than it felt.

"Good heavens, sir. What a dreadful thing. I'll have Martin see to it at once," said the butler, as if Dominick had said nothing more shocking than he'd gotten a spot of mud on his coat. Perhaps Dominick was overreacting and this sort of thing happened all the time in the country. Or perhaps the butler just did a better job of hiding his worry than Dominick could.

"Breakfast is just being laid out, sir," Mr. Howe continued, the matter already resolved or at least doing a good job of pretending it was.

"Thank you, Mr. Howe."

Dominick wasn't sure he could eat, but he didn't know what else to do, so he followed his nose towards the breakfast room.

By the time he arrived, the smell of eggs, bacon, and freshly baked bread had almost driven the horror from his mind. Certainly his stomach had already forgotten, and growled in anticipation as he stepped into the room.

The pale green walls glowed in the morning light that streamed in through the French windows, their gleaming white trim seeming ready to float free. The windows looked out now onto the empty garden, but from the final drawings McConnell provided, come spring it would be beautiful.

For all the art and armour displayed throughout the manor, it was this room Dominick thought the most impressive. A room for no other purpose than to have breakfast. It was a luxury he'd never even considered possible. Or necessary. Well, it still wasn't necessary, but it was damned nice.

Feeling a little better, he patted one of the stone lions beside the door and made his way towards the sideboard. Mrs. Hirkins was stood there, just setting down a tray that smelled of such perfectly seasoned kippers that his mouth began to water.

Since their return, he'd eaten like a glutton at every meal, Mrs. Hirkins having taken command of the kitchen like Admiral Nelson stepping onto the deck of the *Victory*, with Agnes as her trusted second-in-command. From what he could tell, Janie didn't put up much of a fight and neither did anyone else after the first batch of Bath buns.

"Good morning Mrs. Hirk—ah, and Agnes." Dominick stumbled as Agnes stepped out from behind her grandmother. He'd seen rather more of Agnes than he needed to the night baby James arrived and neither of them had quite been able to look each other in the eye since.

Mrs. Hirkins scowled. "What kind of a morning can it be when you have a thankless grandchild intent on driving herself into a grave?"

Dominick didn't have an answer for that and sincerely doubted he ever would.

Agnes slammed the toast caddy down. "Oh, you're one to talk! You're retired, gran! How many hours have you spent in that kitchen this week? This morning even? That's not your job anymore. It's mine!"

"You just had a child! You should be resting. Besides, what's to be done with him if you're working? Put him in the cook pot? Let him play with the pretty little knives? 'Oh there goes Old Hirkins' great-grandson. You can tell which one's him by counting the fingers.'"

The women glared at each other. If Dominick laughed now, he'd be back to eating Janie's raw eggs in no time.

"You're lucky Master Alfie offered you this position," Mrs. Hirkins continued. There was anger in her voice, but worry as well. "You think many other houses let their servants have children? Never mind any houses this grand, any houses at all? The least you could do is be thankful I'm making it easier for you."

"I am grateful!" shouted Agnes. "But I'm worried for you too. You should be knitting by a fire, not stirring a cauldron over it."

A small fist appeared over Agnes' shoulder as if to say, "Hear, hear!" Then the crying began.

What Dominick had thought was simply a shawl tied around Agnes turned out to be some sort of complicated sling from which could now be heard the shrill cries of an infant, likely ringing throughout the entire manor. While Balcarres was sprawling, the thick stone walls which usually muffled every sound to an eerie silence carried the baby's cries far further than they should. More than one night Dominick had awoken to hear the wailing and each time it took him longer to fall back asleep. He'd slept through far worse, but there was something haunting about the way the sound echoed through the manor until the cries seemed to come from both within and without.

Those nights, he'd reach across the bed to make sure Alfie was there, that this wasn't some awful dream.

"And now you've woken him," Agnes sighed, shrugging the sling off one shoulder so she could tend to James. The two women ceased arguing then, engrossed in trying to comfort the baby. His face was red and he was having none of it, freeing a second fist from the sling and swinging both as he wailed.

Dominick didn't have much experience with babies, but based on the strength of his lungs, this one seemed healthy enough, so Agnes must be handling things well. But there was no reason not to make her life easier if possible, and the happier she was, the happier Mrs. Hirkins was, and the happier they all would be.

"Gil hired some women to clean out the east wing. They'll be starting soon, but I could have some moved to the kitchen instead," he offered. "More help there should make things easier for you. Or one could even mind him while you worked."

Dominick felt quite proud of his solution. James would be safe, Mrs. Hirkins would stop fretting, and he could continue to enjoy Agnes' excellent breakfasts. His empty stomach growled again in approval.

The two women, however, looked less pleased.

"Sir," Agnes tried but was cut off by her grandmother.

"You think it's all much of a muchness, is it? Airing linens or roasting duck? It's a miracle that Janie girl didn't poison you all. And as for his own personal minder! Why not just hang up a banner in the town square saying, 'His Lordship's mistress has come to roost and his by-blow with her!'"

"Nan!" Agnes shouted, while Dominick was still reeling.

James was *not* Alfie's child. It was impossible for many reasons. Firstly, Dominick himself—that was a major one. And even if Alfie had somehow taken leave of his senses, become a completely different man and thrown Dominick over, he certainly wouldn't do it with *Agnes*.

Not only was Alfie not inclined towards women at all, but Agnes was barely more than a girl. Alfie would never take advantage of a near-child in such a way. And if he had, he certainly wouldn't have survived Mrs. Hirkins finding out about it.

Dominick's confusion must have been clear on his face, because Agnes looked up from soothing James to add quietly, "There've been whispers, sir."

He gritted his teeth. "There fucking won't be any more. Who?"

"And how would that look?" Mrs. Hirkins asked. "The more it's denied, the more it'll spread. Start punishing them who spread it, and it'll go like wildfire. James will be known as the earl's bastard all his life. No. Ignore it and let the gossip burn out on its own."

"It doesn't even make any sense. Any fool who can count to nine months would know Alfie was still here in Scotland when James was…" He trailed off, not knowing how to finish that sentence without getting slapped.

"Gossip doesn't need to make sense," sighed Agnes. "Especially not when it's this good."

Dominick understood. The bachelor earl sending his personal carriage from London to his secluded manor carrying a pregnant woman with her own driver, footman, and an elderly female servant to attend her, then dashing home himself just in time for the birth.

Bloody hell. That was scandalous enough, but to then hire his mistress to be his cook? That was more than just scandalous, that could truly hurt Alfie.

Dominick had seen enough to know reputation was everything with toffs. It wasn't just that he'd stop being invited to parties, Alfie probably wouldn't mind that. But proper folk might not want to do business with him, or his bank want him as a client. All to save their blessed reputations. Not that half of them hadn't done the same or worse. And if they started whispering about that, what other odd behaviours of the earl might suddenly seem worthy of closer examination.

Gil had hinted at such a thing that night at supper. And that sort of scandal—*their* sort of scandal, would do more than just hurt Alfie, it would *ruin* him.

Dominick would never let that happen.

"What should we do?" he asked helplessly. "Just keep on as we have and wait for it to die out?"

"For the best," said Mrs. Hirkins decisively. "And you'll have a crib put in the kitchen—well away from the fires, mind you! And I will let Agnes do most of the cooking when James is in the crib."

She sniffed. "I think that's more than fair."

James seemed to agree, because his crying had gone from shrieking to a mere grumble.

Agnes nodded. "Thank you though, for your concern."

"Move along, Agnes," Mrs. Hirkins tutted. "We've kept him from his breakfast. Much work to do."

With that, they finally moved out of the way of the sideboard and headed off into the house, James bouncing along on his mother's hip. Dominick's worry was momentarily overwhelmed by his hunger and he helped himself to several platefuls. Then the worry returned, and he stewed on that for several hours. But by that time, he'd completely forgotten about telling Martin to fetch a crib from the attic.

He would regret his forgetfulness that evening.

CHAPTER 7

I t was an hour or so before supper and Dominick was in the library enjoying the glass of port Jarrett had already poured before he arrived. He'd been unsurprised to find Alfie and Gil there, sat either side of the chessboard, and was happy to settle into a chair by the fire while they frowned over the inscrutable game, taking turns moving their pieces in patterns Dominick didn't understand, nor care to learn.

"There's an advertisement in the paper that might interest you," Gil said distractedly, moving one of his pieces in a way that made Alfie scowl. "Page four, I believe."

Dominick picked up the discarded paper from the chair beside his, something with the outlandish name of *The Caledonian Mercury,* whatever that meant. He squinted at page four, the tiny print almost impossible to read. He had to read it several times to himself before he was sure of all the words, then groaned and read it aloud.

"Esteemed Architect, CAPTAIN CLYDE MCCONNELL, formerly of the CORPS OF ROYAL ENGINEERS, who has designed such fine works in both the COLONY OF NEW SOUTH WALES and in SCOTLAND, is honoured to announce his latest assignment for the RT HONOURABLE ALFRED PENNINGTON THE EARL OF CRAWFORD at the earl's residence, BALCARRES HOUSE in County Fife. Captain McConnell is assisted by his esteemed wife OLIVE in the construction of both a folly—his finest work—and gardens for the earl that will soon be marked as the most beautiful in the county if not nation."

"Kind of him to mention his wife," Gil added. "There's another in *The Times* and that edition's some weeks old. He must have started running them as soon as the ink was dry on the contract."

Alfie moved one of his black pieces and took a smaller one of Gil's off the board. "I suppose I don't mind him using my name, but I'd have preferred he asked first."

Now it was Gil's turn to scowl at the board. "You wanted to improve your image," he said at last.

"Yes, but I'm not sure it needed improving to the point of being 'the most beautiful in the county if not nation.'"

"I was thinking I'd go offer them a hand tomorrow," Dominick said. "Me being there should improve its looks enough to at least get you best in Scotland."

He remembered too late that they were trying to be discreet, but it wasn't as if the other men in the room would go pointing fingers.

Alfie huffed out a small laugh, but Gil looked pained.

"I'd advise against that," he said evenly. "In line with improving Alfie's image, at best, the cousin of an earl lowered to such physical work upsets the natural order. At worst, it could be seen as taking a day's wage from an honest labourer."

"You're joking."

Gil shrugged. "I'm only the second son to a second son to a barony and while I was certainly put to work as a child to *learn the land*, I haven't been allowed to do so much as hang a painting since I was old enough to ship off to university. Since then the only proper things I can get my hands on are the accounts."

From how fiercely Gil tackled those, they probably wouldn't need to hire any other labourers at all if the man was allowed to wield a hammer.

More toff nonsense.

Dominick read the advertisement again, then glanced through the rest of the paper. The world seemed to be in the same mess it always was and deciphering the tiny letters hurt his eyes, so he set it aside. Watching the chess match quickly bored him, but fortunately, there was a much more entertaining game going on.

Jarrett had taken it upon himself to be unusually attentive tonight. Normally, that would be a trial as Dominick was forced to fend off the man's constant advances, but tonight he found himself being ignored. Thinking back, Jarrett hadn't been nearly as much of a pest these last few months as he'd been before they'd left, and Dominick was starting to suspect why. While he sat ignored with his glass of port nearly down to the dregs, Jarrett had stepped forward to refill Gil's glass any time the man took more than a single sip. And if the soft looks Gil gave him every time were anything to judge by, the poor fool was completely besotted. With *Jarrett* of all people.

Well, well, well. The two had been dancing around each other since before he and Alfie had left for London. Clearly, they hadn't been the only ones having adventures in the last few months.

He tried to catch Alfie's eye so he could share this revelation, but Alfie was too absorbed in his game to notice. So he missed the next time Jarrett leaned in to refill Gil's glass, placing his hand on the back of Gil's collar as he did as if it steady himself, his thumb running over the skin at the back of Gil's neck, the intimacy and intent of the motion unmistakable.

Gil shivered, which was the exact moment the door to the library was violently flung open.

All four men froze in place.

Mrs. Hirkins stomped in, hand on one hip, baby on the other. She took one look at the tableau and narrowed her eyes at Alfie.

"Are you building a *hareem*?" she hissed.

Alfie started, his eyes going comically wide. Then he looked over at Gil and Jarrett and his eyes went even wider. Dominick could see the moment it clicked into place. Alfie gaped, but didn't say anything, his mouth opening and closing like a fish.

Dominick couldn't help it. He laughed, and once he started, he couldn't seem to stop. He'd been wondering how long it would take Alfie to notice their property manager's interests didn't actually lie with women but instead with their valet.

Alfie was one of the smartest men he knew, but utterly oblivious sometimes. Yet Mrs. Hirkins only needed to see them together once, the crafty old bird.

The image of a feathered Mrs. Hirkins looking disapprovingly down her beak made him laugh even harder. Then she turned her narrow gaze on him and suddenly everything seemed less funny.

"I don't know what you're laughing at," she hissed again. "As well he should. Master Alfie can do far better than the useless sod you are. You said you'd sort a crib for the kitchen."

Dominick shrank back in his chair. "I—"

"I, I, I," Mrs. Hirkins muttered. "No crib. No other kitchen staff hired, just a lot of sweaty men digging up rocks in the garden and stealing our water to pour all over themselves without refilling the buckets!"

Jarrett made a noise at the mention of wet, sweaty men, briefly drawing Mrs. Hirkins' ire before she turned her focus back to Dominick.

"Try carrying a raw chicken in one hand and a babe in the other when it's time to start the pot. Not a mistake you'd want to make. So. You said you'd arrange a crib, and here we are. No crib."

Then to Dominick's abject horror, she came over and gently but forcefully sat James in his lap. Dominick's hands came up to cradle the baby's head instinctively, which earned him the briefest nod.

"Not as good a proper crib, but you'll have to do. I'm needed back in the kitchen. Master Alfie, supper will be ready in half an hour."

While Alfie got a smile, she gave the rest of them a long look. Then she sniffed, turned on her heel, and was gone, leaving the library door pointedly open in her wake.

The four—well, five—of them sat there in stunned silence. Then James began to cry.

Dominick looked down as James' face fell. One tiny hand gripped Dominick's sleeve as he gazed back up, his little eyes welling with tears. Dominick's heart tugged. He'd always had a soft spot for poor little things, and James was so small and helpless. Dominick was afraid to move in case he'd fall apart in his hands.

He gave the other men a pleading glance.

Gil raised his hands. "Don't look at me."

"Whisky," Jarrett offered. "I've heard a little on the gums quiets them right up."

"I'm not giving a baby whisky," snapped Dominick, then immediately regretted it when that seemed to make James cry harder.

"Sorry, dove," he whispered, bouncing James gently on his knee. Babies liked to be bounced, didn't they?

This one didn't, so Dominick looked at Alfie, his last hope.

The expression on Alfie's face was one he didn't recognise, but his voice was gentle when he said. "Perhaps some fresh air?"

"We'll see to a crib while you do that," Gil said, rising from his chair and giving Jarrett a pointed look. Dominick imagined they'd be up in the attics for quite a while, coming back down with cobwebs in their hair, having only spent a minute of that time actually looking for a crib. He hoped spiders bit them in unpleasant places.

They filed out, but Dominick remained rooted in his chair.

Alfie rose and stood over Dominick with his hands on his hips, his stance an uncomfortable mirror of Mrs. Hirkins'.

"You knew about this," Alfie said accusingly.

"What, James? He's a bit hard to miss. If I'd known I'd be stuck with him though, I'd have done a better job of remembering that crib."

Alfie shook his head. "Not him. Gil. Why didn't you say anything?"

"Ah. That." Dominick shrugged, careful the movement didn't dislodge his charge. "It wasn't my place to tell."

And it was damned funny watching you figure it out, he didn't add.

Alfie let out a sniff as disapproving as any of Mrs. Hirkins' best.

"I'm still not happy." Alfie's mouth twisted. "But really? Jarrett?"

"You're the one who added him to your hareem. Clearly you and Gil have similar tastes."

"Don't you start. Come on, if we're going to take this one on a walk we'd best start now before it gets dark." Alfie started to walk away.

"Alfie?"

"Yes, Nick?"

"How am I supposed to hold onto this blasted thing and stand at the same time?"

This time, it was Alfie who couldn't stop laughing.

Chapter 8

Alfie wasn't entirely certain what babies required to be happy, but being held against Dominick's chest while the man whispered sweet nothings seemed to do the trick.

He understood completely.

"Lovely little thing, isn't he?" Dominick asked, propping James up a little higher so the babe's head rested on his shoulder. "At least when he's not screaming the walls down."

"An activity which does fill much of his day," replied Alfie, trying not to be jealous of an infant.

Despite his initial protests, Dominick handled the child well. Cradling him protectively as they made their way down the front steps, one large hand holding his head as Dominick took every step with care. James had quieted almost instantly, emitting only the occasional coo as they walked.

Alfie swallowed around the hard lump in his throat. In another life, Dominick could have passel of children if he wanted. Still could in this life, if it wasn't for Alfie.

"Did you ever want children?" he asked. He hadn't meant to, but now that the question was out, it couldn't be withdrawn.

Dominick gave him a flat look as if he knew exactly what Alfie had been thinking. "Don't be daft."

"You could though," Alfie said, unable to resist poking the bruise. "You—that is, you've said before that you, ah, enjoy women as well."

The last part he said in a hushed whisper, mindful of both their circumstances and tiny ears hearing things they shouldn't.

Dominick gasped theatrically. "My God, do I? Then there's no time to waste! Tell Graham to saddle a horse! I'm needed in the village!"

"Be serious."

"Oh, I am," replied Dominick. "I'll have to go to the village. None of the women at Balcarres will have me, they've too high standards. Do you think I should alert the minister on the way in so the first banns can be read, or just start fucking anything in skirts and deal with the formalities later?"

"Language!" Alfie hissed, fighting the urge to cover James' ears.

Dominick rolled his eyes. "That's what you're worried about? I'm sure with Mrs. Hirkins as his great-grandmother he's heard far worse just today."

Alfie felt ridiculous. Not just for chastising Dominick about swearing in front of a child far too young to understand, but for his moment of insecurity. He'd never questioned Dominick's love for him. And he hoped he'd never given Dominick reason to question his in return. To think Dominick would throw him over after five minutes of holding a baby was just that—ridiculous.

"I'm being an arse, aren't I?"

"Language," Dominick grinned. "And you are, but no more than usual. I'm used to it by now though, so I suppose I'll keep you."

"You'd better," Alfie said, but couldn't stop the last little doubt from seeping out. "But still, you're all right with it? It's not as if I'll ever be able to give you a family."

Dominick's grin turned wicked. "I don't know, perhaps we just haven't been trying hard enough."

Alfie's response to that was cut off as they turned at the corner of the house to find Janie kneeling on the ground. She started when she saw them.

"Oh, sirs, I'm sorry! I'm not going out, I swear, I just had a moment to myself and well, I am out, but I wasn't going out. Just out here, sirs."

"Of course. I quite understand," said Alfie to spare them from further explanation. "It is a lovely evening for it. Just needed some fresh air as well?"

"Oh no, sir. Milk."

As if he recognised the word, James began to stir, only to be hushed by Dominick. Janie looked at him quizzically, but had sense enough not to ask why they were playing nursemaid to the cook's child. It was just as well, as Alfie wasn't sure he had an answer to give her.

"Aye, sir," she said slowly. "Bread and milk. Not for myself, that is. But the broonies."

At some point, Alfie's life had made sense, he was sure of it. Just because he couldn't remember such a time now didn't mean it hadn't existed.

Dominick frowned. "Broonies?"

"Aye, the guid folk." At their blank expressions, Janie continued, speaking very slowly, as if she was surprised they had survived so long with only their current amount of wits. "Spirits that come out at night and cause mischief, making trinkets disappear or tangling horses' manes, that sort of thing. But they like milk and bread, so if you leave a bit out for them, they'll do good mischief instead, like returning lost items or getting hens to lay. I heard Mrs. McConnell say she was going to plant lilies, so we'll have something in bloom come spring. If you ask me, the ground is too damp for them. She'd be better off with bell heather. So I'm hoping a bit of milk and bread will get the broonies to keep her lily bulbs from rotting in the earth."

Alfie looked down and sure enough, at Janie's feet sat a small saucer of milk with a roll of fresh dark bread steaming on the doorstep beside it.

"There's more of them about than usual." She held out an empty saucer. "Before they took only sips and barely touched the bread, but lately they've both been gone each morning."

"Well," Alfie tried. He was rarely at a loss for words, but Janie seemed to be expecting some sort of a reply. "Thank you for looking after the household, Janie. Now you'd better be off. I'm sure Mrs. Finley is looking for you."

She bobbed a quick curtsey, then made her way back through the side door, leaving Alfie and Dominick staring down at the saucer.

"I thought the barn cats looked fatter," Dominick said at last.

Alfie shrugged. "If she's willing to steal from a Hirkins' kitchen, she's braver than me. I don't suppose there's any harm in it?"

"I can't think of any. Besides, we're trying to get you on better terms with the locals, why not the local spirits as well?"

Alfie snorted. "I suppose you're right. Perhaps the broonies will work some good mischief on my leg while they're at it. I'm feeling well enough at the moment though, shall we walk down to the main road while we have the time?"

To his surprise, Dominick shuddered. "How about a bit of the path to the chapel and back instead. Found some things on the gateposts this morning. You were busy all day, so I haven't had a chance to tell you."

As they made their way down the forested path, Dominick explained his grisly findings of that morning.

Alfie shuddered, glad the sun was only beginning to settle over the horizon and he didn't have to hear about anything so awful in the dark. He looked at James to make sure he wasn't disturbed by the tale, but he was curled up under Dominick's chin, his little pink mouth open in sleep, and drooling on Dominick's coat.

"What do you think it means?" Alfie asked.

Dominick shrugged. "I was hoping you might know. Just a prank, I'm hoping. Or poachers."

"But knowing our luck..." Alfie trailed off. He slowed to a stop, the forest ahead suddenly looking far less inviting.

Knowing their luck, someone had seen something they shouldn't and this was a silent threat. Hopefully, it wouldn't go any further. But again, knowing their luck...

"We've been discreet," he said at last. "Certainly more than we were before."

Maddeningly so sometimes. It wasn't fair that his own valet was apparently allowed to get his hands all over his overseer whenever he wanted and Alfie couldn't do the same to Dominick. Yes, Alfie clearly valued his life more than Jarrett did, but still.

"Not discreet enough, it seems," Dominick said, rubbing soothing circles on James' back. His thoughts seemed to be following similar lines to Alfie's. "What's the bloo-blasted point in being an earl if you can't do what you want with who you want?"

"Being able to hire the best barristers if you're caught?"

"Mm, let's try not to let things get to that point."

Alfie thought of Dominick's description of the bloody sheep heads and felt a shiver of fear and revulsion. "If they haven't already."

"Maybe it was the broonies?" Dominick offered.

Alfie smiled at the joke, thin as it was, but happy to let the conversation stray to less dangerous grounds. "If these broonies are capable of doing something like *that*, I see why Janie wants to stay on their good side."

"If they're that strong though, I'd rather they be put to work on something more important than Mrs. McConnell's lilies."

"Don't let her hear you say that," said Alfie. "I'd like to remain in her good graces, considering the circumstances. I certainly don't want to risk my chance of having 'the most beautiful in the county if not nation' now that the opportunity has presented itself."

"And we've already seen what damage a vengeful woman with a love of plants can cause," Dominick added. "All right, if the broonies want to protect her garden, I'll leave them to it."

The wind chose that moment to rustle through the leaves in agreement, and Alfie could almost swear he heard the snap of a branch somewhere nearby. He shook off the image of swarms of mischievous spirits listening in from the trees and waiting for darkness to fall before descending upon Balcarres.

He fought down a shudder. "Perhaps we should turn back. I'm sure it's nearly time for supper."

Dominick nodded, hoisting James up a little higher on his shoulder as he did.

"Is he heavy?" Alfie honestly had no idea how much babies weighed. It couldn't be that much, surely? "I could carry him back if you want."

"He is a bit," Dominick said slowly. Then he glanced at Alfie's cane. "But he's asleep now, it might be better not to move him too much."

Alfie tried not to feel hurt at the refusal. Dominick was kind not to say it directly, but he was right. A baby, an uneven forest path, and an unreliable leg were a recipe for disaster. "I suppose only one of us needs to be returning with a collar covered in spittle."

"Did he really?" Dominick tried to crane his neck enough to look and Alfie felt a little better.

"Pampered little thing." Dominick sighed. "What about you?"

"Pampered perhaps, but I'd hardly call myself little."

"No," said Dominick as they turned back, the sounds of the forest dampening their voices. "Did you ever want children? You're an earl, after all. It's expected."

It was, but Alfie had spent a great deal of his adult life ignoring that fact. "I'm sure there are plenty of distant cousins who would be happy to take over the earldom once I'm gone. Hopefully not anytime soon. But no, as sweet as James is when he's sleeping, I never had any desire to be a father."

Dominick hummed. "You should know, word's already spreading that you are. And to this little one."

Alfie stumbled and it wasn't at all his leg's fault. "You can't be serious!"

"I only know what I've heard. We just need to be careful that no one goes digging too deeply to find any other secrets."

He didn't have to say anything else. Despite their increased caution, they'd still been too careless if someone was making threats. And with the household growing by the day, they'd have to be more on guard than ever.

They walked in silence for a bit, the atmosphere heavy as the twilight descended around them.

Alfie tried to lighten the mood. "I suppose I can see the resemblance. Natural sense of command, stunning eyes, flawless skin, entire household at his beck and call, yes, he most definitely takes after me."

Dominick snorted. "Full of shite too, I can smell it coming off the both of you."

Alfie wrinkled his nose. He certainly wasn't in a rush to carry James now.

"Still," he continued. "It's a shame his mother isn't of noble blood. Now he'll never be allowed to inherit."

"Christ no, can you imagine some dirty commoner prancing around pretending to be an earl? Who ever heard of such a thing?"

They both snickered and made their way back towards the welcoming lights of the manor as darkness fell in earnest. Just as well too. He knew it was only his imagination, but after Janie's tale about the broonies, Alfie had felt eyes on the back of his neck the entire walk from the woods, and once or twice, thought he heard the sounds of footsteps following them back.

CHAPTER 9

Dominick might not be allowed to work on the folly, but that didn't mean he couldn't *look*.

"Ah, Mr. Trent, good afternoon. Come to keep an eye on things?"

Captain McConnell was carefully stepping his way along the narrow ledge of earth that stood between the new folly and the sudden drop down the crag. As he approached, he wiped his hands with his handkerchief, then reached out to shake Dominick's hand.

"Captain," Dominick said. He liked McConnell. The man had a plain directness to him that Dominick could appreciate. Probably a good trait in a man who dealt in straight lines and solid rock. "What progress today?"

"It's going a bit slower than I'd like," the captain admitted, looking up at the scaffolding around the tower. "But if a project ever went exactly to plan, I'd probably worry more. If we can get another two feet added to this section of the wall before nightfall, I'll be pleased."

Dominick was pleased as well. He didn't know how long these sorts of things usually took, but at the rate McConnell and the army of workers Gil had found were going, it couldn't be more than another month or two until the folly was complete. The tower itself was nearly twenty feet high and while the walls that extended from the sides weren't nearly as tall, each time he visited they were always a little longer and a little higher, giving the impression that the folly wasn't so much being built as growing out of the ground.

It was tall enough now that the room at the base of the tower was complete, with a wooden door already affixed so it could be used to store tools, and several of the stone stairs that would lead to the top of the tower were already spiralling up to nowhere within.

Captain McConnell looked him up and down. "In fact, you've arrived at the perfect time. We're just about to lay the first stone to mark out the window in this wall. It's a larger piece, and you look like you have a strong back, if you don't mind my saying. Care to give us a hand? You'll be able to say you built it yourself."

Dominick ducked his head. "Am I that obvious?" But he was already pulling off his coat so it wouldn't be damaged.

McConnell chuckled. "Most gentlemen want to put their mark on the work at some point in the process. Usually though, I just give them a trowel and let them smooth a bit of mortar. You don't look like you'd collapse under a bit of real labour, but if you'd rather, there's a whole bucket of trowels right behind you."

"I think I'll manage," said Dominick, failing to pretend he wasn't delighted to be put to work. He remembered Gil's warning about upsetting the natural order, but he'd been invited by the captain himself. It would be rude to refuse.

Within minutes, he was lowering a long rectangular block into place, moving it slightly left and right under McConnell's orders. He could feel the strain in his shoulders and it felt good.

"Left a bit. Bit more. Bit more. There! Down!"

Dominick set the block in place.

"Excellent!" exclaimed Captain McConnell, before turning to direct some of the actual workers to the next step in the process. Dominick stayed there a moment, his hand on the stone. Once the folly was complete, he could stand right here, looking out the window to the sea, his hand resting on this very stone and know that he'd been a part of it. A small part perhaps, but when centuries passed and he was long gone, this stone would still be here, and he'd still be a part of Balcarres.

The thought warmed him, sad as it was. He'd have to drag Alfie up here one day, make him lay his own stone so they could both be a part of it.

"Captain McConnell," Dominick said, when the man rejoined him. He rapped his knuckles against the stone, *his* stone. "I think this deserves a celebration. Will you and your wife join us for supper?"

It was an impulsive question, but it seemed like the sort of thing a gentleman would offer. Besides, now that a crib had been safely delivered to the kitchen, Agnes was able to truly focus on her work and had been outdoing herself. The fact her grandmother was still hovering about the kitchen doing twice as much meant that every meal was a bounty best shared, and Captain McConnell seemed like the sort of man to enjoy a good meal.

"We'd be honoured!" the captain beamed, then his face fell. "Unfortunately, however, we've already accepted an invitation for this evening."

"Invite them along. I can have word sent when I get back to the manor." Dominick offered. Surely no one would turn down the offer to dine with the earl, and he was in too good a mood to delay.

"If you're certain," said Captain McConnell hesitantly. At Dominick's nod, he pulled out a notebook and scribbled a few lines before tearing the sheet out and passing it over.

"Wonderful," Dominick said, tucking the note into his waistcoat pocket and gathering up his discarded coat. "Who should it be sent to?"

Dominick found Alfie in the library, eyes closed in sleep and a book in danger of slipping from his fingers to the floor. Shutting the door softly behind him, he removed the book and set it on a side table before pressing a kiss to Alfie's hair.

"Mm, Nick?"

Dominick gave him another kiss, this one on sleep-softened lips. "Forgive me. I've done something dreadful."

Alfie's eyes flew open, and Dominick put a hand against his chest to keep him from leaping out of the chair.

"Not that sort of dreadful," he added. "No one's bleeding."

That was enough to get Alfie to relax at least a little.

"Go on then. What dreadful thing have you done?"

"I've invited the McConnells to supper."

"That doesn't seem so bad." Alfie wrinkled his nose. "A bit short notice, but to be honest, I probably should have extended an offer weeks ago."

"They already had plans, though, so I told them just to invite the others along as well."

That was enough to make Alfie tense again. He'd known Dominick more than long enough to know he wasn't going to like what he said next.

"Who?"

Dominick braced himself for Alfie's reaction. "The Carnbees."

"Magistrate Carnbee?" Alfie hissed. "Oh, for God's sake, Nick!"

"I didn't know it was them when I offered!"

Alfie groaned. "Well, it's done now. And it's not like they can turn down supper with the earl, even if they think this place is a den of murderers. Tell Jarrett to make himself scarce though, just to be safe."

"I will," Dominick said, kissing Alfie again. "Sorry."

"It's not the worst thing you've done," said Alfie, which was true. No one was bleeding.

Alfie pressed a finger against Dominick's lips, halting yet another apology kiss. "It might even mend some bridges. However, *you* get to be the one to tell Mrs. Hirkins she and Agnes are cooking for seven tonight instead of three."

Dominick groaned, but it was a punishment he deserved.

To say Mrs. Hirkins was unhappy about the new supper arrangements was putting it mildly.

"I'm just meant to pull another two ducks out of the air? Fully plucked ones too, because Lord knows we haven't the time for that! Perhaps in a proper city, but the flea-bitten souse that calls himself a butcher here never delivers half what I ask nor half on time neither!

"Nan, I think we can manage," Agnes offered quietly, but she didn't look any more pleased than her grandmother.

"We might manage, if that girl Janie wasn't filching half the larder for the fairies! I tell you, no English spirit eats as well as these Scottish ones. That means no bread to go with the no meat from the butcher. So you tell Master Alfie that if he's expecting supper for seven on no notice, he can just—"

In the end, Dominick decided against conveying the rest of her message.

As it turned out, it was supper for six instead of seven, but that hardly dulled the wrath of the Hirkins. Gil had begged off, claiming a headache that Dominick suspected was more of an unwillingness to share a table with the man who'd had his lover arrested, which was more than fair. In his place, Dominick would've done far worse. Anyone who laid a hand on Alfie was lucky to still be bleeding by the time Dominick was done with them.

Magistrate Carnbee seemed to be just as unhappy about the situation, slumped into his seat across the table, his great moustache twitching with displeasure as he glared down at one of the finest roast ducks Dominick had ever tasted. Carnbee's much younger wife seemed not to notice his dour mood, dividing her time between catching the McConnells up on local gossip and attempting to secure an earl for her second husband.

"Thank you for inviting us to join you this evening, Your Lordship!" she gushed, placing her hand on Alfie's arm. "It was ever so kind. And with such delightful company! Did you know Captain McConnell designed the rose gardens at Charleton House? I know Catriona Charleton quite well, you know. I believe her husband is your overseer's brother. Or is it his cousin? I can never keep track. Regardless, she and I are practically sisters, so I suppose that practically makes me a Charleton as well!"

Practically a suitable wife for a bachelor earl! was what she meant. For once, Dominick was glad he and Alfie had to hide their relationship. He'd already had poison put in his food once and he didn't want to risk it happening again if Madam Carnbee thought he was in the way of her becoming a countess.

Unless she'd heard rumours and the sheep's heads were her way of warning him off.

Unlikely, but not impossible. He couldn't imagine such a flighty woman determinedly dragging two severed heads down the lane and mounting them on the gateposts. If she had though, she'd probably done it as alluringly as possible, just in case the master of the house happened to be watching.

No, Dominick was probably safe from her for now. The magistrate was on his own though. If he wasn't good enough at his job to notice when his wife was blatantly flirting with other men in front of him, then Dominick doubted he'd notice if she poured his tea straight from a bottle of rat poison.

"Actually," said Captain McConnell, drawing some but not all of Madam Carnbee's attention. "I could never have completed Baron Charleton's gardens without the help of my wife."

"Oh Captain, how gracious you are to say such a thing. You know, I think humility is one of the finest traits in a man," Madam Carnbee said, leaning over so Captain McConnell had an uninterrupted view of the lush acreage of her bosom. Apparently, if she couldn't have an earl, a renowned architect and former military man was good enough.

Despite himself, Dominick was impressed. If he'd been half as good as she was at flattering men back when he was working the streets, he'd have had himself a nice set of rooms in Mayfair as a kept man and not that hovel in Spitalfields.

"I'm only telling the truth," Captain McConnell said, oblivious to Madam Carnbee's charms as he gazed at his wife in complete devotion. "I don't think I'd be able to find my socks in the morning if it wasn't for Olive, never mind build gardens or follies or anything larger than a stack of toast."

He reached out and Mrs. McConnell took his hand. Wrapped in his, her hand looked even more delicate. For a moment the two of them just smiled at each other. Dominick knew the look on their faces and couldn't resist a glance at Alfie, knowing his love would be looking at him just the same way. Some things were worth being a little indiscreet, and absolute adoration was one of them.

Then the magistrate harrumphed and the spell was broken. "I'm sure you're exaggerating."

A look of irritation crossed Madam Carnbee's face. Dominick changed his mind. If she poured rat poison into her husband's tea, he'd pass her the spoon to stir it.

Captain McConnell shook his head.

"Not at all. In fact when we met..." He stopped then, and something passed between him and his wife. Then he gave her hand a squeeze. "Why don't you tell it, my dear? You're far better at this sort of thing than I."

"Very well," said Mrs. McConnell, finally drawing her hand back. "Clyde and I met when he was just a young engineer in Australia."

"Young and foolish," the captain interrupted, with a wink at his wife.

She smiled. "Indeed. Foolish enough to forget to bring enough water when they sent him out to survey the bushland. I found him wandering half-dead and nursed him back to health. When I was certain he could walk without tripping over the nearest snake's den, I showed him which trees meant there was water nearby and which berries would give him... a most debilitating sickness. Then I let him go. I was more surprised than anyone when he stumbled back again a few months later, still alive and survey completed."

"And right then and there," Captain McConnell added, "I decided I quite literally couldn't live without her. So I asked her to keep me on the right path for the rest of my life and she agreed."

Madam Carnbee sighed longingly. "That's so romantic."

"My husband exaggerates," Mrs. McConnell said fondly. "He did nothing then except thank me for saving his life. The rest didn't come until we met again by chance some months later on the ship back to Scotland. He had the entire voyage to make up his mind as to my usefulness."

Madam Carnbee shook her head. "That's even more romantic! Brought together by fate in a hostile land, not once, but twice! Is it quite a beautiful place, Australia? I suppose it would have to be, to make up for all the snakes and poison berries. Never mind all the convicts! Were they quite frightening? I can't imagine living in a place where half the population are filthy criminals. Although I suppose they were all locked up. Did you build many prisons while you were there, Captain?"

"No," said Captain McConnell. "For the most part, it's Australia itself that serves as the prison, cut off from the rest of civilization as it is. Most of the convicts are assigned work to do and live as decent lives as they can. As for the beauty of the place, I think I brought the best of that home with me."

Mrs. McConnell rolled her eyes at that, but the entire table couldn't help but smile at the sweetness of his words. All except for Magistrate Carnbee. Dominick couldn't fully tell what was going on under his moustache, but it looked like more of a sneer.

"Sounds dreadful," Carnbee said. "I suppose you didn't have a choice in going, McConnell, but I can't imagine what would possess any decent Englishwoman to live there."

Never mind handing her the spoon, if Madam Carnbee poisoned her husband, Dominick would hold the boorish lout's mouth open and make sure he drank every drop.

"I didn't have a choice either," Mrs. McConnell said. Her voice was soft, but it would take a greater fool than Carnbee to miss the steel underneath. "When I met Clyde, I was married to a farmer. It was his land Clyde was stumbling across when I found him. *His land,* I say again, not my own.

"A farmer's wife has little choice but to work the lot she is given and hope for the best. And that lot is a hard one, especially in such an untamed land. It claimed the life of my first husband and left me a widow.

"But if it comforts you, Magistrate, as soon as my husband died, I boarded the first ship to leave Australia I could afford. It was the most fortunate coincidence of my life that Clyde was aboard that same ship."

An awkward silence descended then, made no less awkward by Martin's arrival to remove the dishes and set out the next course, thick slices of apple cake nearly drowning in cream. Dominick was delighted not only for the cake itself, but because it meant the meal was nearly done.

"How are you finding County Fife, Mrs. McConnell?" Alfie asked, changing the subject. "Is it much as you remember it?"

"Very much so or perhaps even more lovely," she replied, perfectly pleasant once more.

"I don't remember things being quite so far apart though," the captain chimed in. "I swear I lose an hour's work each day just walking up from the inn, and that's before climbing that damned crag! Apologies for my language."

Madam Carnbee looked shocked. "You've not been staying at the inn all this time! Why, I'd assumed His Lordship had put you up here. How dreadful! You simply must come and stay with us."

"No!" cried the magistrate and Mrs. McConnell in unison. They looked at each other in surprise before quickly glancing away.

"What I mean is—"

"I'm sure they don't—"

The two began to talk over each other and Dominick had to wonder if Captain McConnell had been so quick to accept his offer of supper because they hadn't wanted to deal with the magistrate alone. Dominick could understand. But had they been supposed to offer the McConnells lodgings as part of their employment? Gil hadn't said as much, but perhaps he'd assumed they knew.

It didn't matter now. They hadn't offered, and now that Madam Carnbee knew, it wouldn't be long until the entire county knew the Earl of Crawford was a poor host. It wasn't the most scandalous thing a man could be, but it wasn't exactly reputation-building either. There was only one thing for it. From the grimace on Alfie's face, he knew it too and wasn't any happier about it than Dominick was.

Alfie schooled his face into something slightly more welcoming. "I completely apologise for my oversight. Allow me to make it up to you by offering one of Balcarres' guest rooms for the remainder of your time with us."

"That's very kind," said Mrs. McConnell. "But we couldn't possibly impose."

"Oh, but you can't stay another night in that dreadful inn!" interjected Madam Carnbee. "Our home isn't a lordly manor, of course, but if you won't stay here, you must stay with us."

Caught between a rock and a hard place, the McConnells shared a look before the captain cleared his throat.

"Thank you for your generous offer, Madam Carnbee," he said. "But logistically, I suppose it would make more sense to sleep where we work, as it were. If you're sure that's quite all right, my lord."

"Quite," said Alfie, not sounding nearly as defeated as Dominick felt. Two more sets of eyes and ears to worry about. "I'd be delighted for you to stay here."

Before the McConnells could give their politest thanks or—as Dominick would prefer—make up an excuse to remain at the inn, Madam Carnbee let out a shriek.

Dominick and Captain McConnell were both on their feet instantly. The magistrate seemed more interested in the contents of his glass and Alfie was hampered by the amount of Madam Carnbee suddenly clinging to him.

Dominick's hand went for his dessert knife. "What is it?"

"It was the most dreadful thing!" exclaimed Madam Carnbee as Alfie did his best to keep her from hiding her face in his lap. "There was something dreadful at the window. A man, I think, but he looked so ghastly. He must have been some awful spirit! It was terrible!"

The McConnells were both seated on the window side of the table and the captain immediately went over, cupping his hands against the glass to peer out into the night. Dominick joined him, but couldn't see anything in the darkness. What little moonlight there may have been was covered by clouds and he couldn't even see the end of the terrace, never mind any lurking spirits.

"Nothing out there," Captain McConnell said at last.

"What did this man look like?" asked Dominick with a sneaking suspicion.

"Oh, simply awful!" Madam Carnbee replied, her hands pressed against Alfie's chest in despair. "The ghost had the most wicked look about him. He must have truly been an evil man in life! He had sneer, aye, and... and oh, a scar! A most dreadful scar! Perhaps he wasn't a ghost at all, but some frightful murderer! It can't be safe to travel tonight. You don't suppose—"

Carnbee harrumphed. "It was just your imagination, dear. Those silly novels you're always reading are to blame, I'm sure. I don't know how you can stand such nonsense."

Despite the magistrate's boorishness, Dominick decided he wouldn't help poison the man's tea after all. He'd stopped his wife before she could invite themselves to stay the night. Besides, if he died, there would be nothing to stop her campaign to become an earl's wife from turning into an all-out war.

Alfie had finally extracted Madam Carnbee from his lap, much to her dismay. "It *was* real! A real ghost, right there. I'm overwhelmed just thinking about it."

She appeared about to swoon herself right back into Alfie's lap. Dominick debated helping him, but his cake had been neglected far too long. He returned to that instead. Alfie could fend for himself.

"In that case, perhaps we should be getting home," the magistrate said, knocking back the last of his wine. "Captain McConnell, can we offer you both a ride? To either the inn or our home, whichever you'd prefer."

"Actually," the captain said, with a look at his wife, "I believe we'll take His Lordship up on his kind offer to stay here, if that's quite all right?"

"Of course," replied Alfie, sounding only a little strangled.

"But we do need to go collect our things," Mrs. McConnell added.

Madam Carnbee placed her hand on Alfie's arm again, not realising how close she was to getting Dominick's dessert fork stuck in it. "My Lord, if you send a servant for their things now, they wouldn't have to return to the inn at all and we could *all* stay much later. I'm sure I shouldn't be travelling so soon after witnessing such a terrible apparition. Do you have a pianoforte, my lord? I'm told I'm quite skilled on that... or any other instrument you have that I can get my hands on."

Dominick nearly choked on a bite of cake. It was all too much. Spluttering, he left the table with an excuse about finding Martin to go collect the McConnells' things. As he abandoned Alfie to his fate, Dominick caught one last look of utter betrayal before he made his way out into the hall, his howls of laughter muffled by his sleeve.

Chapter 10

That night, with supper long behind them and Dominick asleep beside him, Alfie lay awake, listening. The manor was utterly silent for once, no crying babies or murmured thanks from unwelcome guests or the hushed footfalls of servants echoing down the halls. Even the wind had died down, leaving a stillness that felt unnatural, an eerie calm before the storm.

Sleep continued to evade him, so he rose, going to the window and looking out. The moon was full and in its light, the cleared top of the crag was especially barren. The scaffolding around the folly was silhouetted like a gallows against the sky. He could almost see the heads of traitors mounted on pikes like Dominick's description of the beheaded sheep on the gateposts. Or perhaps a head bearing the monstrous face Madam Carnbee had described. At the time, it'd been easy to see through her attempt to acquire an invitation to stay, but in the small hours of the night it was easier to believe in all sorts of horrors watching from the dark.

He wrapped his arms around his bare chest, wishing he'd had the forethought to grab his banyan. He was about to go look for it when he heard a strange noise. A low, haunting cry unlike anything he'd ever heard.

He held his breath and strained his ears, but couldn't hear anything but Dominick's soft breathing. Then it came again, a long 'Ooooooooo' that slowly grew higher in pitch until it was as sharp and high as a fox's cry.

It raised the hairs on his arms. He'd never heard a ghost, but that was exactly what one would sound like.

He leaned closer to the window, peering out to see if he could spot what was making the ghastly call. The ancient glass was warped, and cold against his cheek, but he couldn't see anything other than the folly, its moonlit shadow casting strange shapes down the face of the crag.

"Wha' is it?" Dominick mumbled.

"Shhh," Alfie hissed, but the sound didn't come again.

He looked over to see Dominick with his face half-buried in the pillows, one arm stretched out over Alfie's empty half of the bed. When he looked back out the window, the moon had gone behind the clouds and all was dark again.

"Nothing," he said. "Just the wind."

"Then ge'back here," said Dominick without opening his eyes. "You're thinking too loud. Keepin' me awake."

Alfie chuckled, sliding back into bed and pulling the covers up around them both. Dominick hummed appreciatively and pulled Alfie up against him. His body was warm and despite the heaviness in his voice, there was one part of him that was definitely awake.

"Oh, you just wanted me to stop thinking, did you?" Alfie said, wrapping one hand around Dominick's cock. It was already half-hard and firmed even further as he began to stroke slowly along its length. "Nothing else you wanted from me?"

Dominick cracked open an eye. "I might be able to think of a few things."

"Just a few?"

"To start. You can keep at that for now."

"Thank you, I believe I will," Alfie said, enjoying the heat of Dominick's prick in his hand. It had been damned cold by the window, so Alfie indulged himself by burrowing up against the great furnace that was Dominick, his chest hair tickling Alfie's nose.

Dominick hissed and Alfie stilled his hand. "Did I do something wrong?"

"I swear to God I'm going to glue your slippers to your feet," Dominick grumbled. "You can't have been out of bed five minutes. Why are they always so cold?"

Alfie had no idea what Dominick was talking about. His feet were quite warm actually, tucked between Dominick's own.

He slid his thumb over the head of Dominick's cock, making him hiss for an entirely different reason.

He kept on like that, slow pulls punctuated by the occasional twist or unexpected attention to the head when he felt Dominick might be growing a little too complacent. One of Dominick's heavy arms was slung over his waist, idly tracing the dimples in the small of Alfie's back. It was lazy, comfortable lovemaking to match the hushed stillness of the night. He didn't even know if Dominick's eyes were open. His weren't, but why would he need to see when he could feel Dominick, smell him, and hear his breathing as his chest rose and fell against Alfie's cheek? It was heaven.

His arm was trapped between them as he worked, knuckles brushing Dominick's belly, but the awkwardness of the angle was worth it as with just a shift of his hips, he could add his own cock to his grasp. Dominick was leaking profusely by now, and the slick slide of his length against Alfie's was unbearably good.

"Fuck." Dominick's hips bucked against his, and the hand on Alfie's back slid lower, teasing the crease of his buttocks.

"I've thought of another thing I want from you," Dominick whispered.

Alfie was still a little sore from earlier in the night, but it wasn't as if they were short on oil. Dominick would be gentle with him... if that's what Alfie wanted.

Dominick chuckled. "I can hear you thinking again. You might be up for all that, you strumpet, but I'd actually like to get some sleep tonight. I was thinking of this."

Without any warning, Alfie found himself being bodily lifted. He let out a squawk as he was rolled over Dominick's body, thudding down onto the mattress on the other side of him.

"Was that entirely necessary?" he asked, a little breathless. Dominick being able to so easily manhandle him shouldn't be nearly as arousing as it was.

"Mm, entirely." Dominick had deposited Alfie on his side, facing away from him and was now nosing at Alfie's nape, his breath tickling the delicate hairs there. "Couldn't do this on your other side, we'd crush your leg. Besides, oil's on this side of the bed anyway. Now you can reach."

Alfie blinked. In the darkness, he could just make out the bottle of oil on the small table next to the bed where they'd left it earlier in the evening. When he reached out to grab it, Dominick ran his nose down the top of his spine, nearly making Alfie drop the damn thing.

"You did that on purpose."

Dominick didn't respond, but Alfie could feel him grin against the back of his neck. Then Dominick kissed him there, a soft whisper of a kiss that was to be the first of many. He ran a line of them up to Alfie's shoulder and back, maddeningly gentle, before burying his face in the crook of Alfie's neck where he was especially sensitive.

This time Alfie did drop the bottle. It vanished into the bed linens as Dominick lips, tongue, and teeth all came into play against the side of his throat. Every swipe of Dominick's tongue against his pulse stoked Alfie's arousal higher and each bite sent a bolt of heat straight to his cock. He wished Dominick could bite him hard enough there to leave marks, but had to contend with the agony instead of teasing nips that were almost—but not quite—enough.

The sensation was unbearable. He tilted his head back for more.

Dominick's hand came down heavily on his flank, pinning him in place.

"Stop squirming," Dominick whispered, but his voice was far too smug to be an admonishment. He punctuated his order by licking the shell of Alfie's ear in a slow, devastating swipe that only made him squirm more.

"Bastard," Alfie whispered back. He tried to pull away, just to see if he could, but Dominick's grip was unrelenting. It was as if he didn't even need to make an effort to hold Alfie in place.

The thought was as thrilling as it was completely unfair. What must it be like to have such strength so readily at his command? But if he was as strong as Dominick, he might not appreciate Dominick's ability to toss him about so much. Or would it be worth it to be able to do the same right back? Quite the dilemma.

Dominick sighed in his ear. "You're thinking again."

"So make me stop."

"I'm trying, you maddening creature, but you're being too stubborn for your own good."

"Then why don't you—" But Alfie forgot what he was going to say when Dominick used the hand on his side to pull Alfie backwards on the bed, his body slotting perfectly against Alfie's back and his hard cock pressing against the globes of Alfie's buttocks, parting them just slightly to make more room for himself.

Alfie hadn't even been paying attention to Dominick's other arm, until the pillow under his head moved and he realised he'd been cradling Alfie's head on his upper arm this entire time. Alfie turned his head into it, burying his moan into his inner elbow. Dominick smelled like sweat and candle smoke, and more than a bit like Alfie himself.

The hand on his side teased its way down past his hip. Dominick dragged his fingertips as he went, leaving trails of fire, until *he* was the one with his hand around Alfie's cock, pulling slowly but firmly. He rubbed his own cock against Alfie's arse in time with his hand, leaving Alfie unable to decide whether he wanted to move forward or back.

Dominick had been the one complaining about needing to get to sleep, but it seemed now he had all the time in the world to slowly drive him mad. The head of his cock brushed over Alfie's rim more than once, making him gasp, but Dominick didn't change his angle to fuck him, instead keeping up his leisurely torment until Alfie thought he might shiver out of his skin with want.

But Alfie's arse was just a little too sore and Dominick's hand was just a little too dry. Soon he was squirming again.

"Nick," he panted. "I need."

Dominick's voice was rough. "Oil's by your hand."

Alfie groped around, but couldn't seem to find it.

"No, here."

Dominick leaned over, taking Alfie with him and for one glorious moment he was pinned to the bed, Dominick's weight pressing him down into the mattress as he reached over Alfie to grab the bottle himself. Alfie thrust his aching cock against the soft sheets, needing to relieve some of the pressure. He nearly sobbed when he was rolled back, now denied both the sheets and Dominick's hand.

The glass of the bottle was cool against his stomach, Dominick's palm holding it there even hotter by comparison.

"You're such a beautiful wanton, aren't you?"

"Shut up and give me that," Alfie snarled, trying to pry the bottle from Dominick's grip.

"No. I want to do it." Dominick pressed another achingly sweet kiss against Alfie's shoulder. "Will you be good and hold still for me?"

His words made Alfie's hips jerk of their own accord. This man was going to be the death of him. The motion had the pleasing effect of rocking him back against Dominick's cock, so he did it again intentionally.

Dominick's breath stuttered and he moaned against Alfie's neck. Good. If Alfie was going to be driven mad, he could at least drag Dominick down with him.

"Why do I even ask?" Dominick muttered, but he was uncorking the bottle.

Alfie stilled. If it got Dominick in him again sooner, then he supposed he could behave, just this once.

Unfortunately, Dominick needed both hands to pour and catch the oil, so Alfie lost his pillow. He could hear Dominick shifting around behind him, but he was taking his bloody time about it, so Alfie picked up where his lover had left off, wrapping his hand around his prick and pulling. After all, Dominick hadn't said he needed to be *perfectly* still.

"Christ," Dominick swore. Then Alfie felt exactly what he'd been waiting for, Dominick's oiled fingers against his arse. He arched his back, shoving back against those fingers, but instead of pressing in, Dominick instead slid his hand up and down, slicking Alfie's crease. Then his hand dipped even lower, and suddenly that hot palm was oiling Alfie's inner thighs, slicking the tight space where his legs met his body.

"Need more, love?" Dominick asked. He pulled his hand away before Alfie could respond, pouring more oil in his palm before reaching back between his legs, lifting Alfie's upper thigh as he coated the inside of it.

Alfie tightened his grip on his prick, squeezing tightly to keep from coming on the spot. Dominick's hands—rough, scarred, fighter's hands—were like silk with the oil coating, flowing over all of Alfie's most intimate areas without any question as to whether they had a right to be there. That surety—that Alfie would let Dominick do whatever he wanted with his body and Dominick knew it—took his breath away and he missed the sound of the bottle being recorked.

He didn't miss Dominick settling down against his back or lifting his injured leg again, so gently. And he certainly didn't miss Dominick sliding his cock between his thighs.

Alfie gripped the sheets tightly with his free hand. Dominick's cock felt larger, hotter than it had before. And if Dominick's oil-covered hands felt like silk, then his cock felt like something meant for only emperors and kings that had somehow fallen into the bed of an urchin-turned-earl instead.

He intended on keeping it there.

"That doesn't hurt, does it?" Dominick asked, pushing down a little on his leg. His voice was strained but still he didn't move, waiting for Alfie's reply.

He'd had Dominick inside him more times than he could count, but there was something about this act that made him feel even more possessed. Perhaps it was because like this, Dominick could change his mind and decide to fuck him at any moment, but chose not to. Or perhaps it was because it was one of the first things he'd ever learned men could do together, from the dirty jokes and hushed laughter of other boys.

Whatever it was, he answered Dominick's question by reaching back and tugging on Dominick's thigh until it was over his, pressing down and making the channel between his legs even tighter, hotter for Dominick's use.

"Christ," Dominick whispered again, and then he was moving. The feel of him was dizzying, holding Alfie in place as he took his pleasure. Then that oil-slicked hand was around Alfie's cock again, even better than before.

Alfie thrust into it. He was too wound up to even try to match Dominick's pace as Dominick rutted against him. He had to bite back a shout as the head of Dominick's cock tapped against his bollocks. Dominick let out a grunt before releasing Alfie's cock to cup them instead, holding them in place as he continued to rut. The knuckle of his thumb rubbed against the base of Alfie's cock, but that wasn't nearly enough, and he was so close.

"Nick, please. Please, Nick, please."

Dominick could have kept him like that, ignoring Alfie's needs to chase his own desires, but he immediately moved his hand back to Alfie's prick, jerking fiercely, the combination of his slick hand and the rough treatment bringing Alfie right to the edge. Then his wicked thumb swiped over the head of Alfie's cock, using his own tricks against him, and that was it.

Everything went very bright and then very dark as pleasure surged through Alfie, Dominick's hand working him through his climax, making him shudder as wave after wave rolled through him.

Finally, it was too much and Alfie batted his hand away weakly. It didn't go far, settling on his hip as Dominick continued to thrust. Each time his cock thrust through Alfie's legs, striking his bollocks again, Alfie keened, so over-sensitive now that the feeling walked the line between pleasure and pain. Still, he tightened his legs until they ached, wanting to give Dominick just that little bit more.

Dominick was panting, exhaling wetly against his neck, so Alfie reached back, twisting his fingers into Dominick's hair and pulling him impossibly closer.

"Nick," he said again. "Please."

Dominick's hips stuttered and then he spent, the hot rush spilling between Alfie's legs making them both groan. He continued to thrust after he'd finished, the roll of his hips less urgent as he spread his come over Alfie's thighs. Alfie let him, even as he felt some trickle out from between his legs and run down his backside.

Dominick might as well enjoy it while he could. After all, he was the one who was going to have to brave the cold floors to fetch the washcloth while Alfie stayed cuddled up in their bed, now thoroughly warmed.

◆○◆

"Can you stop thinking and sleep now?" Dominick asked with a contagious yawn sometime later. Even as he closed his eyes, he was rubbing soothing circles on Alfie's leg around and around the scar where he'd been shot, knowing where it was without needing to see.

"I'll try," said Alfie, yawning right back. He was warm and clean and sated. That was enough to make him forget some of the troubling thoughts that had been keeping him awake, at least for now. "I suppose I have to. Busy day tomorrow. The workers will be back and the McConnells want to meet to look over some final designs for the gardens. And that means meeting with you too, not just me, so you'd better not go riding off after breakfast. Dominick, are you listening to me? Repeat back what I just said."

"Tomorrow. Look. Better. Breakfast." Dominick slurred. "E'rything looks better after breakfast."

And like that, he was asleep.

⸺◆⸺

The next morning, Dominick was proven right. With the bright morning sun and a belly full of tea and eggs, everything did look better. The eerie sounds of the night before seemed like little more than a bad dream.

At least until the screaming began.

Chapter II

Dominick rushed out of the breakfast room with Alfie only moments behind. They stopped in the hall, trying to locate the source of the screams. As they did, the house fell into silence, as if the entire manor was breathing in, filling its lungs for the next terrible shriek.

Alfie laid his hand on Dominick's arm, the gentle pressure a reassuring comfort.

Then came a sound, not a scream, but a distant sobbing.

"To the right," Alfie said. "Front hall?"

When they made it to the front hall it was empty, but the sobbing was louder and coming their way. Dominick took a deep breath as they headed into the oldest part of the house, where sounds echoed in the strangest ways. They turned a corner, Dominick in the lead, so he was the one who crashed into the grey figure.

He had a moment to imagine some ghostly apparition before Mrs. Hirkins was wrapping her arms around him, the grey wool of her dress coarse against his silks and linen as she sobbed.

"Mrs. Hirkins?" Alfie asked, panic making him sound far younger than he was. "What's wrong? Are you hurt?"

She shook her head against Dominick's chest. Despite everything she'd been through, he'd never seen this strong pillar of a woman crumble before and if it was scaring him, it must be terrifying Alfie. Mrs. Hirkins was the closest thing he had to a mother and here she was, weeping inconsolably.

"He's dead!" she cried at last.

Dominick's heart turned to lead. He could barely get the question out. "James?"

Many children died young, especially babies, that was just life, but he'd been there when James was brought into the world, and the idea of him being gone so quickly was impossible to fathom. Never again holding that struggling weight in his arms, or hearing the pleased babbling that followed Agnes around the house from his sling on her back. Even his little baby wails, so heartrending, were all the worse now that he'd never hear them again.

When Mrs. Hirkins shook her head *no*, his legs went so weak with relief that he had to cling onto her right back.

"Not James." She sobbed. "Thank God! That architect man. Captain McConnell. It was horrible. His poor wife. Oh God, she's still there!"

"Where?" Alfie asked, one hand hesitating over Mrs. Hirkins, before settling it on her back and stroking in a manner that was likely meant to be comforting. "Where is she?"

"The drawing room."

By this time, the commotion had drawn several of the servants, thankfully including Mrs. Finley, who stepped forward.

"Come now dear, I've had the same thing happen to me. Finding a body's a dreadful shock, isn't it? Let's get you some tea. That will put you to rights."

Dominick transferred Mrs. Hirkins over to Mrs. Finley's care as Alfie addressed the other servants who'd assembled.

"Martin, go to the stables. Tell Frank he needs to go into town and fetch the doctor. Have Graham ready another horse as we may need the magistrate as well. Mr. Howe..."

Alfie hesitated then, and Dominick couldn't think of what else should be done either, other than keep everyone away from the drawing room.

"Perhaps I should gather the maids, sir? Agnes and Janie? Ensure they're all right?"

Alfie nodded. "Make sure James is with Agnes, and add Davey to the list. Keep them somewhere away from windows. If something terrible has happened, I don't want them to see it."

"I'll find Gil," Jarrett offered without prompting.

"Good," replied Alfie, too distracted to say more. "Thankfully, the staff from the village haven't arrived yet. You and Gil keep them outside, and stop any builders you see from going up the crag until we know what's happened. Dominick?"

Dominick didn't need to be told where his place was—at Alfie's side, as always. If the situation wasn't so dire, he'd be pleased at the way Alfie took control. It wasn't quite effortless, but in the end a plan had come together. He knew his lover feared he'd never be more than a shadow of an earl, but even if he hadn't fully mastered the art of command, he was the most noble man Dominick had ever met.

Orders given, the servants scattered as Alfie and Dominick made their way towards the drawing room and whatever horror awaited them there.

⊷◦⊶

The door to the drawing room gaped open. Beyond it, Dominick could see an arm stretched across the rug, the body it belonged to hidden by the settee. Instead of the sturdy frame of Captain McConnell, however, the arm appeared quite delicate. As he reached the room, it was clear the body on the floor wasn't the captain at all, but his wife.

Dominick rushed in and knelt down beside her. Mrs. McConnell's sensible skirts had billowed out around her and her prim bun was thoroughly mussed, but he could see no blood.

"Well?" asked Alfie.

Dominick cupped a hand over her nose and mouth, then placed his fingertips against her cheek. "She's breathing and her skin is warm. I think she's just fainted."

"Thank God." Alfie sighed. "Where's her husband?"

Dominick rose. The room wasn't a large one by Balcarres' standards. There wasn't anywhere to hide a dead body, no hidden nooks, or large chests, or even secret passages as far as he knew. Yet Mrs. McConnell was the only one here. He checked around the settee, just to be safe, but the room was empty. The only thing out of place—aside from the collapsed woman—was a small end table that had been knocked onto the floor beside her, the stack of papers that had been on it now scattered across the rug. One moved, fluttering over its fallen companions as it was caught by a breeze.

Dominick turned his attention to the windows. They gave a clear view of the barren gardens, but due to the angle of the house, most of what lay beyond was woods and the crag, the half-built folly on top perched like a bird of prey above them all.

He could see all this quite clearly because the windowed doors were open, the floor-length curtains on either side billowing in the morning air.

"Could he have gone for help?" Alfie asked. "Perhaps he wasn't as dead as Mrs. Hirkins thought."

"But dead enough to frighten his wife into a faint?"

When Alfie didn't answer, Dominick peered into the garden beyond, looking for a sign of the captain. "I'll go check. Just in case."

"Nick."

Dominick looked back at Alfie, who was now kneeling stiffly beside Mrs. McConnell. With a nod, Alfie tossed his cane at him. Catching it one handed, Dominick nodded back.

I'll be careful.

"I don't like this," Alfie said.

Dominick flicked the catch on the cane, revealing the sword within. He didn't like leaving Alfie without a weapon, but he was right, there was something wrong here, and the cane had saved their lives before. If he was going to be running out into Christ-knew-what, he was glad to have the weight of it in his hand.

He took one last look at Alfie, then headed out in search of a dead man.

The gardens were empty and grey, punctuated only by the piles of brush. He nearly had to hack his way through one to get out to the gardens from the drawing room doors, but there was no sign of Captain McConnell anywhere. He kept his eyes trained to the ground, but the earth was too hard for any footprints, and there were no other signs he could make out—no drops of blood or conveniently torn fabric caught on a rose bush.

He called out the missing man's name, but the only response was the rustle of the wind through the trees and the cries of birds wheeling above. Hesitantly, he stepped into the forest, sword held at the ready, but turned back when the climb grew too steep. If Captain McConnell was so injured that Mrs. Hirkins thought him dead, he'd never be able to manage the path to the top of the crag, resurrection or not.

He shouted for the captain again, but hearing no reply, turned back to Balcarres. If Captain McConnell was alive but wandering somewhere injured and befuddled, there were too many forest paths for Dominick to explore alone. And if Mrs. Hirkins was correct and he was dead, then Dominick had some questions about his damned disappearing act. And the only place he'd find answers was back at the manor.

Chapter 12

Within the hour, the doctor had been fetched and was attending to Mrs. McConnell, who had yet to come out of her faint. As Doctor Mills hadn't wanted to move her more than necessary in her state, Dominick had helped lift her onto the settee, turning the drawing room from the site of a disappearance into a sick room.

As Alfie returned from organising search parties to check the forest and any outbuildings for the captain, be he dead or merely disappeared, he saw Dominick beside the closed drawing room door, standing guard as the doctor examined the patient within.

"Any change?" Alfie asked.

Dominick shook his head. "She mumbled a bit when the smelling salts were brought out, but that's all. I don't know how she didn't jump out of her skin at them right under her nose. I was halfway across the room and they made my eyes water. How about you?"

"Anyone who finds Captain McConnell is to report back immediately, but nothing yet. There's a lot of places he could be, but hopefully, he'll be looking for us as much as we're looking for him. If not—"

Alfie was cut off by the drawing room door opening and the doctor slipping out.

"Ah, Your Lordship." Doctor Mills gave a jerky bob of his head. "The patient is resting now. I believe she should be coming around shortly. However, she has had quite a shock."

"Thank you, doctor. Will she be all right?"

The doctor bobbed his head again. "Aye, I'm most certain of it. Still, perhaps you could have a maid sent to keep her company."

"Of course." Alfie hesitated. Mrs. Hirkins hated to be fussed over, but she'd had a shock as well and was of advancing years. He'd rather she deride him for being a fusspot and find out she was fine than ignore the opportunity to have a doctor look her over and have there be something truly wrong.

He told Doctor Mills as much, and received yet another rabbit jerk of his head.

"If she was able to flee under her own power, she's likely well enough, but I'll be happy to make certain as soon as Mrs. McConnell awakes."

"I'd appreciate that," said Alfie. "I'll go determine where she is and have a maid sent for Mrs. McConnell."

With that, the doctor ducked back into the drawing room.

"If you're going to tell Mrs. Hirkins what to do, you'll need this back," Dominick said. He handed Alfie his cane, the blade returned to its hiding place within.

Alfie rubbed a hand over his face. "Forget the bloody cane. I'll need more firepower than that. That's why I'm bringing you with me."

Unsurprisingly, they found Mrs. Hirkins in the kitchen. She seemed to have channelled her nerves by turning the female staff into her own personal battalion, rocking baby James in her arms while giving orders to Agnes and a few of the new cleaning maids. Most of the new staff looked even more uncomfortable in the kitchen than Janie, who'd been placed off in a corner to peel vegetables.

Mrs. Finley had escaped the press gang, and was sitting beside Mrs. Hirkins. Instead of tea, she was pouring her drink from a very familiar and highly illegal bottle of the local whisky.

Alfie relieved a thankful maid of her duties and sent her off to join Doctor Mills, then sat down at the kitchen table beside Mrs. Hirkins.

"Are you all right?" he asked softly.

"Just fine," she snapped. "But I won't be if that girl overbeats the eggs. They've suffered enough! Let them be and start folding in the sugar."

Alfie looked up at Dominick helplessly. He'd never seen Mrs. Hirkins as frightened as he had that morning, and he'd seen her through fire and murder and the worst of his adolescence. She wasn't one to show her fear and he didn't know if all this was embarrassment or still shock.

Dominick stepped forward, taking her drink for himself and downing it in one.

That got her attention.

"It was going to waste just sitting there," Dominick said, but refilled the glass. Mrs. Finley took that as her cue to leave, going over to keep Janie from losing a finger and giving the three of them a bit of privacy.

Dominick took her seat and held the glass out to Mrs. Hirkins. Without so much as jostling James, she took it, finishing it in several quick sips.

"There you are," said Dominick, holding the bottle out, but relenting when she shook her head. Then she reconsidered and he refilled her glass.

"'Come to Scotland,' you said. 'Nice quiet place to retire,' you said. 'No murders at all.' Ha!"

Alfie had never made that last promise to her, but wished he could have.

"Ah, but you'd be bored if it was otherwise," said Dominick.

Mrs. Hirkins glared at him.

"We're actually not sure there has been a murder or even a death at all," Alfie offered diplomatically. "Captain McConnell has yet to be located."

"Nonsense," she said. "Corpses don't just get up and walk about."

"Are you sure he was a corpse?" asked Dominick. "Perhaps you just didn't get a good look."

This was why he'd brought Dominick with him. Alfie wouldn't have survived the glare Mrs. Hirkins was levelling at him now.

"I've seen more of life than a squeaker like you. And I know death when I see it."

"Perhaps you can tell us exactly what you did see," said Alfie gently.

She huffed. "I was coming down the hall when I saw Mrs. McConnell wandering this way and that. I know how many times I've gotten turned about in this bloody warren, so I figured she was the same. I asked if she was looking for the breakfast room, and she said no, she never breakfasted, it disagreed with her digestion. Her husband had gone to fetch some papers from the drawing room and hadn't returned, but she didn't know the way. I said I'd be happy to show her.

"But when we get to the drawing room, no sooner had I opened the door than she lets out this almighty shriek and cries out, 'My husband!' I look, and there he is in the centre of the room, lying stretched out on the floor and the rope still wrapped tight around his neck, knotted at the back like a noose. He's as dead a man as I've ever seen, but I don't get more than a look before she grabs my arm and faints dead away. Well, I'm not going to be standing there with a dead man and a woman gone out of her senses, so I go off to find help. The rest you know."

Alfie made eye contact with Dominick, but they both let her get away with omitting how clearly rattled she'd been by the whole ordeal.

"Were the windows open?"

She stared at Dominick as if he was mad. "There was a dead man at my feet and Mrs. McConnell was halfway there herself. You think I gave a poxy whore's arse about the fucking windows?"

James burped at that and she paused her obscenities to wipe some spittle from his face. Alfie shared another glance with Dominick, but he only shrugged.

"I'm sorry you had to see that," said Alfie.

She harrumphed.

He couldn't seem to find any more comforting words. What else was there to say? Instead he laid his hand over hers, feeling the faintest tremble as she patted a cloth to James' lips. He risked a brief squeeze.

"If there's anything you need, Mrs. Hirkins, let me know. Please."

She nodded. He gave her hand one last squeeze before rising.

"By the way," he said, "please don't go anywhere. The doctor will be down to check on you shortly."

Then he left the kitchen with further curses ringing in his ears.

CHAPTER 13

"What are we doing here?" Dominick asked.

Alfie sat down heavily on one of the tombstones. "I don't know. I thought, 'Where might a dead man be?' I suppose it's silly."

The stones of the chapel ruins were as grey as the skies above, and the wind held a definite bite. Alfie wrapped his coat tighter around himself and stared at the overgrown graves of generations of earls before him.

"I suppose I should have this restored next, after the gardens. Gil will have to find another architect for the folly. Do you think they'll be able to work from the captain's plans or have to start again?"

Dominick leaned against the chapel wall beside him. "I don't think you need to be worrying about that now, love."

"At least those are problems that make sense. All this?" Alfie waved a hand before dropping it dejectedly. There was still no sign of Captain McConnell. The search had moved indoors, in case he'd collapsed in some back hall, but Alfie couldn't stand to be trapped inside another minute with everyone looking to him for answers and him finding none.

If what Mrs. Hirkins said was true, there was nothing for any of them to find. But dead men just didn't go off on their own. So where was he?

"You don't think she made it up, do you?" he asked at last. "Or not made it up but... got confused?"

Dominick hummed and Alfie wasn't sure whether to be comforted or concerned that he didn't dismiss the idea out of hand. But there hadn't been a corpse, hadn't been any blood. If not for the unconscious Mrs. McConnell, Alfie might have believed Mrs. Hirkins' mind had betrayed her. As it was, he still wasn't sure.

"She was there when you were first taken in, wasn't she?" Dominick said slowly. "That's been how long?"

Alfie scrubbed a hand over his face. "Fourteen years? Give or take. And she wasn't young then."

"She still seems sharp enough to me. Her tongue still is, at any rate. But I suppose you never know. There was an old man I knew in Spitalfields who seemed perfectly sane and could carry on any conversation just so long as you called him Lord Nelson. Was absolutely convinced he was the admiral himself. He could talk all about the tactics he used in every battle and was happy to tell you how he survived his wounds at Trafalgar. Never been to sea at all, as far as I ever knew, but as long as you indulged him in that, he was as sane a man as any other."

Alfie kicked a rock at his feet. "You think Mrs. Hirkins had a delusion?"

"I might if it was just her word," said Dominick, frowning and picking at a bit of flaking mortar. "But we both saw Mrs. McConnell."

"And there had to have been *something* in that room that caused her to faint. Her husband's dead body would certainly make sense. And if he really looked as horrible as Mrs. Hirkins described with the rope around his neck, that suggests he wasn't just dead, but murdered."

"You're thinking about the headless sheep, aren't you?"

Alfie had been trying very hard not to think about the headless sheep. Because if he did, he'd have to think about the fact that if they were indeed a warning meant for Dominick and him, then Captain McConnell might not have been the killer's intended victim.

"The sheep. The cut from the farmer. Hell, even Madam Carnbee's ghostly face at the window."

"You think that was more than just an attempt to get into your trousers?"

Alfie gave Dominick a flat look. "I don't know what to think. All I know is that someone doesn't like us—worse, I think it's safe to assume they *hate* us—and the night after we open our home to guests, one of them ends up dead."

Dominick swore. "You're right. So either the captain was killed as another threat to us—"

"—Or it was meant to be one of us and they killed the wrong man. But if he's dead, then where *is* he?"

"I don't know." Dominick held out a hand, palm up, and gazed up at the sky. As he did so, Alfie felt the first heavy drops of rain land on his shoulders. "And I don't know about any of the rest of it either. But I do think we should go back and see how things are going with the others searching inside."

Alfie sighed. "I suppose so." He kicked out at one last rock, but to his surprise, it gave under the toe of his boot. He leaned over and picked it up.

"What have you got there?"

"Just a crust of bread." Alfie tossed it into the woods. "A rat must have dragged it up. We need to tell Janie to stop leaving out bread and milk for the broonies or we'll be overrun."

"The cats must like it though," said Dominick as they made their way out of the chapel's clearing. "Bit of meat with their milk. Do you think it was the broonies that carried the captain away?"

"Don't even jest about that. You don't think he brought it up here, do you? Could he be nearby? Although why would a man who was near-dead stop to pick up a piece of bread that'd been left out all night? None of it makes any sense!"

"Here now," Dominick stopped him with a hand on his arm, then looked around. Content with their privacy, Dominick leaned in and kissed him. When he tried to pull away, Alfie reeled him back in, kissing him again before letting out a sigh and resting his forehead against Dominick's. The rain was falling heavily now, but he didn't want to move.

"You're all right," Dominick whispered. "Don't get yourself all tied up in knots about things we don't have enough pieces to puzzle out just yet. This will all be sorted soon enough and the answer won't be broonies, or giant rats, or even Lord Nelson, I promise."

"Why do you always have to be so reasonable?" Alfie asked. Going in for a final kiss, he could feel Dominick grin against his lips.

"I'll remember you said that the next time you complain about me stealing the blankets. It's reasonable that I need more of them because I'm bigger. Now come on, we'll be soaked to the skin if we don't head back now. With any luck, Captain McConnell will be waiting for us to return, full of apologies for the misunderstanding and with a bottle of port for our troubles."

⎯⎯◦⎯⎯

Captain McConnell was not waiting for them to return, but Mrs. McConnell was.

She was sitting up on the settee in the drawing room, a blanket pulled over her lap and Doctor Mills' fingers on her wrist, timing her pulse against his pocket watch.

"Are you feeling better?" asked Alfie.

"I am," she said softly. "Or at least, somewhat. Doctor Mills has informed me of what happened, but I'm afraid I can't quite believe it."

Dominick raised an eyebrow at this. Doctor Mills finished his counting, and apparently satisfied with the results, put his watch away.

"I'm afraid Mrs. McConnell is a wee bit confused about this morning's events," said the doctor. "It's quite common for ladies of refinement following a great shock. Now that she's regained consciousness, bed rest is the best thing for her."

"You don't remember anything?" Alfie asked incredulously.

She shook her head, then winced at the movement. "I remember following Mrs. Hirkins to the drawing room and her opening the door, then seeing... Oh, but it's too awful! I can't have seen that, could I? Doctor Mills says you can't find my husband, but I saw him on the floor."

She took a deep breath. "My husband was dead. I saw him. But that's all I remember and now I'm told you can't find hi-his body. What's going on?"

Doctor Mills tutted. "There now, don't get over-excited."

"I don't know what's going on," said Alfie. The pained confusion on Mrs. McConnell's face was heartbreaking. "But I promise you we're going to find out. You're welcome to stay here until you're better, of course."

"I'll be staying longer than that."

Alfie was taken aback by the strength in her voice. "I beg your pardon?"

"Well, I'll have to stay, won't I? To finish the work on the gardens and the folly. Unless you'd prefer I return to the inn."

"N-no, of course not," Alfie stuttered. The inn might be safer, but he didn't like the idea of her taking that journey through the woods every day if she was determined to return to Balcarres. "But I assumed—that is, if the worst turns out to be the case—that another architect from your husband's firm would be taking over."

She waved a hand. "Nonsense. All the technical planning is done, and I can read his blueprints as well as any man—better, I would say, when it comes to his handwriting. I won't leave his finest work to anyone else. And if Clyde is still here, one way or the other, I can't leave him."

Her voice waived on the last sentence, and Alfie didn't have the heart to argue. "Very well."

Dominick spoke up. "We can offer you a maid while you're here alone. For, um, pro, prop?"

He looked at Alfie for help.

"Propriety." Alfie should have thought about that, given the other rumours Dominick had mentioned about him corrupting young kitchen maids from London. A freshly widowed woman staying by herself at the bachelor earl's manor would hardly put those rumours to rest. Especially since it was his manor where she'd been widowed.

If half the county already thought Balcarres was a den of murderers, surely the other half would once they heard about that.

"There's a girl employed here named Janie," he offered. "A bit excitable, but I have no doubt she will make an excellent companion for you. Although, of course, I hope Captain McConnell will be found alive and well soon enough."

She smiled gratefully. "Thank you, that would be very kind."

They left the doctor to explain his instructions to Mrs. McConnell. As soon as they were in the hall with the door closed behind them, Dominick punched him in the arm.

"Ow! What was that for?"

"Janie? Don't you think Mrs. McConnell has suffered enough?"

"I don't know any of the new girls' names!" Alfie protested. "So unless you wanted me to offer Agnes and have Janie go back to the kitchen, it was the best I could think of."

Dominick's silence made clear how much he absolutely did not want that to happen.

"Besides," Alfie added. "Perhaps being around a grounded, sensible woman will benefit Janie as well. They might each help each other."

That time, Dominick's silence had quite a bit more to say, but Alfie ignored him. A flighty maid was the least of his worries.

"Come along," he said. "Let's see if all the hidden passages have been searched yet. Knowing our luck, he'll be trapped between our bedrooms and won't that be fun to explain."

Chapter 14

Over the next week, no sign of Captain McConnell was found, and the household fell into a strange new kind of normal.

Magistrate Carnbee had arrived some hours after Doctor Mills and stayed only long enough to drink the brandy that had been brought out to warm those who'd been searching for the captain all day in the cold.

Carnbee had harrumphed a bit around the drawing room, then harrumphed even louder when Mrs. McConnell declined to see him, citing her poor health. As he'd then gone on to loudly proclaim no crime had been committed and Captain McConnell had simply absconded for his own reasons, likely the attentions of another woman, it was just as well she hadn't had to endure the magistrate's miserable excuse of an investigation.

Even by Carnbee's standards, it was a poor showing, but it wasn't exactly as if Dominick could say, "Excuse me, sir, we're pretty sure there *has* been a crime. No doubt you've heard the rumours about me tupping the earl? Oh good, you have. Well, we think someone might have taken against us for that, and the captain got it in the neck by accident instead of us."

Instead they'd let the magistrate harrumph his way back down the road, drunker and more self-satisfied than when he'd arrived, but bringing them no closer to finding the missing captain—or his body.

In the face of her husband's disappearance and possible murder, Dominick had expected Mrs. McConnell to spend several days recovering at the very least, but the next morning she'd been up and directing gardeners with firm orders. She'd even made the trek up the crag to supervise work on the folly.

For a woman who'd seemed so infatuated with her husband, she hid her loss well. Perhaps she was still clinging to the hope he was alive somehow, but as both she and Mrs. Hirkins had seen his body in the drawing room, Dominick couldn't see how that was possible. Although he couldn't see how a disappearing corpse was possible either.

Neither, it seemed, could many of the labourers hired to work on the gardens and folly. Each day, fewer and fewer turned up. Work was still being done, but not at the breakneck pace it had before.

Unfortunately, Gil didn't seem to be having the same problem retaining workers. An army armed with buckets and cleaning cloths had overwhelmed Balcarres and only seemed to grow in numbers by the day. This morning alone, Dominick had been politely shooed from the stables, the dining room, and the entire east wing by scrub bucket-wielding invaders before finally finding refuge in the library.

He looked out the library window, watching Mrs. McConnell talk to one of the labourers in the garden below. He couldn't tell what was being said, but whatever it was, the labourer didn't seem happy about it. Despite the man towering over her, Mrs. McConnell remained resolute.

Finally she turned on her heel, discussion apparently over, and as she went, Janie trailed after. Dominick wasn't sure what a lady's' maid was meant to do, but dogging Mrs. McConnell's every step kept Janie out from under everyone else's feet and, more importantly, ensured that none of the allegedly single men in the household ended up alone with the possible widow, so she was doing a fine job as far as he was concerned.

He was just thinking about going and bothering his own allegedly single man, when Alfie popped his head into the library.

"Oh thank God! I need your help. Gil's explaining crop diversification again. I barely escaped with my life. Hide me."

Dominick snorted. "Where? He knows this house better than either of us."

"Then hide me somewhere else. It's stifling in here."

Dominick knew exactly what he meant. He couldn't describe how, but ever since the captain's disappearance, there'd been a heaviness to the air in Balcarres. Perhaps it was the reminder of the disappearances the year before and the terrible secrets they'd uncovered. Or perhaps they all felt the same unease he had any time he opened a cupboard, that breathless moment of fear that a body would come tumbling out. Or perhaps it was just the changing seasons. October had been settled in for only a few days and already the brilliant flash of colours from September had given way to the grey bleakness of winter.

"We could go to the folly," Dominick suggested. He expected Alfie to groan at the climb, but Gil must have outdone himself today, because Alfie agreed as soon as the suggestion was out of his mouth.

Climbing the crag's steep path, Dominick knew this had been the right idea. He had to slow his steps so Alfie could keep up, but it was worth it to see the flush in Alfie's cheeks, the exertion brightening his eyes as he took deep breaths of the chilly air.

He really was unfairly handsome. His fine features hid the strength within him, just as his lordly bearing hid the mischievous demon beneath. Truly, his beauty was completely wasted on a man like Dominick when Alfie could be inviting any man he wanted to his bed, from dukes to delivery boys. But by some miracle, it seemed the only man he did want was a battered bit of street rough and Dominick was going to do everything in his power to keep it that way.

Alfie stopped to wipe his face with his handkerchief and the ring on his finger caught the weak sunlight. Dominick's ring, where it belonged. A warm tendril of possessiveness curled in his belly.

"Put that face away," Alfie said. "We're almost to the top and I won't have the workers see you leering like a baboon."

"You've never seen a baboon."

"Perhaps not, but you look like one. Stop it. I think I hear Mrs. McConnell's voice. You'll frighten the ladies."

Alfie was right, for as soon as they rounded the last turn of the path, they spotted Mrs. McConnell leaning over a small table, pointing out something on a piece of paper to a man in a plaid coat. Janie hovered over her shoulder, trying to see the paper as well.

Finally, the man in the plaid nodded and headed back to work, taking the paper with him as he went. Despite the narrowness of the ledge between the front of the folly and certain death, his steps were confident and he whistled out to several other workers as he walked, his thoughts clearly more on the task at hand than the drop below.

Janie noticed their presence first and tapped Mrs. McConnell on the arm.

"Ah, my lord, Mr. Trent, what brings you up here?" Mrs. McConnell asked, tucking a pencil behind her ear just as her husband once had.

"Mrs. McConnell," Dominick nodded. "I was wondering if you could help us with something. Some time back, I set one of the rocks into the folly window. I thought His Lordship might do the same so a bit of this was his work as well."

Alfie gave him a betrayed look, but it wasn't Dominick's fault he'd been so eager to agree to climb the folly.

Dominick grinned at him. Several stacks of stone lined the edge of the clearing at the top of the crag, waiting to be fit into place in the folly. The stones were laying atop beams of wood to keep them free of earth and stop them from sinking into the mud when it rained.

He waved towards the nearest stack. "Go on, my lord, find one that appeals to you."

Alfie's look this time said Dominick should be checking his boots for rocks for the foreseeable future, but it was worth it. Besides, it would do Alfie some good to get his hands dirty. Dominick knew he hadn't been doing his leg exercises as often as he should.

It was partially his fault. He should've been making more of an effort to get Alfie back into the gymnasium he'd built them. If nothing else, it would be some escape from the growing number of people at Balcarres. No one would dare bother an earl while he exercised and risk catching him in a less-than-gentlemanly state of exertion.

Perhaps he could use that as a threat: do your exercises or go lift rocks. Gil had said it was a bad idea for Dominick to help build the folly, but he hadn't specifically said Alfie couldn't.

He took a moment to envision Alfie stripped to the waist, trim muscles glistening in the sun with the sweat of an honest day's work, a hint of dirt clinging to his collarbone as he stretched his long body upward, heaving another stone into place.

A cough broke him from his reverie. Alfie was giving him a stern look, then mouthed the word "baboon".

Dominick did his best to school his features and returned his attention to Mrs. McConnell. "Sorry, what was that?"

"I said, I'll wager it was my husband's idea to have you be a part of building it. He likes that sort of thing." Her face fell. "*Liked* that sort of thing, I mean. It's hard to remember he's gone sometimes."

"I'm sorry," Dominick said. He wanted to reach out to her, but knew that wasn't the proper thing. "I didn't mean to bring up sad memories."

"No," she said, shaking her head. "It's a fond memory, just at a sad time. And it's an excellent idea. If you'll accompany me, my lord, I'll see if the workers have something that would suit."

Alfie shot Dominick another look that promised retribution, but dutifully followed, resigning himself to the task of lifting a single stone.

Dominick stayed where he was. He wasn't going to miss the spectacle of Alfie at work, but no doubt Mrs. McConnell would want to update the earl on the progress of his folly first, and that might take some time. He felt a twinge of pity for his lover, swapping Gil's lecture for Mrs. McConnell's, but such was the price of an earldom.

He looked out over that earldom. The view really was spectacular, even on such an overcast day. The sea haze hid the distant shore and painted the land below in soft greys. But the soft blur gave the familiar view a strange, isolated look. It was as if they were on an uncharted island, cut off from the world beyond by a sea of fog.

He was so lost in silly imaginings of a ship made entirely out of mist and crewed by will-o'-wisps that he almost missed Janie coming up to stand beside him.

"I just wanted to thank you, sir," she said, her words quick with excitement. "It's been wonderful working for Mrs. McConnell. She's the most amazing person I've ever met. And her designs, sir! Well, her husband's designs, of course, but they're hers now. Balcarres is going to be so beautiful when she's done with the gardens. Not that it isn't already beautiful, but it's nothing like it will be. And she even took my suggestion and planted the bell heather! The lilies will remain, if they don't rot, but the rest of the garden she's going to plant with bell heather instead. She says she thinks it will be even more lovely that way, and even asked if I had any thoughts about ferns!"

"I'm glad to hear you're enjoying it, Janie. I'll let His Lordship know as well." Dominick dropped his voice so it wouldn't carry. "How is she? Truly?"

Janie's eyes went wide and she glanced over her shoulder. But either the urge to gossip got the better of her or she remembered who she actually worked for, because she finally whispered, "Truly, sir, I'm not sure. I'm with her each day from when she wakes in the morning until she dismisses me at night, and I can see she's sad, but I haven't once caught her crying or anything of that sort. Yet she's collected up all his notes and won't let anyone else touch them. The other day, I found a scrap of paper in the folly and I recognised it as his hand and brought it to her. She wasn't herself at all about it, snatched it from me like she'd caught me rifling through her jewels."

"I'm sure she didn't mean any harm. Was it a love letter?" Dominick asked. "I could understand that. A letter from a dead love would be more precious than jewels."

Janie shook her head. "I recognised his hand, but I was never very good with letters. I've been practising so I can be more help to Mrs. McConnell, sir, but I don't think it's speaking ill of the dead to say his handwriting was truly terrible.

"But I suppose it doesn't matter. Anything he wrote would be worth keeping if they loved each other as much as they seemed. Still, it's unnatural she hasn't cried. Aye, I know plenty of women with husbands they wouldn't cry over, but I didn't think she'd be one of them."

Dominick agreed. "It might not have all hit her yet. When it does though, she'll need someone there for her."

"I'll be there," said Janie fiercely.

She'd stopped wearing her maid's cap when she started working as lady's maid to Mrs. McConnell—yet another secret rule from the world of nobility and their servants that Dominick would never understand. Her bright red hair shone like a flame, wisps dancing around her head. She hesitated, but seemed to draw courage from this new fire.

"There is something else troubling her, sir."

"Oh?"

"The workers. She's angry they've stopped showing up. She says there's no way they'll be finished before winter and she'll be stuck here for months longer than she ought."

Dominick frowned. Mrs. McConnell had seemed so determined to stay as long as her husband's body was missing. But in fairness, that had been on the day of his disappearance. He could understand how her mood might have shifted in the days since, living in the same house where he had likely died, spending every day pouring over his papers to create his great final, unfinished project. And all without even the comfort of a proper burial or even knowing what had happened. The mystery was maddening enough for Dominick, for her it must be torture.

He couldn't even let himself imagine what he'd do if the same thing happened to Alfie. He certainly wouldn't have the courage Mrs. McConnell was showing. He doubted he'd even be able to get out of bed. But she hadn't said anything about changing her mind and handing the job over to another. If she was determined to see her husband's work through, then the least they could do was make it as easy for her, and as quick, as possible.

"We could raise the workers' wages," he suggested. "That might draw some back."

Janie frowned. "Well, I mean, no one would say no to a bit more coin in their pockets, but they didn't leave because of the pay. Unless His Lordship is willing to offer a king's ransom, I doubt you'll get enough back to make a difference."

Dominick fought to hide his smile. He'd never heard Janie speak so plainly to anyone, never mind him. She hadn't tripped all over her words either. Apparently, all she needed to find her confidence was a few days in the company of a woman she admired. Just as well they'd gotten her out of the kitchen before she'd spent too much time with the Hirkins women. If she'd started to take after them, it would probably be easier to just hand over the earldom and be done with it.

"You sound like you have an idea."

"Aye," she said, tucking one of the more violently fluttering wisps of hair back behind her ear. "The problem is, there's been a run of bad luck here, and everyone around knows it. I've been leaving out more and more for the broonies, cheese and apples even, but even though they're taking the offerings and things are sure to change soon, no one wants to risk bringing any sorts of curses or bad spirits home with them. Those Mr. Charleton is hiring on for the household haven't much choice, jobs are hard enough to come by and the chance at a one that might keep them paid for life is worth the risk, but for the men up here at the folly, a few weeks extra coin is hardly worth getting on the wrong side of the spirits.

"It's one thing for Balcarres to be haunted, we all know about that, but when a dead man gets up and walks away, that's more than more than most folk can bear. I couldn't bear it either, sir, except I know how much the captain meant to Mrs. McConnell, so I know he can't mean any harm to her or those with her, but the other workers don't know that. Besides, there's the matter of whatever it was that made him get up and walk in the first place, if you follow me."

Dominick did. He wasn't sure if he believed in curses himself, but the longer they went without finding Captain McConnell, the more reasonable the idea of a walking corpse sounded.

"So," she continued, "I was thinking that what's needed is the chance to get rid of all the bad spirits and let everyone see it being done. It's a good thing then, that we're so close to Samhain."

"What's Sow-en?"

"Samhain," she said again slowly. "The last night of October when the spirits of the dead come back and bonfires are lit to drive back evil. There's all sorts of guising and mumming too, the boys and young men using paints and masks to make all sorts of frightful disguises to scare the rest of us."

Just what they needed, more terror.

"And you think all these reminders of death and evil will make people *less* afraid of Balcarres?"

To Dominick's surprise, Janie laughed. "Aye, it sounds like it shouldn't, but it's all in good fun. A chance for everyone to come together and celebrate the end of the harvest and enjoy a bit of the spoils. There's games and fortune telling, putting two hazelnuts together, naming one for yourself and one for your sweetheart to see whether they jump together or apart when they roast, or peeling an apple to see the first letter of your true love's name for those who read, that sort of thing. Then there's all sorts of food and soul cakes brought from every house. If we add the Hirkins' baking to that, I don't see how anyone could stay away."

The fortune telling and guising reminded him of something a few families he knew in Spitalfields used to do.

"I think I've heard of this," he said. "But I thought it was an Irish custom?"

"Aye, and who do you think they stole it from?" Janie sniffed. "But all that's just a bit of fun to get the people in the village to come. The important part's the bonfire. On Samhain, the fires in all the homes are put out, and everyone gathers to light a great new fire. Then there's all sorts of dancing to bless the fire and the dancers too. They say the brighter the fire and the better the dancing, the more the bad spirits are driven away. At the end of the night, everyone takes home torches to relight their homes for the coming year so we're all warmed by the same flame.

"We've all these great piles of sticks and logs already, put them into one stack and it'll be the largest bonfire the county's seen in lifetimes. No one will want to miss that. And once they've all danced in the ashes and lit their hearths from it, they won't be afraid of coming back to work at Balcarres. How could they, when the fire that protects the manor is the same one burning in their homes?"

He could imagine it now, the lights slowly winking out in the cottages that spread out below as everyone made their way up to Balcarres, then the procession of small lights leading away again in the early morning, carried by those with faces still flushed with heat from the great fire, and the homes finally lighting again, one-by-one.

Janie stopped and Dominick could almost see her shrinking back into the Janie she'd been before. "I know it's silly, and I don't expect His Lordship to believe—"

He cut her off. "No, I think it's a brilliant idea, and I'm sure he will too. Even if it doesn't bring back more workers, we could all use something to look forward to. Speaking of which, want to see an earl get his hands dirty?"

She giggled and they went to watch Alfie place his rock.

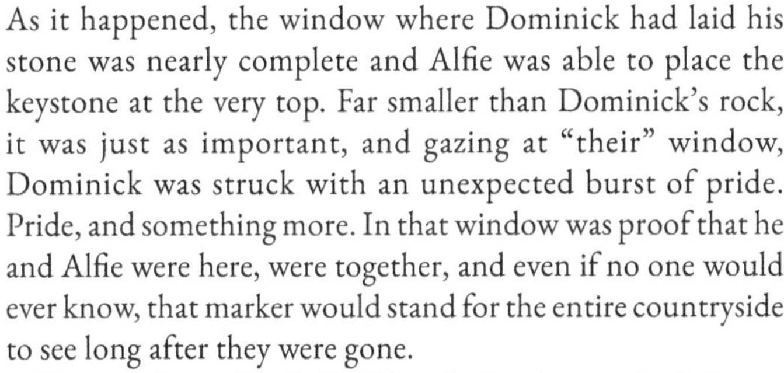

As it happened, the window where Dominick had laid his stone was nearly complete and Alfie was able to place the keystone at the very top. Far smaller than Dominick's rock, it was just as important, and gazing at "their" window, Dominick was struck with an unexpected burst of pride. Pride, and something more. In that window was proof that he and Alfie were here, were together, and even if no one would ever know, that marker would stand for the entire countryside to see long after they were gone.

"Is everything all right?" Alfie asked as they made their way back down the path.

Dominick just nodded, unable to put his feelings into words.

"It's just," Alfie continued, "ever since we got out of earshot of the others, I've been waiting for some terrible quip about how I'll always be on top now. The lack of innuendo has made me worry somewhat. I could start off with one about you forever being on the bottom if that would help?"

Dominick barked out a laugh. "And you're supposed to be the respectable one! Besides, no matter what's running through your filthy mind, that arrangement would never last."

Alfie narrowed his eyes. "Care to place a wager?"

"Happily." Dominick stuck out his hand. "I'll bet you that within a week you'll be begging for my c—"

He stopped at a shout from above. They were now passing directly below the worksite. Following the shout came terrible splintering cracks and rumbles that shook the ground. There was no rain, or each boom could be mistaken for thunder. Instead it sounded like some great beast rushing at them through the forest from above.

Without thinking, he threw himself at Alfie, knocking him back against the nearest tree and sending his cane skittering into the underbrush. He didn't have time to worry about that, because just as he ducked their heads down, pulling Alfie's against his own and sheltering them both with his raised arms, a massive stone tumbled down, striking the path where they'd been standing just a moment before.

It split in two with an almighty *crack*. Immediately, another stone followed it, then another and another, waves of solid rock crashing against each other like the ringing of unholy bells.

Then everything went silent.

Alfie's grip was tight around him, and Dominick wasn't sure whose heartbeat it was he could feel racing in his chest.

"Nick?" Alfie croaked out at last, his breath hot against Dominick's throat.

Dominick had to wet his lips several times before he could respond, his gaze fixed on the pile of rocks that lay in the middle of the path, a small avalanche of pebbles still trickling down behind them. Each stone was the same pale grey of those being used to build the folly and ranged in size from no larger than a hare to no smaller than a barrel of ale. Hundreds of pounds of stone where they'd just been standing.

"I'm all right," he gasped out. But he so easily couldn't have been. Another second more and he—or worse, Alfie...

He couldn't put the thought into words. All he could do was cling to Alfie to prove to himself that the worst hadn't happened. They were both still there, still alive.

But someone didn't want them to be.

Chapter 15

Alfie stared at the bare patch of earth as Mrs. McConnell gave her apologies again and again and the foreman spluttered excuse after excuse.

The stacks of stones still sat at the top of the crag waiting to be used. Now, however, there was a gap like a missing tooth between two of the stacks. Below the gap, a path cut through the foliage as the tumbling rocks had carved their way down towards where he and Dominick had been standing.

One of the beams that had supported the rocks was missing, although stepping a few steps closer to the edge revealed it to be tangled in a gorse bush just a few feet down the rocky slope.

"Alfie…" Dominick called out warningly.

For once, Alfie listened, leaning heavily on his cane as he backed away from the drop below. It had taken Dominick some time to find the cane after the rockfall had finally ceased, but Alfie's nerves were so frayed from their experience, he wouldn't have been able to walk far without it, never mind climb back up to the folly to find out what in God's name had happened.

"My lord," said Mrs. McConnell, her clear voice breaking through his thoughts. "I cannot apologise enough. I assure you, my husband and I have always taken great pride in the safety of our construction process. I have no idea how an accident like this was allowed to happen and I will ensure it does not happen again."

"What *did* happen," asked Dominick lowly. Alfie recognised the danger in his tone. If Mrs. McConnell was a man, she'd stand a good chance of being dangled over the side of the crag until Dominick had his answers.

Mrs. McConnell hesitated, likely sensing the danger as well. "I'm not sure. One of the workers noticed a problem with the scaffolding on the back side of the structure. It was all hands on deck seeing to that. No one noticed the hillside giving way under the rocks until a man on the top of the scaffold gave a shout. By then it was too late. I can only apologise again and thank God neither of you were harmed.

"We'll be dealing with this immediately, I assure you. No one goes home this evening until all remaining rock piles are secured further from the edge. I will be closely observing the work myself to ensure the piles are structurally sound and no longer at risk of collapse.

Alfie wanted to snipe that her husband had been the engineer, not her, but that was far too cruel a thing to say aloud. In the end, no one had been hurt and he wasn't so callous that he was going to lash out at a grieving woman over his fear of what might have been. Besides, she hadn't been in charge of the site when the rocks had been stacked so precariously. That had been her husband and he'd more than paid for his sins.

He pursed his lips, but could find no more to say than, "See it done."

Mrs. McConnell nodded at the dismissal and headed off, no doubt to berate the workers for allowing such a thing to happen. Janie hesitated before following, but it appeared her loyalty to her new mistress was greater than her concern for the health of her lord. Just as well. Alfie was in no mood to soothe someone else's nerves when he was so close to losing hold of his own.

Looking back at the empty space where the rocks had once stood, he hadn't noticed the tension in his shoulders until it eased as a familiar presence joined him at his side.

"What do you think?" Dominick asked.

"I think we were bloody lucky not to be killed."

Dominick hummed. Alfie ached to reach out, wanting to take hold of his hand, needing the simple comfort of Dominick's grip in his, but there were too many people around to risk it.

"What else?" asked Dominick.

"I don't think it happened the way she said it did."

"I don't either. If the ground had given out, wouldn't it look like the ground had given out?"

Dominick was right. Alfie might be new to country living, but he knew mud, and he knew what it looked like when it gave way.

The yard at the workhouse had been nothing but mud, and he could remember how they'd all watched with interest one particularly rainy spring as it had washed away, bit by bit, under a corner of the outhouse, until the entire thing had collapsed, falling into the stinking mess below. Fortunately, neither of them had been inside at the time. Another boy hadn't been so lucky.

"Thinking of the privy?" Dominick asked at Alfie's grimace. "Half of that was hanging in open air before it went."

While there was likely some difference between when filthy London mud and good Scottish ground would give way, Alfie would've expected it to favour Scotland. Yet the earth where the missing stack had been was entirely intact. All the supporting beams, save the one that had tumbled with the rocks, were still in place and ended at least two feet short of the edge of the crag. However, there was a large divot in the earth at the very edge where the missing beam had been.

Alfie pointed with his cane. "What do you think caused that? It almost looks like someone leveraged up the beam."

Dominick nodded. "Could be." He glanced over his shoulder, then squatted down, getting his hands under the end of the nearest beam and lifting it just slightly. The remaining stones on the pile wobbled.

"*Nick*," Alfie hissed.

Dominick set the beam back down and wiped his hands on trousers far too expensive to be treated that way, old habits not yet forgotten.

"It's heavy," Dominick admitted. "But I think I could do it. One big heave."

He mimed lifting the end of the beam up and over his head, then pushing it away from him, up and over the edge. Alfie could envision the far end of it digging into the ground, then the rocks atop it sliding as Dominick's end rose, their momentum carrying them off the crag and crashing down onto the path far below.

And anyone unfortunate enough to be standing there.

He shivered. The rocks hadn't fallen on their own. It hadn't been an accident. Someone had tried to kill them.

But who? One of the workers? Mrs. McConnell? *Janie*? Each option seemed more unlikely than the last.

He looked around the site for any alternative. The clearing wasn't large, but the folly was already well over twenty feet tall. If the workers were all on the back side of it dealing with the scaffolding as Mrs. McConnell had said, they wouldn't have been able to see the rock piles at all. It would've had to have been timed perfectly, but if someone had been waiting just beyond the treeline where the clearing turned back to forest, they wouldn't have been seen as they sprinted out, lifted the beam, and sent death tumbling down towards them.

Alfie stared into the woods, hoping to spot something, but all he saw was leafy shade that grew darker and darker the harder he stared.

"We shouldn't discuss this here."

"No," Dominick agreed. "Someone might overhear. I think I know a place they won't, though. Will your leg carry you back?"

Alfie leaned on it, wincing at the twinge. "Do I have a choice?"

"I could carry you," Dominick offered.

Alfie's mouth dropped open at the absurd suggestion. "Absolutely not."

Dominick grinned. It was thinner than usual, but he was clearly trying. "Sure. On my back, your sword at the ready like a cavalry officer riding into battle."

Then his grin dropped and he leaned in closer to Alfie. "Take my arm at least, once we're in the woods. And keep the sword ready, just in case."

Chapter 16

They didn't encounter anyone in the forest as they made their way back down the crag.

Their progress was slow, save for when they reached the spot where the rocks had fallen. Then, without having to speak, they joined hands and ran across the gap as quickly as Alfie's leg could carry him. By the time they reached the manor, he was limping worse than he had in months and groaned when he realised where Dominick was leading him.

"The gymnasium? Really?"

Dominick raised an eyebrow. "You want to have this talk in front of some maid sweeping out the fire or Jarrett folding up your socks?"

"Fine," said Alfie. "But I'm not doing any of my blasted exercises. I've suffered enough today."

He hadn't realised how much he really had suffered until they were in the gymnasium, its smell of leather, chalk dust, and dried sweat more comforting than it should be. The moment Dominick had the key turned in the lock, Alfie threw his arms around him, gripping him tightly. He didn't realise he was shaking until Dominick's arms came up around him too, crushing their bodies together.

Neither was willing to be the first to let go. Nearly seeing the man you loved die or being killed yourself wasn't a thing someone should have to get used to and Alfie hadn't, God damn it! The look Dominick had given him the moment they heard the rocks crashing down from above was just as terrible as it had been the first time their lives were threatened and had filled Alfie with the same bottomless dread.

And afterwards, he hadn't even been able to hold Dominick's hand.

Well, Alfie would hold him now. He buried his face in Dominick's collar until he could feel the pulse of his throat against his lips, rhythmic proof that Dominick was alive. *A-live. A-live. A-live.*

Finally, Alfie's leg grew too painful for him to ignore any longer. He reluctantly pulled away, not that Dominick was willing to release him, and sat on the nearest chair to hand.

That was unfortunately the chamber horse, an absurd piece of equipment with a bellows for a seat, meant to mimic the motion of riding a horse and help improve the required muscles. The chamber horse let out a protesting wheeze as he sank down, but he was too distracted by the sudden relief in his leg to care.

Dominick didn't go far, sitting at his feet and leaning back against Alfie's uninjured leg. He wrapped his hand around Alfie's ankle, and even through the boot, the pressure was grounding. When he dropped his head back against Alfie's knee and closed his eyes, he looked like a fallen angel.

Alfie took the opportunity to run his fingers through Dominick's hair, working through the sweat-dampened tangles until the blond strands parted around his fingers like water. They stayed that way for some time, him petting Dominick and the gesture soothing both of them. Dominick sat so still and his breathing grew so heavy, Alfie began to wonder if he'd fallen asleep.

"I'm tired of people trying to kill us," Dominick said at last, his voice thick.

Alfie huffed. "Me too."

Dominick stayed silent for several more minutes. Alfie began to wish one of them had thought to light the small fireplace before settling in, if nothing else so that he could see Dominick more clearly. The windows in this wing of the house did very little to keep the chill out while also never letting enough light in.

Finally, Dominick spoke again. "If they're going to keep doing it, the least they could do is tell us *why* they're trying to kill us."

"Any ideas this time?" Alfie asked.

Dominick shook his head against Alfie's knee. "Could it be more of that 'cut' nonsense that farmer on the cart did? Not liking the new earl at Balcarres?"

"Or the new bugger at Balcarres," Alfie offered. "Or the new bastard-maker at Balcarres, depending on which rumours are going about. Captain McConnell surprised the murderer the first time and was killed instead, so he tried again today?"

"And since that didn't work either, he'll likely try again," Dominick said darkly. "You do believe the captain was murdered then?"

Alfie groaned. "I keep going in circles. If he's dead, where's his body? If he's not dead, where is he?"

"And what did his wife and Mrs. Hirkins see?"

"Precisely. And I'm still not certain, but too many strange things have been happening for me to think he just decided to walk off on his own.

"So yes, for the sake of argument: He's dead. And if I accept he's dead, I accept the rest of what Mrs. Hirkins saw, so he was likely murdered. Perhaps the murderer carried him off, or stuffed him up the chimney, or made him disappear into smoke. At this point I neither know nor care. Regardless, he was murdered and today someone tried to murder us. Why?"

As he spoke, Alfie had stilled his hand without thinking. Dominick butted his head against his knee like an enormous cat until Alfie began stroking his hair once again, pulling a little more meanly on the tangles this time.

Dominick all but purred. "Well, I do care. Bloody strange for a body to walk off on its own, and I won't pretend otherwise. Stranger still that we can't find where it went. And I'll say I care a great deal less about *why* someone is trying to kill us if we can stop the *who* before he has another chance. McConnell's death was his bad luck. Today was our good luck. I don't want to see whose luck it is a third time."

A sudden thought struck Alfie and his hands stilled again. This time he ignored Dominick's nudging. "What if we're wrong, and McConnell was the right victim in the first place?"

"Then what was today?" Dominick asked, but he didn't seem to be discounting the idea. "Do you think he developed a taste for killing after strangling the captain? Or is it a second killer who just happened to show up at the same place and time as the first, only with eyes for us—or one of us, at least—instead? That sounds like a bigger coincidence even than those rocks 'accidentally' falling."

"I don't know," Alfie admitted, but now that he'd had the idea, he couldn't shake it. "I don't like to think someone's killing purely for the enjoyment of it. But if it is two persons, could today have been *because* of Captain McConnell's death? Retribution of some sort? Could someone be blaming us for that?"

"Mrs. McConnell didn't seem to," Dominick said slowly. "But she was on the crag when the rocks happened, and those men are her men. There's no chance she could have lifted that beam herself, but one of them might have on her orders."

"Or he might have done it on his own, if he was loyal to the captain. He saw his opportunity when everyone was distracted at the scaffold and took it. Or perhaps even two of them together, one to cause the distraction and one to act. I should have taken better note of who was there. I suppose it's not too late to go back."

Dominick gave his injured leg the briefest squeeze and Alfie couldn't fight back the hiss of pain.

"You're not going anywhere," Dominick said, his point made.

He craned his head over Alfie's leg to get a look at the window. The sun was already beginning to set, its long rays creeping over the floor, drawing ever closer. "They'll all be off by now and halfway to the village. We could ask Mrs. McConnell for a list of names..."

"But if she was part of it, she wouldn't tell us the truth."

"Janie then?"

"Unless she's also switched allegiances."

Alfie scrubbed his hands over his face. He could feel a headache coming on, his temples pounding in time with the throbbing in his leg. If only they were having this conversation in the library, or his office, or any other room in this bloody house with a properly stocked cellarette.

He slumped against the wall behind the chamber horse, the change in angle making it give another wheeze.

"I feel like we're coming at this from the wrong end. Or that we're either making too much of it or not enough."

"How do you mean?"

Dominick wrapped his hands around the heel of one of Alfie's boots, working it forward and back until he'd loosened it enough to slide off. Alfie hadn't realised how much the damn thing had been hurting him until it was gone. Then Dominick had to ruin it by running his fingers along the underside of Alfie's foot where he was far too ticklish and the bastard knew it. He jerked away and cuffed Dominick lightly upside the head for good measure.

"Arse. I mean, either today was a complete accident and we're seeing conspiracies where there are none, or there's more going on here and we're only focussing on a small part of it."

Dominick hummed and began work on Alfie's second boot. "I see what you mean. All right, let's have it out. First, just to get the ridiculous out of the way, let's say it was an accident. What then?"

"Then the rocks fell on their own. Perhaps they were unbalanced by uneven ground or a gust of wind at just the wrong angle. They happened to drag the beam with them in a manner that looked suspicious but was actually quite natural.

And we happened to be directly below them at just that time, and everyone else happened to be looking the other direction."

Successfully removing the second boot, Dominick set them both out of the way, far more careful with Alfie's things than his own. "Put all together it doesn't sound bloody likely."

"No, it doesn't," Alfie agreed. "What are you doing?"

"Getting rid of your socks next. If you were sitting as close to them as I am, you wouldn't be asking why. Although I'm not sure I need to bother; they'll walk off on their own if we give them a minute."

Alfie rolled his eyes, but didn't fight back when Dominick flung each sock across the room dramatically. One caught on a stand of dumb bells, which were decidedly more Dominick's domain than Alfie's. It would serve him right if it was forgotten there, only to spring out at him on some unsuspecting later date.

Then Dominick's hands were around his foot, pressing too firmly to tickle, knuckles working deep into all the right places. Alfie took back every mean thought as his aches began to unwind under Dominick's clever fingers.

Dominick chuckled and Alfie realised he hadn't been keeping his noises to himself.

"Focus," he said sternly and more to himself than Dominick. "So we agree it wasn't an accident?"

Dominick squeezed his toes just a little too tightly before releasing a heavy breath. "No. It wasn't."

"Then not only is someone trying to kill us, but it likely has something to do with the captain's death and subsequent disappearance—either as a consequence or continuation of the act. Let's start there."

Dominick shook his head. "No, start at the beginning. First was the sheep."

"The sheep?"

"The sheep heads on the posts. At the time I hoped they were just a sick prank, but with everything else?"

"Not a chance. Even if I'm not the most popular person in the county at the moment, that's a bit much just to make me feel unwelcome. But if you look at it as a threat..."

"It's a damned good threat. Two sheep's heads though. You think that was just for looks or is one for me too?"

Alfie had been relaxing under the rolling of Dominick's hands working not only his sore foot, but the tight muscles of his calf as well, digging in his knuckles in a way that hurt even as it soothed. But the thought of Dominick being under threat was enough to make him tense again.

"I hope not," he said honestly. "No matter what rumours may be spreading about the Earl of Balcarres, hopefully as far as anyone else knows, his 'distant cousin' is just that—his cousin."

"And no one with noble blood has ever fucked his cousin."

Alfie yanked Dominick's hair. "I'm saying that with any luck, rumours haven't actually spread about us at all. I'd think Gil, or Jarrett, or even Mrs. Hirkins would have warned us if they'd heard anything. And our own fears aside, we don't really have any proof they have. Aside from what happened to both of us today. And the fact there were two heads."

"Aside from all that," Dominick said. Alfie didn't need to see his face to know he was rolling his eyes. "I'd say that was plenty of proof someone noticed us and didn't like what they saw."

The idea was terrifying.

"I don't suppose there's any other reason someone would want both of us dead?"

"A toff's a toff." Dominick shrugged. "That was reason enough for the French. And a distant cousin to a toff is still a toff."

Dominick grunted and gave Alfie's leg a shake. "Ease up, you're undoing all my work."

Alfie tried, but it was hard to relax at the thought of the man he loved being in danger. His own safety was a worry, yes, but if someone killed him, it would very rapidly no longer be his concern. But if someone killed Dominick, it would destroy him for the rest of his life.

However, Dominick had made it very clear that the feeling went both ways and if Alfie ever allowed himself to be killed, Dominick would never forgive him.

He tried to push thoughts of either of their deaths from his mind. The best way to keep them from happening would be to figure out what the devil was going on.

"All right, it all started with the sheep. Unless you can think of anything strange before that."

Dominick snorted and removed one hand from Alfie's ankle to give an all-encompassing wave of, *Look around. What about our lives isn't strange?*

"There was the farmer who wouldn't look at you, but I don't know if that's the kind of strange we mean. Or Janie leaving food out for the spirits. Or me helping to deliver a baby. Or the three-legged cat in the barn. Or—"

"Yes, yes. I see your point. Of that list, I'd say only the farmer is possibly strange in a *malevolent* way, but even that might just be local hostility."

"Local hostility's gotten men killed before," Dominick pointed out. "Although Janie thinks she found a way to solve that problem at least."

"Oh?"

"A Scottish tradition she told me about. Called *Samhain*. At the end of October, everyone in the village douses the fires in their homes, then lights them all off the same bonfire for the next year. After a good deal of drinking, dancing, and free food, of course. Janie suggested we use up some of the felled wood to do the bonfire at Balcarres.

"It's also supposed to keep the evil spirits away or some such, although she's also been raiding the larder to keep her broonies fed. They're getting more than just milk and bread now, so we should be expecting a boon from them soon. Unless Mrs. Hirkins catches her at it first.

"One way or another, hosting a Samhain bonfire might bring some of the workers back. And make them in the village less likely to think you're up here cavorting with the Devil to bring down ruin on their heads."

"Well, I'm not doing the second part, but I can't guarantee the first." Alfie tugged Dominick's hair until his lover was forced to tilt his head back to look at him. "They say the Devil is very handsome. I may have been seduced."

Dominick grinned and shook his head free. "If I was the Devil, we wouldn't be locked away afraid of the servants seeing. I'd have you out in the front hall on that bear rug, doing whatever I damn well please to you and to hell with anyone who tried to stop me."

The image was certainly visceral. Alfie would never be able to walk in his own front door again without seeing that rug and thinking of it. The thought of being out in the open like that, completely exposed and at Dominick's mercy made him shiver.

"Are you certain you're not the Devil?" he asked hoarsely.

Dominick grinned again, then turned his attentions back to Alfie's leg, working his way up from his foot, digging into every painful knot until the tension finally unspooled, then moving onto the next.

It was heaven. It was hell. But if Dominick really was the Devil, Alfie had thrown his lot in with him far too long ago to change his mind now. He might as well enjoy his damnation.

"So you agree to the Samhain party?"

"Yes, you bastard. Whatever you want, as always." Alfie hissed as Dominick's hands found a particularly sore spot just behind his knee. The bright flash of pain was enough to momentarily clear his mind and remind him of exactly why his leg hurt so much. He'd been run off his feet because someone had tried to kill them today.

The thought was a sobering one.

"Do you think such a celebration is safe?" he asked. "There's already one man dead. If the killer wished to strike again, which judging by our encounter today, he very much does, then we couldn't be creating a better opportunity for him to do so."

From the way Dominick tilted his head, Alfie could tell he was mulling the thought over.

At last Dominick spoke. "That's a good point. Whoever they are, they wouldn't need an excuse to get close. They'd be expected to show if the whole village was there. Add to that the darkness and drink and chaos of it all—never mind, it's too much of a risk. I'll tell Janie you said no."

"Unless..." Alfie started, before trailing off in thought.

Dominick growled. "I don't like that *unless*. It sounds like something that's going to end with one of us shot, or poisoned, or disappeared."

Alfie waved a hand Dominick couldn't see. "*Unless*, we use the celebration as an opportunity. As you said, all potential suspects will have to be there. We could keep an eye out for anything suspicious. Catch him before he strikes again."

The risks of such an idea were obvious, but the reward of catching whoever killed Captain McConnell and tried to kill them couldn't be ignored. Nor could the chance to show everyone that whatever was wrong with Balcarres wasn't a spirit or a curse, but a flesh and blood *man*. And more importantly, a man who wasn't Alfie.

How they were going to do all that in one night was a question he didn't yet have an answer to, but they had a few weeks to come up with something.

"It's worth the risk."

He rested his hand on the back of Dominick's neck, feeling the tension there. As his touch, Dominick bowed his head, but Alfie knew better than to take that as a gesture of acceptance.

"We'll be careful," he continued. "Stay in eyesight at all times, no following strangers off into the woods, no accepting anything to drink from comely local maids. And it doesn't need to be just us, we can ask others we trust to help."

Dominick huffed out a humourless laugh. "And who do we trust?"

Alfie didn't answer him at once. The chill of the room began to curl around his bare feet. The bright warmth of Dominick's hands, wrapped loosely around either of Alfie's ankles now, thumbs rubbing absently against the juts of bone, only made the cold worse by contrast.

The sun had finally set, but the night must be a clear one because the silver glow of moonlight came in through the windows. It was barely bright enough to see by and washed everything in an uneven grey. Even the gold of Dominick's hair was dimmed, the shine of it tarnished in a way that made Alfie uneasy.

Who did they trust?

"Not Janie," he said at last, breaking the unbearable stillness. "Not if this was her idea. If it is a trap, I won't make it that much easier for her."

Dominick hummed in agreement, but then asked, "You think she could do it? Not just if she's strong enough, but you think she's capable of killing a man?"

"I don't know," Alfie answered honestly. "And in fairness, I'm not sure she's physically strong enough either, but I'm not going to take that chance. Samhain celebration or not, someone tried to kill us and she was there when it happened."

"The same is true of Mrs. McConnell," Dominick offered. "Not only that, she found her husband's body. Either of them, even if they couldn't lift that beam themselves, could have had one of the workers do it and we've seen women kill before. Still, I can't really see either of them cutting the heads off sheep just to warn us off."

Alfie couldn't either. Not wide-eyed Janie, her curls fluttering around her as she sawed through bone. Mrs. McConnell wiping blood from her face, her sensible skirts soaked red as she lifted the head aloft before slamming it down onto the gatepost.

He shook the visions away. As impossible as they seemed, he'd underestimated women before and nearly lost his life because of it.

"Surely someone would have commented on their absence," he offered weakly. "Captain McConnell certainly, or Mrs.

Finley if it was Janie. I don't know how long it takes to behead a sheep, but someone would have noticed the blood if nothing else."

Dominick hummed again, noncommittal. "I *might* trust Mrs. Finley. I can't imagine what she'd have to do with any of this. Same for Agnes and Mrs. Hirkins. I don't doubt they *could*, mind you. But if they wanted us dead, we would be. And if they had reason to kill Captain McConnell, he likely deserved it. We could have them keep watch at Samhain."

"No," said Alfie immediately. "I won't put any of them in harm's way."

The idea was unthinkable.

Dominick let out a long sigh and tilted his head back. Alfie widened his legs and let Dominick's head fall between his thighs, resting on the leather of the chamber horse seat and looking up at Alfie.

Under other circumstances, it would be quite the view. Alfie couldn't resist at least leaning forward until he could run his hands over Dominick's shoulders, the wool of his coat giving way to the silk of his waistcoat, his shirt hidden beneath a wilted cravat. Idly, he began picking at the knot of the cravat, Dominick tilting his head back even further to let him.

It was an unbearably vulnerable position and Dominick put himself in it without a thought, trusting Alfie completely. That trust—that love—made Alfie swallow hard, the weight of Dominick's ring on his hand feeling heavier than ever. But it wasn't the weight of a burden dragging him down. It was the weight of an anchor, holding him safe and secure whenever the world was trying to dash him to pieces.

Dominick smiled softly up at him, then said, "You're such an arse sometimes."

Alfie squawked and tugged the cravat more forcefully. So much for love and trust.

Dominick's smile turned to a full grin. "Such an arse. Won't put little old ladies or new mothers in the path of a killer. So be it. What about the babe himself? We could have James and Davey keep armed lookout."

Alfie seriously considered tightening the cravat around Dominick's throat, only barely deciding to unwind it instead, tossing it aside.

"Don't even jest about that."

Dominick turned his head and pressed a quick kiss to Alfie's thigh in apology.

"You're going to have the same problem with any of them, you know. If something happened to Graham and Davey was left without a father, you'd never forgive yourself. Gil would never forgive you if something happened to Jarrett. God knows why. And it's my throat Jarrett would slit if you let something happen to Gil. I still can't believe it took you so long to notice, by the way."

Alfie groaned. "What about Mr. Howe? Can I feed him to the wolves?"

"You could, but you'd find some reason not to. The same with Frank and Martin. Likely you'd see it as a waste for them to have come all the way up from London only to be killed. Of course, that's assuming you trust any of them not to be the killer in the first place."

Alfie hesitated. "I'd like to..."

"I'd 'like to' too," Dominick said, more solemn than before. "But I don't 'like to' enough to bet your life on it. Or mine."

"Then that just leaves all the new servants, most of whom's names I don't even know yet, not to mention the gardeners and the labourers up at the folly."

"And don't forget, all of these things happened outside, or near enough with the open door when the captain was killed. It might all be someone from the village we've never even met. Or it could be Carnbee or, bloody hell, even Madam Carnbee. They were here the night before McConnell was found dead, remember. Carnbee hates most everyone in this whole bloody manor. And if he caught that wife of his getting up to no good with Captain McConnell in the drawing room? Well."

Alfie groaned and leaned even further forward until his forehead was resting against Dominick's. The murderer could quite literally be *anyone* and they didn't have the faintest idea of where to begin. They didn't know exactly when the murder had even taken place, or why. Hell, they didn't even have a *body*.

"We don't have a choice, do we?" he whispered. "We need more to find out whoever is behind it. If you have a better idea than this Samhain one, I'll take it. But we have to do something. He's targeting our home, Nick."

Dominick raised himself up enough to brush his nose against Alfie's. It was a silly, childish gesture, but the sweetness of it made tears prick the corners of Alfie's eyes.

"We won't let him," said Dominick. His voice was low but fierce. "We'll use the party to tempt him up, but we'll be the ones laying the trap. We've weeks to figure something out. Between your toff education and what we learned in the workhouse, I'd wager my money on us any day over some coward who runs away after doing his dirty work. Wouldn't you?"

"Any day," Alfie agreed. "Including Samhain."

He stayed curled like that over Dominick until the strain on the muscles in his back became too tortuous to ignore. He sat upright with a groan, hearing the pop of his spine as he did. Dominick didn't seem inclined to move, just looked up at him, an inscrutable little smile on his lips.

"Come on," said Alfie at last. "We'd best go get cleaned up for supper."

"Fuck supper."

After everything, Alfie had to laugh. "I beg your pardon?"

"Fuck supper," Dominick said again. "We can have plates sent up later. What's waiting for us at the supper table? Only more apologies from Mrs. McConnell and Gil's concern when he drags the story out of us. Then his complaints when we tell him he has less than a month to organise a party for the whole village. After the day we've had, do you really want to face that?"

Just thinking about it was exhausting.

Alfie slumped back down on the chamber horse. "I suppose we can excuse ourselves and have plates sent up, just this once."

"Later," Dominick chided. "I said we'll have them sent up *later*. For now, we've got a locked door, a reason to be shut away, and I've only just gotten your socks off. And I'll need more off than just my cravat for what I'm thinking. *A lot* more off."

Suddenly, Alfie didn't find himself exhausted at all. He licked his dry lips. "More than just a cravat, you say? You can't mean your coat as well?"

Dominick's upside-down grin turned wicked. "That sounds like a challenge."

CHAPTER 17

Despite his bold talk, Dominick wasn't actually sure he could do any of the things he wanted to do to Alfie with his coat on, at least not without tearing every seam. From the way Alfie was looking down at him with his eyebrows raised and his lips pursed in amusement, the little devil knew it too. Still, a challenge was a challenge and he'd do far worse to knock that smug look off Alfie's face.

Although considering he was currently sitting between Alfie's legs, there was at least one very obvious thing he could do.

He rolled up onto his knees and shouldered Alfie's legs further apart, making room for himself between them. He took a moment to run his hands over Alfie's thighs, enjoying the feel of lean muscle beneath his buckskins, then went straight for the buttons on his fall.

Above him, Alfie sighed dramatically.

Dominick paused, only a single button undone. "Is something wrong?"

"No, no," said Alfie, before sighing again. "It's just that, well, I suppose I was expecting something more... creative?"

Dominick looked up at him in disbelief. "You're saying you don't want me to suck your prick?"

Alfie gave a shrug of his shoulders that conveyed how put-upon he was by all this and how very brave he was for continuing to endure, but his eyes sparkled with mischief.

"I suppose that's fine. It's just, there was that wager we were about to make on the crag. Something about me begging for your... Well, it doesn't matter anyway. We were interrupted before we shook on it, so really, I can't expect you to abide by your word."

Interrupted by a rockfall that was meant to kill us. But apparently now that the danger had passed, Alfie had greater concerns. Like being an absolute menace.

Dominick growled and grabbed Alfie's cravat. Alfie looked far too pleased with himself at this turn of events, so Dominick used the fabric to yank him down and kiss the expression off his face. He had to raise himself higher on his knees to get a better angle, because menace or not, there were few joys in the world greater than kissing Alfie.

His lover draped his arms over Dominick's shoulders, proving he'd gotten Dominick exactly where he wanted him. Dominick nipped his lip in punishment, but that only made Alfie bolder, snaking his tongue into Dominick's mouth. He lapped at the roof of his mouth, a feeling that always made Dominick bristle even as it sent all his blood rushing straight to his cock.

But the point of this had been to make Alfie less smug, not more, so Dominick pushed back, taking control of the kiss as Alfie melted against him. As it was no longer needed to hold Alfie in place, Dominick released the cravat and put his hands either side of Alfie's hips to steady them both. As soon as he put any weight on them though, there was a long wheezing noise, like the fart of an old dog.

Dominick pulled back in surprise. Alfie looked equally startled.

"Excuse you," said Dominick.

"Excuse yourself," Alfie snapped. "That wasn't me. It was the chair."

To prove this, he bounced slightly and the chamber horse made an even more comical noise.

Dominick snickered, and couldn't resist pushing down on the seat himself, delighting when it made the noise again.

"If you're done amusing yourself," said Alfie, who'd gone distinctly pink, "I believe you had a wager to lose?"

He lifted one of Dominick's hands from the seat and placed it directly over his cock. Even through the buckskins, Dominick could feel how hard he was already just from a little flirting and kissing. His own cock throbbed in sympathy, aching to be released.

Instead of freeing Alfie immediately, however, he traced the outline of his cock through the material, watching Alfie's face all the while. His eyes had gone very dark and that pleased mouth parted in a soft "o" as his breaths came more quickly.

He looked like the lordling that had followed Dominick into that alley last year, too brave and too artless for his own good. But that Alfie would never have done anything as brazen as putting Dominick's hand exactly where he wanted it. Such boldness should be rewarded.

Dominick returned his attention to Alfie's buttons. Needing both hands, he lifted the other from the seat. At the removal of his weight, the chamber horse rose several inches, the sound it made this time high-pitched and almost apologetic.

Dominick laughed loudly and after looking annoyed Alfie did as well. When they began to quiet down, Alfie bounced again and the noise started another round of laughter.

"I can't, love," Dominick said at last. "If it makes that sound while I'm on you, I'm going to choke."

"You'd better find an alternative then," Alfie said, grinning all the while. "Promises were made."

Dominick glanced around the room. In the dim light, most of the exercising equipment looked like mediaeval torture devices, which was probably a little more "creative" than Alfie was looking for. At least without discussing it first.

"Come on. The mats will have to do."

He got Alfie to his feet and helped him limp over to the large span of mats that had been placed on the floor so Dominick could practise sparring without worrying about injury if he knocked his opponent to the ground.

"I need to get you on these more often."

Alfie grinned. "I thought that was what you intended to do now?"

"To work on your fighting, you lecher. I need a sparring partner, you need to practise fighting without your cane, and it will give us another excuse to be in here. Besides, isn't boxing meant to be a gentleman's sport? Be a gentleman."

"I'll be a gentleman later," Alfie said, as they lowered him down onto the mat. "After you make me beg for your cock."

He lay sprawled at Dominick's feet, leaning back on his elbows and looking like temptation itself. Aside from his bare feet, he was still fully dressed and this position made it very clear that the brief interruption hadn't lessened his desire.

Dominick fell to his knees, sending up a small cloud of dust. He crawled up the length of Alfie's body, feeling the heat rising from him, but being careful not to touch. He stopped with their lips a hair's-breadth apart. This close he couldn't see Alfie properly, but he could feel his shivering need as he exhaled.

"There's only one problem," Dominick whispered.

"Oh?" It sounded less like a question and more an invitation. Alfie brushed their lips together as he spoke.

"No oil in here."

That took the wind from Alfie's sails. He craned his head back, peering around Dominick into the dark corners of the room as if a bottle might magically appear.

"We could try—"

Dominick shook his head. "Absolutely not." Spit was enough for a finger or perhaps two, but even with the most extensive preparation, more than that was uncomfortable, and he wasn't going to subject Alfie to it just because of a bet. Besides, he was limping enough already.

Alfie looked disappointed, then brightened. "At least that means I win the wager."

Dominick tucked his face into Alfie's neck, enjoying both the scent of him and the way it made him shiver.

"No," he said, kissing the underside of Alfie's jaw, then setting his teeth lightly against it, feeling the scrape of stubble as Alfie swallowed. "I'll still make you beg for my cock. It just means that no matter how much you want it, you won't get it."

He pushed Alfie down onto the mat. Alfie let out a whoosh of breath as he landed, but Dominick didn't have time to watch what effect his words had on him, already shuffling back to attack Alfie's fall with renewed vigour.

The buttons parted eagerly and within moments Alfie's cock sprang free. If Alfie had been temptation before, he was absolutely obscene now. He'd seen Alfie naked gloriously often, but to have him like this, nearly fully clothed and aching for attention, was irresistible.

If Dominick was a poet, he might be able to wax on about the contrast of Alfie's bare self against the fineness of his fancy clothes, or the way the silky head of his prick brushed against the real silk of his waistcoat. But instead all he knew was that the sight made his mouth water.

He didn't waste a moment more and swallowed Alfie down.

Alfie muffled a shout into his sleeve as Dominick worked. He'd been holding off too long for any finesse, swallowing around Alfie's cock, holding it in his throat as long as he could before the need to breathe became too much.

Alfie jerked and thrashed, so beautifully responsive to every touch. When Dominick released him, his cock fell back against his belly with a wet *thwap* that was both deliciously loud in the quiet of the room and likely to stain the fine linen of his shirt.

Dominick licked his lips, enjoying the taste of Alfie's pre-spend—salty and faintly bitter. Alfie keened into his coat sleeve, a muffled noise that sounded suspiciously like Dominick's name.

"I think you're cheating, love," Dominick said, before tracing the vein that ran along the underside of Alfie's prick with his tongue. It was a beautiful prick, long and lean as Alfie himself and just as irresistible. "How will I know you're begging if I can't hear you?"

Alfie swallowed. "You'll know if you do it right. Don't forget you have to leave your coat on."

Dominick grinned. His coat was the least of his worries. He took Alfie in again, hearing another muffled shout from above, but he didn't go quite as deep this time, licking and sucking around the head and using his hands where he couldn't comfortably reach. He was drooling, and he began to feel a familiar soreness in his jaw, but it was worth it to feel the wetness—his and Alfie's both—running down the length of Alfie's cock to pool in the dark auburn curls below.

Blindly, he unfastened the remaining buttons at Alfie's waist and yanked the buckskins down his legs. He had to stop to untangle them from around Alfie's knees, but he finally got a single leg free, and that was all he needed. Alfie spread his legs, canting his hips up in obvious invitation.

At the sight of him, Dominick suddenly realised that he was painfully hard, his cock straining against the tight confines of his own buckskins.

"Let me see."

Alfie's voice was hoarse, but when Dominick replied, his wasn't any better. "Ask nicely."

Alfie shook his head, and Dominick hadn't really thought it would be that easy, but he couldn't bear it any longer. Unfastening his own fall, he gasped when his cock was freed, the cold air of the room against his hot skin making him shiver. And if he felt that way, how must Alfie feel with Dominick's spit rapidly cooling on him? Best to warm him back up.

"Nick, Nick, Nick!" Alfie groaned as Dominick got his mouth on him again. One of his hands tangled in Dominick's hair while the other scrabbled for purchase on the mat, finding none.

Holding Alfie's hips down with one hand, Dominick took his bollocks in the other, rolling and gently tugging them in his palm.

"Plea—" Alfie whined, cutting himself off by biting his lip before he could complete the word.

Good, but not quite good enough. Dominick released his bollocks, and after running a finger though the mess of spit, traced even lower, pressing it against Alfie's entrance and just holding it there, not breaching him, but not moving either.

"Ohhhhh." Alfie gave a heavy sigh, but didn't say any more.

With his lips still wrapped around Alfie's cock, Dominick couldn't see his face well, but from the tremors running through his legs, Alfie wasn't far from climax and still no begging. With that in mind, Dominick pressed his finger in slowly.

Without oil, there was more resistance, and he pulled out again after barely more than an inch, collecting more spit before pressing further. He repeated that time and time again until he could get his entire finger in, stroking Alfie's inner walls in time with his sucking.

Alfie was rolling his hips and pushing down on Dominick's head, trying to get even more of him. Dominick's own woefully unattended cock bobbed in the air as he worked his hips, shuddering every time Alfie muffled an especially indecent moan into his sleeve.

He was about to give up and accept that Alfie won the wager just so they could both come, when he heard the faintest, "Please."

Alfie's prick fell from his lips with an obscene *pop*. "What?"

"Please, Nick." Alfie begged, the sound of it almost enough to make Dominick spend completely untouched.

"Please what?"

Dominick might be about to go out of his mind with lust, but he wasn't going to let Alfie cheat and say later that he hadn't actually lost because he hadn't said all the words.

From the fierce blaze in Alfie's eyes, he'd been hoping to do exactly that. "Fuck. Please, Nick. I want—I want your cock."

Dominick grinned. The satisfaction of victory was nothing compared to the satisfaction of a needy Alfie begging for him. How fortunate he had both.

He pushed his finger in a little further. With a single finger, he couldn't quite reach that spot inside that drove Alfie wild, but it was still enough to make him throw his head back against the mat and swear.

"Fuck! *Please!*"

"I told you before, no matter how much you beg, you can't have it." Dominick was going to make sure that was changed first thing tomorrow. He'd be stocking the gymnasium with oil himself. If anyone found the bottles, he'd claim it was for rubbing down muscles or some such.

"Yes, I can," Alfie said. "Get up here."

Alfie rolled over on his side, and it took a moment before Dominick understood what he meant.

"Oh Christ," he said, and wasted no time in shuffling around, lying down on his side, facing Alfie. In this new position, they were mirrored top-to-toe. Alfie's prick was still within reach of his mouth, but now *his* prick was also in reach of *Alfie's* mouth.

"Finally," Alfie muttered, before taking Dominick in.

Alfie couldn't go as deep as he could, but that hardly mattered as Dominick's neglected cock was engulfed in tight, sucking heat.

Now it was Dominick who was muffling his shouts into his sleeve, before realising there was a better way to silence himself right in front of his face.

Every lick, every suck, that Alfie did to him he did right back, a wheel of pleasure turning through them both, ratcheting them both higher as they went. It was unspeakably good, and he knew neither of them could last much longer.

Then he felt one of Alfie's spit-slick fingers press against his entrance.

That was all it took. He groaned around Alfie's cock as he pumped his hips, filling Alfie's mouth as he came, and came, and came.

Either that or the vibration of his groans was enough to set Alfie off as well. Before Dominick could catch his breath, his mouth was filling with hot fluid, the taste of Alfie overwhelming him. He swallowed as much as he could, but there was still some on his lips when he wiped his face with a shaking hand.

He rolled onto his back, panting up at the ceiling he couldn't quite see.

"You win," croaked Alfie at last.

Dominick licked his lips, tasting him. "What's my prize?"

"My God, don't you think you just had it?"

The leg beside Dominick's head twitched. It was the one that still partially had the buckskins wrapped around it, so he heaved himself up to start untangling them.

"I kept my coat on too."

Alfie groaned. He was bare from the waist down and wonderfully dishevelled from the waist up. "Yes, you must think you're very clever. Mine, however, may need to be burned."

Dominick finished untangling the buckskins and tugged them back up Alfie's legs. He found one of Alfie's discarded socks and wiped them both off before re-fastening their falls to make them at least somewhat decent. Then he collapsed down next to Alfie, their shoulders bumping.

"I suppose we should see about getting that tray sent up," he said at last. "Supper must be over by now."

Alfie groaned again. "Even if it isn't, I'm afraid we've put off our responsibilities long enough. Help me get straightened up. We need to inform Gil he has a Samhain party to plan."

Chapter 18

Dominick wandered the fringes of the crowd of revellers, searching for a murderer.

A search that would be a great deal easier if he knew what this murderer looked like. So far, the killers they'd met had ranged from brutal thugs to beautiful women. It would be nice to know which he should be searching for tonight.

A group of farmers stood together in a ring, heavy mugs of ale in their hands. Could they be plotting a massacre? A young woman ran past them, the ribbons in her hair already unfurling from her dancing. Was she chasing her next victim? Or should Dominick be keeping an eye on the old woman sitting alone by the punch bowl, ready to poison it when no one was looking? Or perhaps one of the musicians would suddenly cease beating his drum to beat someone else instead.

He shuddered. The weeks since they'd decided on the Samhain party had flown by. He and Alfie had been kept busy with preparations, disappearing together into the gymnasium when it all grew too much, sometimes to plan, sometimes for sex, sometimes—miracle of miracles—to actually exercise Alfie's leg. Occasionally, he'd even gotten Alfie to agree to act as a sparring partner, an excellent way to both work out his frustrations and also reassure himself that if the worst was to happen, Alfie could defend himself.

In all that time though, they'd barely been able to come up with much more of a plan to catch their killer than, "Keep a sharp eye out."

The problem was that there was just so much they didn't know. If their murderer even existed, who was he? What had he done with McConnell's body? Why was he trying to kill them and which of them he was targeting? Had he been trying to kill Alfie with the rocks off the crag, or Dominick, or would he have done the same to anyone else passing below given the opportunity?

If they'd known even one of those things, they might have been able to plan, but as it was, they had nothing, leaving Dominick on edge, his fists clenched so tightly he had to shake them out to keep feeling in his fingers.

He wasn't going to take the risk that Alfie was the target. Even as he circled, he kept an eye on his love at all times. At this point, it was practically a habit. He'd been keeping an eye on Alfie since they were children. What was one more night?

It wasn't as if it was a hardship to watch Alfie either. By firelight, his auburn hair shone like polished copper and the shifting shadows cast his features in strange new ways that were just far enough from the familiar that Dominick was struck by his beauty all over again.

As the days had passed without a plan, they'd stopped burning the discarded branches and logs in the garden, instead just adding and adding to the pile until it was impressively sized. When Gil had started making noises about the age of the manor and the terrible destruction that fires had wreaked upon it in the past, they'd stopped growing the main pile and begun a ring of smaller ones to be burned before the grand finale when the great fire would be lit.

Only the smaller fires were lit now, and around each danced the boys and girls from the town, the bravest of them leaping over the flames, risking setting their trousers or skirts ablaze in the name of good luck.

As the garden was little more than dirt and rocks at the moment, it had been deemed the best spot for such a celebration. With the dark forest surrounding the bare patch of earth and the lights in all the homes extinguished, leaving the ring of fires the only remaining light for miles around, Dominick could understand why Janie believed in her broonies.

There was something otherworldly about it all, especially when most of the village boys, as well as many of the men, had either painted their faces or wore masks of wood, cloth, and paper. Some designs were merely to hide the wearer's identity, some resembled animals, yet others were so twisted in their features as to be completely unrecognisable as anything from this world. In the light of fires, it was easy to believe some of them weren't guised villagers at all, but spirits come to toy with mortals.

He shook his head. He'd told Alfie too many fairy stories when they were younger to be the one falling for them now.

He kicked away a smouldering stick that one of the dancers had knocked a little too close to the central, unlit pile in their leaping. The main pile of logs and branches that would become the bonfire from which all the homes in the village lit their hearths was massive, easily taller than two men, and at least three or four across. Dominick had to give Janie her due, not only should the Samhain celebration help Alfie's reputation with the locals, but it would neatly dispose of the remaining trees felled by the building of the folly. Assuming someone didn't get murdered before the bonfire could be lit, of course.

With that thought in mind, Dominick glanced at Alfie again. Alfie was doing his best to strike up conversations, but it was clear the locals might be comfortable drinking their lord's ale, but not yet up to talking to him about it, and certainly not ready to confess to murder. Gil appeared at his elbow, likely to try some of his own charm, but wasn't there for more than a moment before darting off. The reason for that became abundantly clear when Dominick noticed Magistrate Carnbee elbowing his way towards Alfie.

"Christ," Dominick muttered under his breath. The murderer would have to wait. He had to rescue Alfie from this buffoon first.

By the time Dominick made his way to his side, the farmers Alfie had been trying to speak to had vanished, no more willing to endure the magistrate's presence than Gil was. If only they had the same luxury.

"Ah, there you are, Mr. Trent," harrumphed Carnbee. His moustache was in disarray and even in the firelight, his nose looked red. The sun had only just set, but he'd clearly been taking full advantage of the free ale. "I was just telling His Lordship what an *interesting* idea it was to hold a Samhain celebration at Balcarres. You do know that's never been done before."

Dominick bristled. From his tone, it was clear the magistrate didn't like that it was being done now. After everything that had gone into planning it, Dominick could secretly understand why the previous earls hadn't bothered. The last few weeks had been a blur inviting, cajoling, and outright bribing the locals to attend. It wasn't until word got around that Alfie had purchased nearly every bottle and barrel in the inn's cellars and enough food to go with them that anyone seemed enthused.

Of course, actually preparing that much food nearly led both Hirkins women to riot and Mrs. Finley had spent the entire time alternating between sighing loudly about the extra work this meant for the household and blatantly crossing herself to protect from the "all manner of ungodly things" such a celebration would invite.

The only members of the household who'd seemed truly excited were Janie and Davey. Janie was pleased because the whole thing had been her idea in the first place, but Dominick hadn't understood Davey's excitement until just a few hours ago.

The townspeople had come up from the now-darkened village, the sound of pipes and drums announcing their approach with wild music signalling the beginning of the festivities. They'd been led by a pack of boys in their guises with their faces painted or masked, all carrying even more food for the feasting table, a proud Davey at the front of the mob with a towering platter of soul cakes.

Dominick watched a group of younger boys as they leapt over one of the smallest fires. As the magistrate droned on about the fine lineage of the Crawford family and the many far more *esteemed* gatherings that had been held by earls past, jumping over—or into—a fire to escape him began to sound like a good idea. Or perhaps just tossing the magistrate himself in.

Now that held definite appeal. It wasn't as if he'd even be too singed. At Gil's hand-wringing insistence, Mr. Howe had located every bucket in the manor to fill with water, clearly foreseeing how an evening involving both fire and free ale was likely to end.

"Thank you for the history lesson, magistrate," Dominick heard Alfie say at last. "It really was most illuminating. If you'll excuse us, however, I've just spotted the minister and we have urgent business to discuss."

"We do?" asked Dominick as they made their escape.

"Lord no, I doubt he's here at all with all this 'pagan nonsense'. But even Carnbee can't complain about being passed over for God. Have you seen anything suspicious?"

"A lot of couples disappearing off into the trees, though I don't know if that's suspicious to anyone but the girls' mothers. You?"

"Nothing, although perhaps attempting to gather information on a night where both costumes and mischief are encouraged was not our finest idea."

Dominick snorted. "We've had worse."

"Yes, which means you can judge precisely how terrible an idea this was."

"It's not all bad," said Dominick. "One of the couples I saw go off included Madam Carnbee."

Alfie gasped and wheeled around, craning his neck to look back to see where her husband, the magistrate, had now ensnared Doctor Mills in a lecture. "And who? Curse you, Nick! And who?"

Dominick grinned. "Seems like you weren't keeping as sharp an eye out as you thought. Still, at least that's two of the locals who'll be more likely to think well of you. Perhaps three come next summer."

Alfie barked out an entirely ungentlemanly peal of laughter, but no one seemed to notice, caught up in their own revelries. At least the night hadn't been a complete waste if it got Alfie to laugh like that.

He'd been understandably worried of late, the burden of an earldom, the new staff, and an unknown murderer weighing on his shoulders. His brow had been furrowed over one concern or another increasingly often. If he wasn't careful, he'd wrinkle.

Not that Dominick would mind. With any luck, he'd be there to mark each new wrinkle and laugh line Alfie developed until they were both wizened old men, looking like blanket-wrapped prunes as they reminisced about their younger days by the fire. The thought made him smile.

And speaking of the wizened elderly, it was past time they sampled some of the treats Mrs. Hirkins had prepared. The feast tables were overflowing with the best both Balcarres and the village had to offer—decorated cakes and glazed pork sharing space with hearty bannocks and bowls of roasted chestnuts. Dominick helped himself to a tart, before spotting a plate of shortbread half-hidden behind a basket of apples that smelled so sweet that they must have still been on the tree that morning.

"I believe congratulations are in order."

Dominick turned around, wiping shortbread crumbs from his lips as discreetly as possible.

"Ah, Mrs. McConnell," said Alfie. He had a cup of syllabub in his hand. His favourite. Even seeing it used in Bath to deliver deadly poison hadn't been enough to put him off the dessert. And now that he'd found it, the rest of them would have to risk his sword cane if they wanted any for themselves. "How did work go on the folly today? Apologies for taking over your garden for so long. You'll have it back tomorrow, albeit a bit trampled."

Mrs. McConnell smiled politely. She was dressed in another of her plain, practical dresses, but perhaps in deference to the celebration, had a sprig of gorse pinned to her coat. Half a step behind her stood Janie with a blanket-wrapped bundle in her arms that, from its squirming, was either one of the barn cats or James.

"It's your garden to do with as you wish, my lord," Mrs. McConnell said. "And in truth, a bit of hard-packing will only help where I intend to lay the pathways. As for the rest, there's only so much that can be done this time of year other than plan for spring. For which I must say Janie has had some wonderful suggestions. Her knowledge of what grows best locally has been invaluable. But gardens do require patience to see one's plans come to literal fruition. However, the folly is progressing well. I believe we'll be finished within the month, especially if tonight proves successful in bringing back more of the labourers."

"That's excellent news."

The conversation faltered there. Neither Alfie nor Dominick had forgotten the rockfall. It seemed impossible that Mrs. McConnell could have been the one to cause it, but that didn't mean Dominick was going to turn his back on her any time soon.

While the firelight enhanced Alfie's beauty, it had the opposite effect on Mrs. McConnell. Her features, though never what he would call pretty, were harsher in the firelight and more fixed, as if even the dancing of the flame couldn't coax anything out of them. Her eyes, always sharp, held a wariness to them he didn't recall, like a deer just hearing the snap of a twig under an unseen hunter's foot.

He tried to dispel the eerie idea, but it lingered. It must just be the strangeness of the night and his own wariness getting to him. As he understood it, Samhain was the night for such things. A night for peculiar happenings, ancient customs, the telling of fortunes, visits from spirits, and the night the souls of the dead returned to either bless or curse the living.

There were plenty of dead in his past and none who'd be blessing him.

It wasn't something he wanted to dwell on. And certainly not tonight.

"Janie," he said, searching for anything to break the uncomfortable silence. "I see you've been pressed into child-minding service this evening."

Janie nodded shyly. "Yes sir, I'm not to say anything, but Agnes and Mrs. Hirkins have been working on something grand for after the bonfire is lit and asked if I'd keep an eye on him."

The stone of Mrs. McConnell's face softened for just a moment as she gazed fondly down at the baby. "Janie has been quite the natural. I'm not sure I've ever seen a more well-behaved infant. It seems she has a skill with all growing things, not just plants."

The firelight couldn't hide Janie's blush.

"He's a bit fussy," she admitted. "He should be in bed already, but I didn't want to miss the lighting of the bonfire."

"Would he like a bit of syllabub?" Alfie asked. "That always puts me in a better mood."

Then to Dominick's shock, Alfie actually made as if to share his treat, spooning out a tiny dollop and offering it to the wriggling blankets. Alfie had never offered *Dominick* any of his syllabub.

Perhaps it was his own surprise that made him notice, but the conversations around them had stopped. Everyone close enough to listen in had ceased talking, their eyes darting to Alfie and then away, as if they didn't want to be caught staring. Even the musicians had halted their playing, leaving confused revellers looking their way as well.

Oh Christ.

In all their other concerns, they'd forgotten the rumour that James was Alfie's bastard. If the Earl of Crawford was going to feed the babe with his own spoon in front of all his tenants tonight, he might as well march into Parliament tomorrow and demand legitimate standing for his heir.

Dominick narrowly stopped himself from knocking the spoon from Alfie's hand, compromising by placing his hand on Alfie's arm to stop him.

Dominick winced. If other rumours were going around, this wouldn't help, but sometimes discretion had to be sacrificed for the sake of stopping Alfie from doing something monumentally stupid.

"It's time for your speech as lord of the manor." Dominick leaned in and whispered, "The *childless* lord of the manor who wants tonight to go well, not start a whole new wave of bloody rumours."

Alfie leapt back as if Janie held a dangerous animal. In a way, she did.

"Yes, my speech. Very well." Alfie jerked, torn between the manners trained into him and the instincts to escape that had been beaten into him. Dominick solved the problem by gripping his wrist firmly and tugging him away.

"Mr. Howe has the torches," Dominick said, overly loud. "Let's go find him so the bonfire can be lit."

⸺◆⸺

If the scene with James was good for anything, at least it meant that by the time Mr. Howe was located and Alfie's torch had been lit, everyone had assembled around the largest pile in the centre of the garden. Despite their best efforts, not everyone in the village and surrounding lands had come, but there still had to be several hundred people waiting to hear what their young lord had to say for himself.

Dominick swallowed. He'd never been more grateful Alfie was the earl, not him.

Although Alfie looked as if he'd happily trade places with him—or possibly even Jarrett or the man whose job it was to collect night soil from the privies. He stood on the terrace overlooking the gardens, just a few steps higher than the crowd, but enough to be seen. Behind him, the unlit hulk of Balcarres crouched like a great beast watching over his shoulder, the ghosts of centuries looking down on them all.

"F-friends," Alfie started. His voice was uncertain, but they'd spent hours rehearsing this. He tried again, and this time Dominick could hear his love's stubbornness covering any lack of confidence.

"Friends. Thank you all for coming. I know it has been many years since my family has resided in Balcarres. My father travelled the world, but never thought to bring me here, the seat of his earldom. In the short time I've spent here, I've already come to regret his decision to keep me from such a fine place for so long."

Gil had written most of the speech, knowing both how to sound sufficiently noble and also what those who lived around Balcarres would want to hear. He seemed to have done a good job, as those closest to Dominick nodded with local pride while still looking suitably awed that an actual earl was taking the time to speak to them.

"I intend to make Balcarres my home. And it is in this spirit of making up for the mistakes of the past that I would like to continue forward. Tonight then, let us extinguish the flames of the old year and start anew. Let the same fire that burns in my hearth burn in yours, and may its warmth bless us all for another year to come."

With that, Alfie raised his torch aloft. As he walked down the steps to the unlit bonfire, the only sound was the crackling of the flame and the soft click of his cane on the stones.

Dominick looked around to see the entire crowd focussed on Alfie's solemn procession. All of them, save for Mrs. McConnell.

She was staring at a man who stood apart from the rest of the crowd, closer to the woods than the bonfire pile. He wore a mask that was rougher than the others, little more than a thin piece of wood on which had been painted a menacing grin, the features twisted with some terrible glee. The mask looked to have been drawn with charcoal and a black slash ran down one side of its face.

The man was staring back at her. Then he reached up and lifted the mask. To Dominick's horror, the ghoulish face on the mask was almost an exact copy of the one beneath it. The man was smiling, but there was no mirth in it, only cruelty. And where the charcoal slash had been on the mask, a long scar cut down the side of his face.

A shout distracted Dominick, the villagers cheering as Alfie touched his torch to a pile of rags and kindling at the base of the pile with the reverence of a priest. In seconds, they caught, and soon that corner of the bonfire was crackling merrily as the flames spread outward and upwards.

Dominick looked back, but the man was gone. Mrs. McConnell was staring at the place he'd been and in the rush of sudden light, she looked deathly pale.

Dominick tried to get Alfie to look her way and see what he was seeing, but when Alfie finally turned to him, seeking Dominick out above everyone else in the crowd, it knocked everything else from his mind.

Even cast into shadow by the growing blaze behind him, Alfie was beaming with pride. Dominick's chest felt as if it would burst and he couldn't stop grinning. Alfie had been superb. One speech on its own might not be enough to make his people fall in love with him, but Dominick had a claim on that already. When Alfie had lit the fire, he hadn't looked like some Spitalfields orphan trying on the coat of a nobleman, but as if he'd been born to wear the title. Dominick had always known it, but from the look on Alfie's face, it seemed like *he* finally believed it too.

That was when Dominick noticed the smell.

At first, he thought it was the surprise from the kitchen Janie had mentioned. He looked around, expecting to see the Hirkins women carrying out a giant platter of roast venison or braised boar. But there was a terrible metallic sweetness to the smell, that of a meat that had not been bled after the slaughter. And over that, the bitter pungency of burnt hair.

A confused clamour rose all around the fire, then a woman screamed.

"There's a man! There's a man in there!"

Dominick watched as the pride in Alfie's face turned to horror.

"The buckets!" someone else called. "Fetch the buckets!"

As if freed from a spell, Dominick dashed towards the line of buckets, grabbing the first one he saw. It knocked against his thigh, water soaking his trousers as he ran.

By the time he reached the bonfire, it had grown even larger, flames licking over his head. But through the flames he could see it. The unmistakable figure of a man was now visible amongst logs as the smaller branches that had been hiding him were burned away.

Dominick threw the water on the flames, not even looking to see how much was extinguished before running for more.

When he returned, Alfie was standing beside the fire. With his injured leg, he was unable to run with the buckets himself, so he was directing the other men where to aim theirs.

"There!" He pointed with his cane. "Don't try to put the whole thing out, just enough so we can reach him!"

By Dominick's third trip, there was a noticeable dent in the blaze. By his fifth, the fire was beaten back enough that the man was within reach. Dominick grasped for him, gripping a sooty coat and pulling in tandem with a man he didn't know, but who had the scorched face and broad shoulders of a blacksmith used to such heat.

For one awful moment, it seemed like the fire might topple down on them, a flurry of embers blinding him as the still-burning logs around them cracked and splintered. Then with a furious heave, he and the blacksmith tugged the man free.

The man lay unmoving on his stomach, his skin horribly blackened in some places, but untouched in others. Much of his clothing had burned away, but what remained still smouldered. Coughing from the smoke, Dominick frantically patted the embers out, ignoring the pricks of pain against his palms.

"Out of the way! Out of the way!" came a shout. The crowd that had closed in around them was elbowed aside, then Doctor Mills was kneeling beside Dominick, clicking open his ever-present medical bag.

"My God," Alfie whispered. "He can't have survived that, can he?"

Dominick didn't know. Had some villager had too much to drink and crawled in to sleep it off without anyone noticing? Had the man been burned alive in front of them all?

Horrified, he remembered Alfie touching his lit torch to the kindling and starting the blaze.

"Turn him over," the doctor grunted.

Dominick and the blacksmith did, rolling the man further from the flames. It would be a long time before Dominick forgot the greasy, overheated feel of his skin. The man's head lolled on his neck the way no living man's would. One side of his head was horribly burned, one ear all but gone and his hair ending in blackened stumps, but his face was still recognisable.

A heartrending wail split the night air.

Dominick looked up to see Mrs. McConnell crumple, caught only at the last moment by one of the new footmen.

"Clyde!" she wailed, her voice filled with unbearable sorrow. "My Clyde!"

Dominick looked down at the body of Captain McConnell in front of him.

The dead came back on Samhain after all.

Chapter 19

Alfie knew he should be doing something but he had no idea what that something might be.

He stared down at the body of Captain McConnell. After the incident with the rocks, he'd been more worried about the killer striking again than the strange disappearance of McConnell's body. And of all the places for it to reappear, there were few worse than in the middle of the Samhain celebration. *His* Samhain celebration.

Good Lord.

He ran a hand over his face. If he didn't have a clue what to do next, hopefully someone else did. He looked around for Mrs. McConnell. She needed to be taken away from such a horrible sight, he knew that much. He caught sight of her being led into the house, flanked by Janie and several of the other servants, James' unhappy cries announcing their departure.

Most of the villagers were gathering up their things and leaving, mothers covering their children's eyes as they streamed out the garden gates. Should he try to stop them? He could order them to stay, but then what? Ask them one by one if they'd stashed a dead body in the bonfire? If the murderer hadn't already made his escape, he'd only lie.

Dominick and Doctor Mills were kneeling by the body, far too close to the still-blazing bonfire for Alfie's liking.

"For God's sake, put that out!" he roared, directing his anger at the cluster of men and boys who'd gathered around the body, peering over each other's shoulders for a better look.

To his surprise, they snapped to at once. Within a few minutes, nothing was left of the bonfire other than sodden and smoking embers. The ring of smaller bonfires remained lit around them, giving Alfie the feeling that he was at the centre of some dark ritual.

"Isn't that the architect fellow?"

Magistrate Carnbee. Wonderful. It was his duty to investigate, but by God, Alfie did not want to deal with him right now. At least they'd be able to eliminate whatever pompous nonsense he came up with to explain the body's reappearance. With Carnbee's record, whatever he thought had happened most assuredly hadn't.

"Yes. Captain McConnell. You dined with him here a while back. He went missing and you said he'd simply run off on his wife. The weeping one who was just led away."

Carnbee's next harrumph sounded more intoxicated than usual. "Haven't seen him for some time, now that you mention it. Why's his body in your fire?"

A headache was building behind Alfie's eyes. "When he disappeared, his wife and one of the servants saw him dead on the ground, but by the time they fetched help, he was gone. We didn't know what happened to him."

"Well, this solves that then," Carnbee said. "He wasn't quite as dead as he looked, stumbled off not knowing help was on the way, collapsed into the wood pile, and here we are."

Carnbee clapped Alfie on the shoulder. "Poor luck for you as well as him that he chose this pile to fall down and die in."

As much as Alfie hated to admit it, what Carnbee said made sense. If McConnell had only had some sort of emergency and wandered off, that meant there was no mysterious killer carting his victims away. The rocks coming down off the crag could have been an accident, the sheep's heads some poorly thought-out mischief. They'd been chasing shadows this whole time.

Doctor Mills shook his head.

"If you'll pardon my saying so, sir," he said nervously. "This man hasn't been dead for weeks. I'd say, two days at most."

"What?" Alfie, Dominick, and Carnbee all cried in unison.

Doctor Mills twitched like a coney looking for the nearest hedge. "Well, perhaps three. I'd have to examine him further to be certain and these are hardly ideal conditions. But no, he certainly hasn't been dead for as long as he's been missing and from the bruising here..."

Alfie had to look away as Doctor Mills prodded the flesh of the dead man's throat.

"From what didn't get burned, I'd say his death wasn't an accident. This blackening here, you see? It isn't from the fire. It appears to be bruising, although from rope or hand I can't say without more thorough inspection."

"Strangled," said Dominick with grim certainty.

The doctor nodded. "Again, I'll need to examine him, but I'd say, most definitely."

Mrs. Hirkins had been right when she'd described seeing a rope around the captain's neck when she found him in the drawing room. But if he'd been strangled back then, why was he only dead now?

The magistrate grumbled, but no new theory was forthcoming from his quarter. Finally he grunted. "Very well, make whatever arrangements you need. I assume you can provide a cart, my lord?"

Alfie looked around for a footman to alert Graham when he spotted the stablemaster himself emerging from the woods, followed moments later by a dishevelled Madam Carnbee.

"There you are, my dear," said Carnbee upon seeing his wife. "No, no, don't come this way. Absolutely dreadful. Ah, you there! See our carriage is brought 'round, then fetch a cart for the doctor."

Magistrate Carnbee didn't spare Graham a second glance, too busy with his wife who was demanding to know what was going on. Graham gave a heavy shrug of his shoulders, then headed towards the stables to fetch the carriage and cart as instructed, his thoughts on the matter hidden behind his bushy beard.

Alfie cleared his throat, then did it again when he couldn't think of anything to say.

"Is there anything else you need, doctor?" he asked finally.

Doctor Mills shook his head. "Nothing more to be done until I take a proper look at him. I imagine you have quite a bit to handle yourself. Shame he was found tonight of all nights. I was rather looking forward to the celebration.

"Which does remind me. Mr. Trent, before I go, allow me to examine your hands. I'm afraid you may have burned yourself dragging him out of the fire."

Chapter 20

As it turned out, Dominick had burned his hands. Not badly enough to cause permanent damage, thank God, but badly enough to turn the skin an angry red in places. The doctor had warned they might blister before coating Dominick's hands in some sort of ointment and wrapping them in bandages.

"I feel like one of those mummies you hear about from Egypt," Dominick said idly from where he sat on the edge of Alfie's bed. Just his fingertips were bare, and he used them to scratch the bandages on his other hand. "Perhaps we should stop there when we travel. See if we can't find some long-dead Egyptian king's tomb filled with treasure."

"Stop scratching," Alfie snapped. He couldn't bear Dominick being injured at the best of times, and this was hardly the best of times.

It had been a long night. After the body had been seen to, there were the remaining villagers to be dispersed, the ones who didn't see why a little thing like a murder should come between them and a free drink. Then he'd had to face his own servants, send someone to check on Mrs. McConnell, have the remaining food brought in, ensure the other fires were doused... The list went on and on. Gil and Mr. Howe helped with the organisation, ensuring no one went outside except in pairs after

Alfie insisted, but the clock had been chiming in the early hours before he and Dominick finally made their way up to bed.

In some ways, the distractions had been welcome, giving him no time to think about Dominick's injuries, the captain's murder, or the killer they now knew for certain stalked Balcarres.

"Who do you think—" Dominick began, but Alfie didn't let him finish.

"No," he said firmly, placing one knee on the bed beside Dominick's hip, then the other, until he was seated in his lap. Dominick wrapped an arm around him to keep from falling back. "Tomorrow. We can discuss it tomorrow. I don't want to think about who or why or anything else tonight. I don't want to think at all."

Dominick looked up at him. This close, Alfie could see grey flecks of ash caught in his golden hair and he didn't want to think about that either.

Then Dominick gave him a sly grin. "I think I can help with that."

Alfie took Dominick's face in his hands and kissed him. As he rubbed his thumbs over Dominick's cheekbones, he could feel something gritty caught in his stubble. He pulled back, and saw streaks of soot rubbed into his skin.

Dominick frowned. "What's wrong?"

Alfie shook his head. He wasn't going to think about it, but he couldn't look at it either. "Wait here."

He went and wet a cloth in the wash basin. When he returned, Dominick tried to take it from his hand.

"Absolutely not, you'll soak your bandages."

Dominick huffed, but tilted his face as Alfie directed and let himself be scrubbed. There was something soothing about washing the evidence of the night from him. Alfie ran the cloth over Dominick's hair for good measure. It wasn't as good as a real washing, but it would do for now. On a whim, he did the same for himself before dropping the cloth back into the basin. He couldn't tell if he'd done a thorough job, but

Dominick wasn't complaining and being close to him felt far more important than being perfectly clean right now.

He returned to the bed to find Dominick scowling down at his hands on his chest.

"What are you doing?"

"Trying to get this bloody waistcoat off, but I can't manage the buttons."

"Stop that," Alfie said, grabbing his wrists and pulling his bandaged hands away. "You're going to injure yourself further."

Dominick grinned up at him. "Going to undress me yourself then? Or should we call Jarrett back in here to do it? He'd love that."

"If you're not careful, I will," said Alfie. "And I'll let you be the one to explain it to Gil in the morning too."

The jest was forced, but it felt better than the fear that had been consuming him. He tried another. "Or perhaps I'll send for Madam Carnbee. Unless you don't think you can compete with Graham for her attentions. The magistrate's wife and the stable master, who would have suspected?"

Dominick laughed. "I knew you'd want to find out for yourself. He's a bit of a *dark horse*, eh?"

"You're terribly unfunny."

"Yet you love me anyway."

"I do." The words came out more tenderly than Alfie had intended, but he couldn't help but be serious about his love for Dominick, especially at times like this when he was reminded once again how easily love and lives could be lost.

But he wasn't thinking about that tonight, God damn it.

Clearly sensing his change in mood, Dominick put his bandaged hands over Alfie's. "I love you too. Shall I show you how much?"

Alfie scoffed. "You'll do nothing of the sort. You'll let me undress you, get in bed, and not do anything to risk damaging your hands, understood?"

"I do enjoy when you take control," Dominick said, and stuck out a foot so Alfie could remove his boot.

Alfie stripped him quickly, but not without care. It wasn't the sensual tease he'd done before, but it was impossible not to find the act of removing Dominick's clothes arousing, peeling off layer by layer until he revealed the man only Alfie got to see.

The coat was a bit tricky, the tight sleeves too small to easily pull the bandages through. Dominick hissed in pain more than once as they went, but after that, the rest went smoothly. Once the cuffs were unbuttoned, the shirtsleeves had plenty of room, and the waistcoat wasn't an issue at all. He'd winked when Alfie had removed his trousers, but climbed into bed when directed. And if Alfie had caught himself staring at Dominick's bare arse as he did, that was only fair.

He went to double check the door was locked, then crossed through the passage into Dominick's room to check that lock for good measure. Confirming they were tucked away safely for the night, he made short work of his own clothing.

"Something occurs to me," Dominick said as Alfie was piling his clothes on a chair for Jarrett to sort in the morning.

"Oh?"

Dominick was sitting up in bed, watching him. "It occurs to me that I might not be able to use my hands, but there's nothing you can't do with yours."

He looked pointedly down at where the blankets were pooling in his lap. "Nothing at all."

Alfie snorted and Dominick took his amusement as encouragement.

"Think about it," Dominick said. "Who knows how long I'll have to put up with these bloody things? Denied even the use of my own hands? They say men can die from that, you know."

Alfie didn't want to hear anything about men dying, even as a joke. "And you're already in peril, are you? After only a few hours?"

"Desperately. Only you can save me, love."

Alfie went back to rolling up his used cravat. The idea was ridiculous. Dominick was ridiculous. But hadn't Alfie been looking for a distraction?

He set the cravat down on top of the pile.

Dominick straightened, clearly sensing he'd won. He looked even more delighted when Alfie went over to his dresser and pulled out the bottle of oil within.

"Lie back," Alfie said.

Dominick did as he was told at once, beaming as Alfie came and stood next to the bed. He pulled down the blankets to find Dominick already half-hard and waiting for him.

"I was expecting just a quick…" Dominick moved his hand in a way that would probably be more obscene if Alfie could see his fingers. "But bringing out the oil? You're too good for me."

"Oh, this isn't for you," Alfie said. Then he climbed onto the bed, straddling Dominick's hips again.

Before Dominick could ask any questions, Alfie uncorked the bottle and poured a decent amount over his fingers. Then, making sure Dominick's eyes were watching his every move, he reached back and slid one inside himself.

"Christ." Dominick's whisper was reverent.

Alfie thrust slowly, stretching himself until the finger was buried to the knuckle. Then he added another.

The good thing about doing this himself, rather than having Dominick do it for him, was he could tell exactly what he needed and when he was ready for more without being so blinded by lust he forgot how to form words.

He realised he was rocking back and forth. It felt good, doing this to himself, but it was nothing like the overwhelming sensation of having Dominick in him, preparing him.

He felt a hand on his thigh, then the ends of bandaged fingertips brushed his cock.

He batted Dominick away with his other hand, spilling some of the oil on his chest in the process. He set the bottle on the table beside the bed for safekeeping.

"Ah, ah, ah. No touching. We can't risk your bandages getting dirty."

Dominick's eyes went wide and Alfie saw the exact moment he realised the predicament he'd just gotten himself into.

"You're a devil."

Alfie hummed, scissoring his fingers inside himself. "You should, ah, you should have thought of that before you got into bed with me."

"Christ," whispered Dominick again, thudding his head back against the pillows.

Before Dominick, Alfie never would have dreamed of doing anything so wanton. But here he was, pleasuring himself in the most forbidden way as his lover watched, naked and now fully hard beneath him, but unable to touch.

Just the idea of it had Alfie's eyes fluttering shut. He thrust his fingers harder, seeking that perfect spot. He cried out when he hit it, waves of pleasure radiating outwards. He struck it again. He was fully hard now too, without even putting a hand on his prick. For a mad moment, he wondered if he'd be able to climax just from this alone.

Then someone else's hand was on him, fingertips tracing the length of his cock.

Alfie slit his eyes open the barest fraction. "What did I tell you before?"

Dominick gave him a cheeky smile, fingers following the vein along the underside of Alfie's cock all the way to the head. It was nearly impossible to keep from leaning into Dominick's touch, but Alfie resisted. There was a point to be made.

"Oh no," said Dominick, completely unrepentant. One of his fingertips taped the very tip of Alfie's prick, bringing up a bead of liquid and making his hips jerk. "I must have forgotten. What are you going to do about it?"

Alfie removed his fingers from his arse, wincing at the loss, and climbed off the bed. Hardly believing his own brazenness, he snatched up his cravat.

"If you can't follow instructions for your own good, you'll be made to follow them. Hands out."

Dominick didn't move from his sprawl on the bed. He stared at Alfie with wide eyes, and for a moment Alfie was afraid he'd gone too far.

Then Dominick licked his lips. "For my own good?"

Alfie nodded, afraid to say more.

Then Dominick stuck out his hands, his wrists pressed together. "Well, if it's for my own good."

It took Alfie longer than he'd have liked to tie Dominick's wrists together. His fingers were slick and his hands trembled with excitement. Finally though, he got a knot to hold.

"All right? Not too tight?" he asked.

"Perfect."

About to return to his earlier spot, Alfie gave the knot a last tug. But it hadn't been centred, and one end of the cravat trailed out in a long tail. Without giving himself time to think, he used the tail of fabric to lift Dominick's arms over his head and tied it through one of the decorative carvings on the headboard.

This new position accentuated the heavy muscle in Dominick's arms. It was intoxicating to see all the power that Alfie had just contained—that Dominick had let him contain.

"All right?" he asked again, his mouth dry.

"Fuck, Alfie. I don't deserve you. Yes, it's bloody all right. Now get back to whatever torment you have next, devil."

Alfie resumed his position over Dominick's hips. He shifted, but he didn't think he needed any more fingers. What he needed was Dominick. From this angle, he looked even more imposing, the muscles of his arms flexing as he tested his bonds, elbows slightly bent and his shoulders spread to their broadest by the angle of his arms. He looked like some hero or god from a myth and Alfie was the wicked monster who'd captured him.

Better make the best of him then.

He ran his hands over Dominick's chest, gathering up the remnants of the oils that had spilled there. There was enough to coat Alfie's dry hand, the one wearing Dominick's ring, and he used both hands to slick Dominick's cock.

Dominick bucked up, but Alfie had been expecting it and waited him out, swapping hands when it suited him, or using one to tease Dominick's bollocks.

Dominick gave a wordless moan and closed his eyes. That wouldn't do at all.

Alfie shuffled forward, rising up on his knees and feeling a twinge in his leg that said he'd likely regret this in the morning. He stopped moving his hands, still holding Dominick's prick beneath him, but no longer stroking or teasing.

Dominick took several deep breaths, then opened his eyes. "Why'd you—"

Alfie didn't let him finish his question before sinking down on his cock. He probably should have used a third finger first, but the stretch of Dominick inside him, just this side of pain, was worth it. He was thick, and the burn of trying to make room for all of him had Alfie gasping.

He rode out the feeling, fingers clenching and unclenching against Dominick's stomach. Then the burn eased, and there was nothing left but *Dominick*.

Alfie rose up, just a few inches, but coming back down knocked all the breath out of him. He did it again, changing the angle a little this time, but it still wasn't quite right.

Leaning forward, he ran his fingers through the golden thicket of Dominick's chest hair and braced his weight on Dominick's chest. This time when he came down, sparks burst behind his eyes as Dominick's cock hit the spot inside him he'd been aiming for.

"Nick," he panted. When he dropped down again, Dominick rose to meet him, his heels digging into the mattress, and the sparks turned to white flame.

"You're so beautiful," Dominick murmured, groaning into another thrust. "So beautiful for me."

Alfie kept going, revelling in the feel of Dominick below him. He shifted his hands, scratching Dominick's nipple with his fingernail and earning him a bitten off shout. So he did it again, scratching, twisting, and teasing until Dominick was less thrusting and more just writhing beneath him.

But too soon, that twinge in his leg became an ache and Alfie found he couldn't lift himself as high as before, then could barely lift himself at all.

"Nick," he said, his voice nearly a sob. "I can't. My leg."

"Fuck. All right. I've got this part. Just touch yourself, love, let me see how gorgeous you are when you spend."

Keeping one hand on Dominick's chest for balance, Alfie immediately took hold of himself with the other. It wouldn't take very long, not with Dominick still thrusting up into him, driving his shoulders down into the mattress as he rose up to give Alfie what he needed. Dominick's strength was incredible and right now, it was leashed, harnessed all for him.

Alfie kept his eyes on Dominick's so he caught the crafty look in them just before he heaved up in hard double thrust, bouncing Alfie on his lap.

That was all it took. Alfie gasped as his climax overtook him. Seeing his spend coat Dominick's stomach and up his chest was enough to get him to spend again. He collapsed down onto the sticky mess, still riding up and down as Dominick continued to thrust into him as best he could. The new angle gave Dominick little leverage and with his hands tied, there was nothing he could do about it. If Alfie wanted to, he could leave him like that, used for Alfie's pleasure and left unfulfilled. The thought was enough to make his prick twitch weakly where it was pressed between their bodies.

"Love, please. I need more," Dominick's voice was fraught. He was so close, but only Alfie could control if he climaxed or not. But more than anything, Alfie wanted Dominick to be happy and he knew one sure way to do that.

Dominick's nipple was right in front of his face. His were more sensitive than Alfie's, in fact, they were one of his few weak spots. Alfie bit down hard, then laved his tongue over the abused flesh.

Dominick's breath caught in his throat and his body went rigid. Alfie bit him again for good measure, and then Dominick was spilling into him. The feeling of the hot spend filling him made Alfie feel possessed and possessive. He clenched down, revelling as Dominick shuddered with aftershocks.

When their breathing returned to normal, Alfie lifted himself just enough for Dominick's prick to slide free, missing the loss already.

Then he reached up and untied the knot that bound Dominick to the headboard. It took even longer to untie than it had to tie, as Dominick's pulling had tightened it, but after picking at it with his fingernails, he was finally able to get him free.

Dominick's arms, wrists still bound together, immediately came down around him, cradling Alfie against his chest.

"Are you sore?" Alfie asked, rubbing Dominick's forearm.

"Not enough to bother me," Dominick replied. "Are you?"

"Not enough to bother me."

It was another few minutes before he could pick apart the knots holding Dominick's wrists together, but finally the mangled cravat pulled loose. Alfie wanted to fall asleep right there in the circle of Dominick's arms, but he could already feel his own come growing cold and tacky between them, never mind the mess of Dominick's. He regretted returning the cloth to the wash basin, but it was only a few steps and with Dominick's hands bandaged, the responsibility of cleaning them up was fully his.

With another groan, this one not containing any pleasure at all, he retrieved the cloth, but could only bother tossing it to the floor once they were clean. Another problem he'd think about tomorrow.

Dominick was already snoring when Alfie sunk back down against him, running his fingers through the slightly damp chest hair, his head cradled on Dominick's shoulder. As Alfie drifted off, he thought he heard a cry in the distance, something mournful but this time, it was also triumphant.

Before he could be certain, Alfie was asleep and the sound drifted off into the night.

Chapter 21

Dominick awoke the next morning to his favourite sight in the world. After cutting it all off to blend in back in Spitalfields, Alfie's hair was finally back to its old length.

The auburn curls, so resistant to taming at the best of times, were at their wildest in the morning, sticking every which way and resembling the nest of creature with a fondness for red but few building instincts. Alfie had his head on Dominick's shoulder, where beneath the unruly mass his mouth was open in a very un-earl-like fashion. He was snoring softly as he commonly did and yet denied completely, giving the outrageous lie that Dominick was the one who snored.

Ridiculous.

Looking down at him, Dominick doubted any man in the history of the world had ever loved anyone more than he loved Alfie. Their bond was unlike anything he'd ever felt before, and Dominick would spend the rest of his life marvelling at being lucky enough to have not only found his perfect match, but to have found him again when they were old enough to appreciate it.

Then Alfie wormed the ice blocks he called feet between Dominick's own and Dominick remembered that this was a demon who had been put on this earth solely to vex him. He reached out to brush the curls away from Alfie's face so he could have a better view of his tormentor and was surprised to find himself wearing mittens.

The events of the night before came flooding back, disrupting the peace of the morning. Not mittens, *bandages* from pulling a burning corpse from a bonfire in front of the entire county. The smell of the scorched flesh had been revolting, but even worse had been the feel of it under his now-wrapped hands.

His fingers flexed at the memory and he hissed as the bandages rubbed against his raw skin. At the sound, the nest stirred against his shoulder.

"M'Nick? S'it morning already?"

The faintest grey light was peeking around the curtains, just enough to illuminate the man beside him, but not truly enough yet to be considered dawn.

"Nearly, love. I should get back to my own rooms. No reason for Jarrett to start his morning with an eyeful."

"I think Gil handles that now." Alfie yawned and wiped his mouth with his hand, eyes blinking open in surprise when it came back wet. "Besides, he can try, but I locked the doors last night. After everything that happened, I just needed to know the outside world couldn't touch us for a few hours. Is that silly?"

Dominick pressed a kiss to his forehead. "Not silly at all. Many grown men hide from their valets."

Alfie slapped Dominick's chest at the jest, then left his hand there. After a minute or so of silence, Dominick thought he'd fallen back asleep until Alfie said, "It really was horrible last night, wasn't it? How are your hands?"

Dominick held them both up for examination. In the weak light, they looked like the wraps he used to wind around his hands before a boxing match. Although these were far more extensive, as if he'd started winding and simply forgotten to stop.

"They hurt, but I've had worse. Looks like you bruised my wrists though. That'll be hard to explain to Doctor Mills when he changes the bandages."

Alfie shot up in bed. "Did I really?"

Dominick grinned. Alfie's knots had been far too loose to cause any actual damage, but that didn't mean he couldn't enjoy winding up his lover. "Terribly. Since I'm unlikely to recover, you might as well do it again."

Instead of searching for a fresh cravat, Alfie just slapped his chest again and settled back down.

"Arse," he said. "You did enjoy it though? It wasn't too much?"

"Bloody hell, Alfie. What do you think? I'm only mad we didn't try that ages ago."

"Oh good." Alfie sounded smug, but Dominick could admit he'd earned it. "It *was* for your own good, you know. So you wouldn't injure yourself further."

Dominick raised an eyebrow. "No other reason? How noble of you."

Instead of laughing, Alfie tensed against him.

"What's wrong?"

Alfie sighed heavily, but only relaxed a few degrees. "Nothing. It's just... I don't feel especially noble. In the very real earldom sense. I tried to throw a celebration for my tenants and gave them a nightmare instead. A man I brought here to do a job ends up strangled. My house is swarming with people I don't know or trust. If Gil tries to explain grain tariffs to me again, I'm going to scream. And to top it all off, a murderer has been terrorising us for months and is growing bolder.

"Oh, and let's not forget that the strangled man was already found dead once, disappeared, then found dead again in a fire. So that's quite the fun little conundrum to puzzle over when I'm too overwhelmed by the rest."

Dominick shifted so he could get both his arms around Alfie, then rolled them so Alfie lay completely on his chest. It was a bit tricky without using his hands, but Alfie obliged him, settling his long body between Dominick's thighs and folding his arms into a pillow on Dominick's chest so he could look up at him. He was heavy, but it was a welcome weight.

Dominick kept his arms looped around him, resting his bandaged hands low on Alfie's back.

"I didn't know it was all weighing on you so heavily," he said. "I don't know how I can help with most of it, but I can toss Gil into the horse trough at least."

Alfie chuckled. Pressed this close, it felt like the sound came not just from him, but from them both.

"As much as I appreciate the image, he isn't exactly the worst of it. It's just frustrating. And every time I feel like I'm failing, I remember I wasn't actually supposed to have any of this and that makes it all the worse."

"Well," Dominick said cautiously. It wasn't the first time Alfie had worried about his less-than-noble blood. While everyone agreed that the careful breeding of the aristocracy made them superior, from what Dominick had seen, it hadn't actually done much but make them prone to large teeth and weak chins. "If it means anything, you're already doing more for Balcarres than your so-called father did, noble blood or not."

"Easy for you to say," Alfie muttered. "You're half-king."

"And half-maid. And all French, which I'd appreciate you never bringing up again."

Dominick took advantage of their proximity to flick Alfie on the nose. Or he attempted to, but due to the bandages only succeeded in batting him in the face.

"You'll get your bearing on the rest of it soon enough," he said. "It's really only the murderer that's the problem. Once we figure out who he is and stop him, the rest will fall into place."

"Is that all?" Alfie sighed. "But you're right. And the sooner the better. What do you make of it?"

"Not much more than I did a few weeks ago." Dominick shifted to a more comfortable position amongst the pillows, Alfie swaying above him like a ship at sea. "Although I can't help but think that our reappearing corpse is the key to it."

"I agree, but that doesn't exactly clarify the matter. As I see it, either Doctor Mills was wrong and Captain McConnell really has been dead since the drawing room. In which case, what happened to his body the first time?"

"Or else Doctor Mills is right," supplied Dominick, "He's only been dead a few days. In which case, what the devil happened in the drawing room?"

Alfie nodded, the motion digging his crossed wrists into Dominick's breastbone. "Either way, that still leaves us with the question of who killed him."

"And why did they try to kill us?" Dominick added. "I don't think there's any arguing that was an accident anymore."

"I agree."

Dominick squeezed Alfie tightly, memorising the feel of his body pressed against Dominick's own. They'd had so many near misses, yet here Alfie was, in his bed and in his arms. He'd never take for granted how lucky he was to have that.

They went through the list of suspects one by one, but little had changed since they'd discussed it in the gymnasium after the rockfall. At least now they knew for certain Captain McConnell was dead, although that was a hollow victory.

"Something strange did happen last night with Mrs. McConnell." Dominick had almost forgotten in the horror that came after.

"Right as the bonfire was lit, I saw her looking at a man in a mask, a villager I suppose, but not one I recognised. His mask was a terrible one, all scarred and hateful, but then he took it off, his face was worse. It might have been nothing, just her eye catching on someone, but she looked frightened. And when I looked back, the man was gone. That's about when the hue and cry went up, so I might be misremembering, but I swear she was afraid *before* we found her husband's body."

"Well, that certainly does add a new wrinkle," Alfie said. "And an important one by the sounds of it. Do you remember anything else about the man? Could he have been one of the workers?"

Dominick hesitated, stroking his fingertips idly over Alfie's back as he thought. "I didn't get much of a look, but I'd swear he wasn't, at least not any of them that I've seen since we started paying attention. I'd remember a face like that."

"Definitely suspicious," said Alfie.

"And makes me wonder about Mrs. McConnell too," added Dominick. "If she knows this man, might she know more she's not telling us?"

Alive hummed. "All right, we've added the mysterious stranger to the list of suspects and moved Mrs. McConnell higher. Are we forgetting anyone? I feel like there's an invisible key hanging right in front of us. It would unlock everything, but we just can't see it."

"What about McConnell?" Dominick offered. "The captain, I mean, not the wife. Let's say, the drawing room was some cruel trick on her. She faints, Mrs. Hirkins flees, and he makes his escape."

"It could be, but why? Just to sneak out of the woods later to try to kill us? He was an engineer. If he wanted us dead, I have to think he'd find a more precise way of going about it."

"And why would he want us dead in the first place?" Dominick pointed out.

"*And*," added Alfie, "that still doesn't answer the question of who killed him. He certainly didn't do *that* to himself. If you consider hanging a form of self-strangulation, fine, that's certainly possible. But how does a man hang himself and then after he's dead, cut himself down, get rid of the rope and shove himself into a bonfire?"

"He had help?" Dominick offered weakly. "But that still leaves who. And why."

Alfie snarled and thudded his head against Dominick's chest several times. "It just doesn't make any sense. And I can't make it make sense and there are so many people relying on me to make *everything* make sense. I'm an earl, damn it, but I don't know what to do about any of it. It's all just so bloody frustrating."

Dominick stroked a bandaged hand over Alfie's ear. It wasn't as tender a gesture as usual, but Alfie still leaned into it.

"You're doing a better job than you think," Dominick said softly. "And you're trying, which is more than most toffs would do. And you know what you've got those other toffs don't?"

"The ability to tell dog meat from rat in a workhouse stew?"

Dominick rolled his eyes. "That, and you have me. You might be an earl, love, but you don't have to be one alone."

Alfie stared at him for a long moment, then leaned forward for a kiss. The motion dug his elbows into Dominick's ribs, but he'd suffer a lot worse for one of Alfie's kisses. When they broke apart, Alfie didn't go far, burying his face in the crook of Dominick's neck.

The moment was interrupted by the growling of one of their stomachs or possibly both, Dominick wasn't sure.

He laughed. "We won't solve anything on an empty stomach. Up you get. Since you've locked Jarrett out, I'll need you to help me dress. Can't do a damn thing with these mittens on."

Alfie looked delighted to be useful, which should have immediately made Dominick suspicious.

In no time at all, Alfie was up and had dressed himself, but was having much more difficulty helping him. It wasn't so much that the process was any more challenging with the bandages in the way, but Alfie was in a playful mood, taking his time slowly pulling on Dominick's shirt, letting his hands skate the length of Dominick's body through the fine linen. The trousers were a torture. The buttoning of his fall even more so. By the time Alfie finally got to his boots, Dominick just leaned back in his chair and threw an arm over his eyes.

"You do know this is only fun when you take clothes off, not put them on?"

"Are you not enjoying yourself?" Alfie asked, which was an incredibly cruel question to ask when he was kneeling between Dominick's thighs.

"I'm just wondering, if there were two of you, would this process take twice as fast or twice as long?"

Alfie narrowed his eyes. "You wouldn't have the first idea what to do if there were two of me."

Dominick grinned. That was far too obvious an opening to ignore. "I absolutely do. It might take a while, but the very first thing I'd do is—"

He was interrupted by a commotion in the hall. First the sound of raised voices, then loud footsteps, then a desperate pounding on the door. Alfie snatched up his cane and immediately pushed himself to his feet. Serious now, he slid Dominick's coat over his shoulders, neither of them breaking stride to do so as they made their way to the door.

Alfie unlocked it to reveal Mr. Howe. The butler's usually neat clothes were dishevelled, as if he'd thrown them on at a moment's notice, and there was a frantic look to him so uncharacteristic of the always composed man that Dominick was taken aback.

"What's wrong?" Alfie demanded.

"My lord," Mr. Howe panted. "It's little James. He's missing."

Chapter 22

They followed Mr. Howe as he raced through the house. Even in his panicked state, he wouldn't do anything so uncouth as running, which Alfie's leg appreciated, but he wasn't exactly strolling either.

"What do you mean, James is missing?" The words didn't make any sense to Alfie. James couldn't be missing. He was an infant. He couldn't even crawl yet, could he? And where would he go?

"Just that, sir," replied Mr. Howe as they descended the stairs to the kitchen. "He was with his great-grandmother as she prepared breakfast. She says between one moment and the next, he was gone. It's just like what happened to Captain McConnell."

"Steady," Alfie said. He wouldn't acknowledge that he'd been thinking the same thing, or how that story had ended. "We don't know anything yet.

"And don't be spreading that around," Dominick added.

They heard the kitchen before they saw it, a sound that Alfie shouldn't be able to identify at all, but had become uncomfortably familiar—the sound of Mrs. Hirkins sobbing.

She was sitting at the table when they entered, her face buried in her handkerchief. Agnes sat motionless in the other chair, her eyes staring dully ahead. Mrs. Finley had her hands on Agnes' shoulders, patting her gently and talking in a soft voice. If Agnes even heard her, she gave no sign of it. Alfie followed her gaze to the crib tucked into the corner of the kitchen. It was empty.

"What happened?"

"Master Alfie!" Mrs. Hirkins cried. "It's all my fault! Oh Agnes, I'm so sorry. Oh James!"

She broke into another fit of sobbing then, and Alfie couldn't stop himself from going to her and taking her hands in his own. Her skin was papery and there was a fine tremor running through her hands. He squeezed them tighter, trying to make it stop.

"Mrs. Hirkins," he said around the knot in his throat. "Please, we need to know what happened."

It took her several tries, but she was finally able to get more than a few words out at a time.

"James was... he was fussing this morning. I could hear him through the wall. I was already awake, but it was early, before sun up, so I took him so Agnes could sleep in a bit. I brought him down to the kitchen with me, thought I'd show him how to make my Bath buns. We had the dough all ready, me showing him how to knead it properly, him babbling away to himself in the crib. But I'd forgotten to get out the currants. He seemed happy enough, so I went to the storeroom to go fetch some more..."

At this, she started crying again and Alfie had to release one of her hands so she could wipe her eyes.

"When I came back, he was gone. Oh James!"

"We'll find him," Alfie said, praying it was true. "We'll find him, but I need your help now. You came back and James wasn't in his crib. Is there anything else you remember? Did you see anyone? Was anything out of place?"

Mrs. Hirkins shook her head, but she seemed hesitant. Dominick spotted it too.

"What was it?" he prodded gently. "Even if you think it's nothing or you were imagining it, we'll believe you."

She cleared her throat. "It was cold. I thought it was just me, but no, it was cold."

Dominick nodded. "Like someone opened the door?"

There was a door that led from the kitchen to outside to take deliveries and make fetching water easier. It was where he and Dominick had seen Janie setting out her bread and milk for the broonies a lifetime ago. Alfie looked over at it now.

In the top of the door was a small window, like a porthole on a ship. In the pre-dawn hours, it would've been dark outside, but the interior of the kitchen would've been brightly lit with lamps and the stove fire—and the shared joy of James and Mrs. Hirkins. No one inside would have been able to see out, but someone watching from just outside the door would have been able to see everything. Including Mrs. Hirkins stepping out for currants, leaving James all alone.

Dominick went and tried the door. "Unlocked."

That seemed to snap Agnes out of her daze.

"What does that mean?" she whispered. Then she asked again, her voice growing louder with every word. "What does that mean? Did someone take him? Who? James! Who took my James?"

She was near shrieking by the end. Mrs. Finley wasn't just comforting her any longer, but trying to hold her down in her chair.

"Easy there, easy there. We'll find the bairn. We'll find him." Mrs. Finley looked at him then. "Won't we, my lord?"

Alfie couldn't answer. Someone had come into Balcarres and taken James. He didn't know what to do. If he made the wrong choice, whoever it was might get away. They might never see James again. The thought of not seeing that gummy grin or hearing those sweet baby coos was awful enough for him; he couldn't imagine how Agnes was suffering. And if something happened to James—something unthinkable—if *that* happened, Mrs. Hirkins would never forgive herself. She'd be in pain for the rest of her life, if the guilt didn't make her heart give out first.

He didn't know what to do, but if he did nothing, all that would happen anyway. He had to at least try.

"Mr. Howe, wake the rest of the household. Search the outbuildings first. When the day staff arrive, have them join you. No! Have half of them join you, the other half search the house, just in case."

Was that the right choice? He couldn't be certain. There was nothing to be done about it now as with a curt bow, Mr. Howe was gone, off to see Alfie's orders were followed, be they the right ones or not.

"He's vanished. Just like Captain McConnell." Agnes said. There was a dreamy quality to her voice that had Alfie and Mrs. Finley sharing a worried look.

"It's not like that at all," said Dominick, but Alfie could hear the fraying in his voice. Could see it too, in the worried pinch of his mouth.

"It is though." Mrs. Hirkins added, nodding frantically. "It is, it is. I saw James and then he was gone. I saw the captain's body and then he was gone too. Poor Mrs. McConnell, I should never have left her there alone when she fainted. The way she cried out for her husband before she collapsed, I'll never forget it. But what was I to do then? What now?"

Something in her words caught at Alfie, not an invisible key, but maybe, just maybe, the handle of one.

"Mrs. Hirkins," he said slowly, trying to puzzle out his own thoughts even as he spoke. "I need you to think very carefully. Please, I wouldn't ask you to relive it if it wasn't for James' sake. Did you know Captain and Mrs. McConnell before that day in the drawing room?"

"I knew they were the architect and his wife, here to mess everything about. I'd seen her darting around the garden and him at a distance a few times, either going out to the folly in the morning or back to the inn in the evening, but we'd no reason to be introduced."

"That's very good, Mrs. Hirkins. You told us that when you found the body, the rope was tied like a noose around his neck. Did you mean it was a hangman's knot?"

Dominick was staring at him quizzically, but even if Alfie was wrong, at least he was distracting Mrs. Hirkins from her worry for a few minutes while the search began.

She shook her head. "I don't know what sort of knot it was. It was more the way it was tied at the back, just behind his ear the way the hangman does right before the drop to snap the neck instead of—"

She cut herself off then, overcome, and Alfie gripped her hands more tightly. "Just a bit more. That morning, Mrs. McConnell found you in the hall. She needed help finding the drawing room so you showed her the way. Then what? Tell me exactly what you remember."

"I showed her the way," Mrs. Hirkins repeated. "I didn't blame her for not knowing how to find it in this warren. We got there. The door was closed. She thanked me for helping her and dismissed me. I said it was my pleasure and opened the door so she could go in. When I did, there was something lying in the middle of the room. I didn't understand what I was seeing at first, but then Mrs. McConnell cried out 'My husband!' and I realised it was the captain's body I was looking at. Facedown on the rug with that rope... as I've said. Then she fainted, and I ran for help."

And there it was, the key. Alfie could see it clearly now, and he was pretty sure he knew what it unlocked.

"Is that exactly what happened?" he asked. "Those words, that order, everything?"

She took a moment, then nodded, certain.

Alfie leaned down and pressed a quick kiss to her knuckles.

"Thank you," he whispered. Then he rose and turned to Mrs. Finley. "Watch over them both. A pot of tea wouldn't hurt. Nick?"

He didn't wait for Dominick to respond, knowing he trusted Alfie enough to follow wherever he led.

When they reached their destination, Alfie didn't bother to knock before throwing the door open. His way was immediately blocked by a flurry of skirts and bright red hair.

"You can't come in!" Janie screeched as she rushed to the door. She gripped either side of the doorway with her hands, using her body to stop Alfie from going any further. "Sir, you can't come in here! This is Mrs. McConnell's room! It's not proper!"

Normally, Alfie would agree, but James' life might depend on the woman in that room.

"To hell with proper! Let me in this instant!"

Janie's eyes were wide, torn between following orders and following propriety.

"Sir…" she whined.

"Alfie?"

He raised a hand to stop Dominick before he could say anything more. Dominick didn't know it, but without him, Alfie would never have figured it out.

"Janie, this is an emergency. I'll give you to the count of three. One. Two."

"That won't be necessary."

Mrs. McConnell appeared behind Janie in the doorway. She was fully dressed, but her hair hung loose about her shoulders. Janie had not yet had the chance to brush it into its tight bun for the day. She looked older, as if all the years had caught up with her in a single night, and her eyes were red from crying.

There was no time for condolences. "Where is your husband?"

Janie gasped, but Alfie was watching Mrs. McConnell.

"My husband is dead," she said.

The invisible key turned in the lock. It clicked open.

"No," said Alfie. "*Clyde McConnell* is dead. Despite what you made us believe, *your husband* is alive. And he has James."

Chapter 23

Dominick watched the colour drain from Mrs. McConnell's face.

He had no idea what Alfie was talking about, but from her reaction, he was absolutely right.

For a moment, he thought Mrs. McConnell might faint again as she had when she'd discovered her husband's body in the drawing room. She *hadn't* actually discovered his body though, had she? Not if Doctor Mills was right and the captain had only been dead a few days.

None of it made any sense to him, but if Alfie had worked it out, Dominick trusted that whatever conclusion he'd come to was the correct one.

Mrs. McConnell gathered herself up and straightened her shoulders. "I suppose I'd better explain."

Then she turned and walked back into her chambers. Alfie went to follow, only to be stopped again by Janie.

"Sir!" She squeaked, looking shocked at her own courage. "That's her bedchamber! It isn't proper!"

"Damn proper, a baby is missing." Alfie growled, then made his way past the maid.

"Come along, Janie," said Dominick. "You can chaperone. And the more of us who find out what's going on, the better."

Janie didn't look convinced, but Dominick didn't have time for her crisis of morals. As Alfie said, James was missing.

The guest room was large and when Dominick entered, Mrs. McConnell was sitting in a chair by the fire. She waved them both towards the settee opposite her. Alfie remained standing, however, an angry scowl on his face, and Dominick followed his lead.

"May I ask what gave it away?" Mrs. McConnell said at last. To Dominick's surprise, when she spoke, her accent was no longer a bland, unplaceable, unremarkable English, but distinctly Irish.

Alfie nodded, as if he'd suspected as much. "Mrs. Hirkins said that when you found the body in the drawing room, you shouted, 'My husband!' Yet when we pulled the captain from the fire, you shouted his name. Clyde. Not remarkable on its own, perhaps, only none of the rest of it made sense. A disappearing body, a man who'd been assumed dead for weeks only being a few days deceased, your lack of mourning after the first 'death' compared to your reaction last night...

"And then the things no one even suspected were related. Janie's broonies' sudden increase in appetite for one, but I imagine there's more. I assume that's how he kept himself fed all these weeks. Was it your idea for Janie to start leaving them more than just bread?"

Dominick had almost forgotten Janie was in the room until she gave a small gasp, as if the revelation that a man had been eating food meant for the fairies was the worst of it.

"None of it made any sense with just one husband," Alfie continued, "but as soon as I had the idea there might be two—that Clyde and 'my husband' were two separate men—it explained everything. Well, nearly."

It explained damned all to Dominick. He forced himself to focus on the conversation at hand and not that he'd been the one to suggest the thought of having two of his husband—or as close a thing to his husband that Alfie could be—just that morning and under what circumstances. Bloody hell, if that was what had given Alfie the idea, he'd never be able to explain it in court.

Mrs. McConnell's hands were clenched tightly in her lap, but to her credit, she kept her head up. "It might be best if I start at the beginning."

Dominick began to protest, but she held a hand up. "I'll be brief. But if you're going to rescue the babe, you need to know what sort of man you're dealing with. And exactly what he's capable of."

She took a deep breath. "I was sentenced to transportation in 1806. My crime is irrelevant now, save that it was enough to earn me a seven-year sentence. After that I would be free, if you could call it that. Trapped on the other side of the world with no money and no way to get home.

"After an eight-month journey in the dark, stinking hold of a ship, packed in amongst the bodies of my fellow unfortunates, we arrived in Botany Bay and I was assigned my duties. At first, I felt lucky. I'd escaped further detention or being put to work at a prison factory and was instead assigned to a farm. My family were from County Galway, so I thought at least the work would be familiar to me. I hadn't accounted for the farmer, Daniel Rutherford."

Mrs. McConnell stopped here, as if just saying the man's name caused her pain. The knuckles of her clasped hands had gone white with strain, but she continued on.

"Rutherford was also a convict. By the time I arrived in Australia, he'd already been there over a decade. He'd been on one of the first transport ships and knew how to survive in the bush better than any other white man. His crimes in England had earned him a life sentence. I soon came to find out what those crimes were."

Dominick could guess. Usually, petty thieves were sentenced to seven years, horse thieves to fourteen. Only rapists and killers received a life sentence.

"Are you familiar with tickets of leave?" Mrs. McConnell asked.

Both Alfie and Dominick shook their heads. Janie sat down heavily on Mrs. McConnell's bed.

"A convict may earn a ticket of leave for good behaviour. They aren't pardoned, but they have greater privileges, such as owning their own businesses and keeping the money they earn. In Rutherford's case, he was allowed a distant patch of land to farm, far from any soldiers or guards to keep him in line. He was also allowed to take a wife.

"At first, he was charming, but it didn't take me long to realise that by marrying him, I had turned my seven-year sentence into a lifetime of misery. Not that it would matter, as I doubted I would even survive seven years. Then after two years of hell, the most extraordinary thing happened. A man stumbled out of the bush, completely lost and near death. My Clyde."

She smiled softly to herself and Dominick couldn't help glancing at Alfie. His lover still had the fierce energy that had propelled him since they learned of James' disappearance, but he was leaning on his cane as if weighed down by her story. Dominick wanted to tell him to sit, but before he could, Mrs. McConnell resumed her tale.

"The rest is much as we told you that night at dinner. Except I didn't see Clyde just once more, but again and again. Over the next year, Clyde and I saw each other frequently as he surveyed the land around the farm. It became impossible to hide my husband's cruelty from him, but there was nothing he could do about it.

"Following the Rum Rebellion, Clyde was disillusioned by the actions of those he'd devoted his career to serving. So when he was recalled in 1810, he had no issue with breaking the very laws he'd been sent to uphold. He sold his commission to the first man in Port Jackson to want it. As a civilian, he used the money for two tickets back to Scotland, smuggling me aboard as his wife.

"We did fall in love on the journey, that much was true. I didn't expect it, or even want it, but it happened. We were married as soon as my feet touched Scottish soil."

"But your first husband wasn't dead," Alfie said firmly.

"We didn't think that mattered. He was serving a life sentence in Australia and we were here. And we were happy. Until two years ago. There was an article in the paper about escaped convicts having stolen a ship from Botany Bay. Against all odds, they sailed it to the Dutch East Indies, where they disappeared into the crowds. None captured.

"The article had a list of names. As soon as I saw *Daniel Rutherford*, I knew he was coming for me. For months, we looked over our shoulders, going from project to project, never knowing when one of the new faces around us would turn out to be his.

"I thought I saw a glimpse of him in Edinburgh and was terrified. The very next day, we received your letter about building the folly and believed it was a sign. We were tired of running. We thought we could lay a trap for him here and be done with him once and for all."

A memory came to Dominick of a quiet evening by the fire months ago.

"That was why you put the advertisement in all the papers! The one thanking Lord Crawford for the job at Balcarres House and listing exactly where it was. You wanted him to find you!"

Worse than that, they'd wanted Rutherford to find them *here*. At Balcarres, Dominick's home and home to the only other people in the world he gave a damn about. The McConnells had lured Rutherford here, knowing exactly how dangerous he was, and said nothing to warn any of them.

Anger rose up in Dominick. He clenched his fists, hissing as the bandages tightened around his blistered skin. Mrs. McConnell's next words only fanned the flames higher.

"We also used both our names and put the advertisement in papers all over Britain, so there would be no chance he could miss it. It was only a matter of time. Then one night, I heard a coo-ee and knew he was here. He didn't just want us dead. He wanted us scared, wanted us to know he was coming. That's what the coo-ee was—his warning and his promise."

"So were the sheep," Dominick realised.

Mrs. McConnell frowned. "The sheep?"

"Several days before whatever happened in the drawing room happened. I found two sheep heads on the gateposts, but got rid of them before anyone else saw."

"Pity," she said, her tone flat. "Had we known, we would have had more warning. But yes, I have no doubt that was him. Who knows how long he'd been watching us before making his presence known. Rutherford's victim had fought back, leaving him with a scar down his face, but I believe the wickedness Madam Carnbee saw in his face at the window had been there long before that."

The scarred mask of the night before came to mind, as did the cruel face of the man beneath it.

"Coo-ee?" Janie asked faintly. She was gripping the banister of the bed, but Dominick couldn't tell if it was from fear or excitement.

Mrs. McConnell looked at her a moment, then cupped her hands to her lips and threw her head back. Dominick jumped as a call filled the room, loud enough to scare the birds from their branches outside the windows.

"COOOOOOOOoooo EEEeeeeeeeeee!"

There was something haunting about the call, a mournfulness to the way it echoed. By the time it faded away, the hairs on Dominick's arms were standing on end.

"The tribes in Australia use it to announce their presence when entering someone else's land. It can carry for miles. It was useful on the farm, or for locating lost surveyors."

"I heard that," Alfie whispered. "The night before the drawing room. And I thought I heard it again last night too."

Mrs. McConnell's face went hard.

"A warning," she repeated. "And now a promise fulfilled."

"What happened in the drawing room?" asked Dominick.

"We set a trap. Clyde woke early and made a great show of himself being in the drawing room, opening the doors to the terrace, fussing around and acting completely obvious to draw Rutherford's eye. Then he hid. Rutherford is one of the strongest men I've ever met. We knew there was no way Clyde could best him in a fight or even the two of us together. And we couldn't shoot him without alerting the household. But if we could just get a lasso around his neck while he was distracted, we could stop him for good without anyone being the wiser.

"I was supposed to come in after Clyde had time to hide and act as bait while he lay in wait, but I hadn't counted on getting lost in this maze of a house. I was late, so I panicked and asked Mrs. Hirkins for help. I tried to stop her from opening the drawing room door, but it was too late. The moment it opened and I saw Rutherford's body on the floor, I screamed. Even though I'd been preparing for it, seeing him again after all these years, even dead, was too horrible.

"Then the curtains moved. Clyde hadn't been expecting anyone but me to come in and was trying to hide himself in them, but I could clearly see his boots sticking out the bottom. Mrs. Hirkins was still staring at the body, but I only had seconds before the shock wore off and she saw him too and would know he'd committed the murder. So I pretended to faint.

"The moment she ran for help, I was up again. We'd planned to bury him in one of the new garden beds before the workers arrived. There had been so much digging already, who would notice if one of the holes had been filled in? But we didn't have time, so we just shoved his body into the nearest wood pile, intending to deal with it later.

"But that still left the problem of Mrs. Hirkins. She'd seen the body and heard me say 'my husband.' I knew the household would be arriving any moment, so I told Clyde to hide in the woods.

"It was all I could think of. If Mrs. Hirkins heard me call out for my husband but the body was that of another man, everyone would assume I'd meant Clyde was the killer. But if there was no body, then everyone would think it odd, but assume he was the one dead. He could hide until the folly was completed—one last monument in his name—then we'd reunite afterwards, take a ship to America this time and start new lives with new names. That his body was missing would be a mystery, but I'd already heard enough stories about cursed Balcarres. In time, his disappearance would be put down to just another strange happening."

"You thought of all this in the time it took Mrs. Hirkins to fetch us?" If the circumstances weren't so terrible, Dominick would be impressed.

She fixed him with a look. Her intelligence had always been clear in her eyes, but there'd been something in them that Dominick only now realised he recognised. It was the look of someone who'd had no one else to rely on for far too long and had endured terrible things in that time.

His fists had kept him alive in his dark time, but such a small woman wouldn't have had that option. She'd have had nothing but her wits to protect her and she'd honed those into her weapon, as quick and sharp as any blade.

"No," she said. "In that time, I thought of it all *and* explained it to Clyde. There would be little chance to speak after. I couldn't risk sneaking out, but as long as he avoided the searchers that first day, he had a key to the folly and could stay there at night. And of course, he had his pencil, so he did leave me a few notes to let me know he was all right. We couldn't risk any more.

"I thought he'd be safe until the work was done. I wanted to finish Captain Clyde McConnell's last great work before we both disappeared. If I hadn't been so prideful and we'd left immediately, the only truly good man I've ever met would still be alive."

She unclenched her hands and smoothed down her skirts.

"Please, Your Lordship," she said, and for the first time, her voice wavered. "I know you won't still employ me after all this, but please, we're so close to completing the folly. It's his finest work. Please finish it. And his plans for the gardens are truly spectacular. Janie has a rare talent for plants and she knows those plans as well as I do, the gardens would thrive under her care."

"Thank you," Janie said softly. From her blush, she was still no better at accepting a compliment than she'd ever been.

"You're in no place to be making requests" Alfie said coldly. "You're an escaped convict and you knowingly brought danger to this house. Employ you? I should report you to the magistrate. Finish the story. Where is James?"

Dominick had never seen Alfie like this. But usually it was Alfie himself who was in peril, or at worst, Dominick. Both were grown men who'd faced danger before and come out the other side. Now, because of this woman, James was in the hands of a ruthless killer.

Where Alfie was cold, Dominick was boiling with rage. If anything happened to James before Mrs. McConnell got to the damned point, Magistrate Carnbee would be the least of her worries.

Chastened, she continued. "I made it back to the drawing room just in time to feign unconsciousness."

"Not quite," Alfie pointed out. "Mrs. Hirkins can be forgiven for assuming the body on the floor was the captain, she'd only seen him at a distance. But you first 'fainted' when she opened the door. You should have been outside it, yet we found you in the centre of the room. We should have known then."

Despite her circumstances, she glared at Alfie as if he was the one who'd done wrong by daring to point out she wasn't as clever as she thought she was.

"Regardless. I thought my first husband dead in the wood pile and my second safe in the folly. After the rockfall, I began to wonder, but I convinced myself it was simply an unfortunate accident. Then I started to doubt, because if anyone could survive off the land for this long without anyone noticing, it would be Rutherford.

"So I checked the wood pile, but when I didn't find the body, I told myself Clyde had taken it and buried it as we'd originally planned. When I saw Rutherford last night, I knew what a dreadful mistake I'd made even before the bonfire was lit.

"He didn't come all the way from Australia because he wants me dead, but because he wants to punish me. He's a monster. He could have killed Clyde at any time in the last month, but instead he stalked him without him even knowing. He watched from the woods, waiting to strike until Clyde's death would cause the most pain.

"He killed the man I love because I dared to leave him, and strangled Clyde for having the audacity to try to do the same to him. If only I'd found Mrs. Hirkins a minute later, Clyde wouldn't have had to stop and hide before the deed was fully done.

"I heard my husband again last night. Another coo-ee, this one in triumph. If he does kill me, it won't be until after he's destroyed everything I love."

At that, she fell silent. She'd been the target all along, never Alfie or Dominick. And now a man was dead and an innocent child was missing.

"Why James?" Dominick could barely get the words out. "James has nothing to do with you. Now Captain McConnell is dead, Rutherford should have come for you, not him."

She had the gall to shrug. "I don't know. Opportunity, perhaps? As I said, this house is a maze, but the kitchen opens directly onto the lawn."

"I think... I think I might know."

Everyone in the room turned to Janie.

She shrunk back, then lifted her chin and said, "If Mr. Rutherford was watching from the woods, he might have got the wrong impression. Most houses, servants care for the ladies' babies, even for the guests. And of course, no servants have babies themselves. Captain and Mrs. McConnell were here all the time, even before they were offered a room. Since they're the only married couple in the house, he might have assumed James was their son and took him to punish her?"

Janie said the last part as a question, but Dominick had never been more sure of anything.

He clenched his fists again and the pain from his hands was nothing compared to the fear in his heart. Sweet little James, Agnes' son, Mrs. Hirkins' great-grandchild, had been taken by a man who'd left his victim in a woodpile waiting to be lit, knowing the entire village would see his terrible handiwork.

Alfie's voice was as sharp as ice. "Damn you to hell. You lured him to us. A madman, willing to cross seas for vengeance, and you put advertisements in every newspaper telling him to come to our home. And you still haven't told us anything useful. Where would he take James?"

Mrs. McConnell looked on the verge of tears again, but Dominick didn't feel an ounce of pity.

"I don't know."

At her non-answer, something in Dominick snapped. He struck out, his hand finding some ornamental trinket. He didn't even notice the pain as it soared through the air, smashing into satisfying little pieces against the wall. Janie shrieked. If it had gone two inches to the left, it would have shattered the window and gone soaring down into the McConnells' precious garden.

Mrs. McConnell cowered and he heard a worried, "Nick?" from Alfie, but he ignored them both.

The window.

Suddenly, Rutherford's plan was nightmarishly clear.

"He wants to punish you by making you watch him destroy everything you love. Not just your husband, but also his legacy. Alfie, I know where he's taken James."

The morning was bright and clear. From Mrs. McConnell's window, the view looked out over the gardens. If Dominick turned his head a little to the right, he'd be able to see all the way to the sea. But if he looked left, the forest thickened, then began to climb upwards until it reached the crag. And on the top of the crag sat Captain McConnell's finest work. His legacy.

The folly.

CHAPTER 24

As Alfie sped from the room, he vaguely heard Dominick shouting behind him, ordering the servants to lock up the house, to not let anyone leave—or worse, enter—but there was no time to lose. Rutherford had had James for too long. The man's hatred for his wife had turned to madness and Alfie had seen before the evil that men pushed to such a point could do.

He tore past the gardens, the smell of charred wood, spilled ale, and worse still lingering on the air. By the time he reached the treeline, Dominick's footsteps were right behind him. Alfie's leg screamed at him as they began to climb the forest path. He gritted his teeth and tried to run faster.

On a wide part of trail, Dominick overtook him, leading the way as the path wound up the crag. He was easily the faster of the two of them, but Alfie refused to be left behind. By the time they broke through into the clearing at the top, Dominick was less than a dozen strides ahead of him. There he skidded to a stop, staring up in horror.

Alfie followed his gaze, craning his neck back further and further. The folly was nearly finished, stone wings spreading out from a central tower that rose forty feet into the air. The room in its base was complete, as were the windows that marked the path of the stairwell that wound its way up the inside of the tower.

The only part of the folly that remained unfinished was the ring of crenelations around the top. When complete, they would not only serve to make the folly look like the ruins of some forgotten castle, but provide a barrier to keep the unwary from falling off. Without them, the top of the folly was a bare circle high above, with nothing to stop anyone who climbed up there from slipping off the edge.

And at this edge, silhouetted against the sun, stood a man. Rutherford.

Alfie had never seen him before, the murderer had kept himself too well-hidden in the shadows, but there was no mistaking who he could be. His skin was as tanned as leather from the heat of the Australian sun. His scar stood out in a pale stripe against a face aged beyond his years by a life of cruelty and brutality. Even at this distance, Alfie could see the obsession that blazed in his eyes.

Despite these differences from the studied blandness of Captain McConnell, it was no wonder that at a glance and hearing Mrs. McConnell's cry, Mrs. Hirkins had thought the body on the drawing room floor was his. The men were of a similar height and build, but there was no mistaking the strength in Rutherford's frame. The span of his shoulders was greater even than Dominick's and he held himself like a man who'd been fighting all his life.

He stood unwavering on the edge of the folly, not heeding the tiny pebbles that trickled down past his feet. His arms were held out over the open air and in his hands, he held James.

Alfie's heart stopped in his chest.

The baby had his face scrunched against the cold wind and he was wrapped only in the blanket from his crib, far too little to protect him from the chill of November. But James only hiccupped, his face red as if he'd been crying too long and had no more tears to shed.

"Don't come any closer!" Rutherford yelled. "Another step and I'll drop him."

"Christ, Alfie, he can't." Dominick hissed.

Alfie didn't bother to reply. They both knew he could and if they didn't do something, he would.

Alfie raised his hands in the air. He'd forgotten he was still holding his cane and as soon as he noticed it, it was as if his leg remembered as well, nearly buckling under him in a sudden flash of pain. He barely steadied himself in time to keep from sliding back down the path.

"Rutherford!" he called out. "Can we talk? We've heard your wife's side of the tale, but I'll wager there's things she didn't tell us. I'd like to know your side."

Rutherford laughed, an eerie cackling that made cold shivers run down Alfie's spine.

"I bet she told you all sorts of things. A damned liar, that's what she is! But she'll pay for those lies. I bet she told you I want her dead. Another lie and she knows it. I don't want her dead. I want her to suffer for what she did. She was *mine*. And now I'm going to take what's hers."

Rutherford gave James a rough shake. Both Alfie and Dominick stepped forward instinctively, but Rutherford kept his grip on the child. Over the pounding of his heart, it took Alfie a minute to parse Rutherford's words.

Bloody hell, Janie had been right. Who knew what Rutherford had picked up as he spied on Balcarres. What snatches of conversations he'd overheard and misheard that made him think that James wasn't Agnes' son, but Mrs. McConnell's. The sight of Janie, who'd been working as Mrs. McConnell's companion, carrying James around the Samhain celebration last night must have cinched it, the two women looking as natural as any well-appointed woman out with her child's nanny.

Rutherford pulled James back to him and for a moment Alfie felt a flicker of relief. Then he realised Rutherford wasn't cradling James—he was wheeling back to throw.

"Wait!" Alfie screamed.

If Rutherford simply dropped James straight down, the fall would likely kill him, but the folly wasn't high enough that death would be assured. The child might survive. However, there were only a few feet of earth in front of the folly before the ground dropped away down the face of the crag. Rutherford had used that drop before when he'd tried to push the stones down onto Dominick and him. If he threw James beyond that narrow ledge, there would be no hope of survival.

To Alfie's endless thanks, Rutherford hesitated.

"You're a reasonable man," Alfie said, not knowing what words would come out next, only that as long as Rutherford was listening, James was safe. "And you've been hard done by. Forced into a punishment far worse than the crime and then, once you'd made the best of it, to be so cruelly mistreated by Mrs. Mc—by your wife. Who was meant to honour you. Obey you. You came to claim back what was yours. I respect that.

"More than respect that," Alfie continued as Dominick stared at him wide eyed, "There aren't enough men who'd face what you have just to put right the wrongs done to you. I think that sort of determination should be rewarded. As an earl, I can do that. A word from me in the right ear and your record is clean. You wouldn't have to hide in the shadows or worry about ever being sent back to the penal colony. More than that, I can force your wife to go back to you. She wouldn't have a choice, would she? Not now that I know she's an escaped convict. You could settle wherever you wanted and never have to worry about losing your property again."

Just saying the words put a bitter taste on Alfie's tongue. It felt like there was some sort of pungent oil on him that he couldn't get off. He'd *chosen* to be with Dominick and every person, man or woman, deserved to choose who they wanted to spend their lives with, not be forced into a marriage with someone who saw them as no more than an object to be owned—an object that might be admired, but could also be broken.

Still, he'd met enough men like Rutherford in both Spitalfields and Mayfair to know how they thought.

When Rutherford didn't answer, Alfie stepped closer to the folly door, only to be pulled up by an arm across his chest.

"What are you doing?" Dominick hissed.

Alfie craned his back head up. Rutherford was watching them, his gleaming eyes sharp but unreadable.

Alfie spoke softly, pitching his voice low so it wouldn't carry. "Someone's got to stop him. I'll go up there, talk to him, and when he's distracted, I'll snatch James."

"He'll fight," Dominick whispered. "He survived years in Australia, Alfie. Hell, he survived the trip back from Australia. He's strong. And with your leg… We can't risk it. I'll go."

"No!" Alfie winced at how loudly he'd spoken, but Rutherford hadn't moved. He still watched them, ignoring James' tiny hands pushing against his chest. "Your hands, Nick."

Dominick looked down at the bandages wound around his hands, pinning his fingers together. He must have done something to his right hand without Alfie noticing as a foul, yellowish liquid flecked with brown rose up through the cloth along his knuckles.

"You won't be able to grab James," Alfie said. "Not and be sure of holding onto him. It has to be me. And I won't be unarmed, remember?" Alfie rubbed his thumb over the catch that released the sword within his cane, a movement Dominick would understand but was too slight for Rutherford to even see.

Indecision played over Dominick's face, but there wasn't anything for him to decide. There was no other choice. It had to be Alfie.

He wanted to kiss Dominick then, but couldn't give Rutherford another way to harm them. Besides, the gesture felt too much like a farewell.

"I'll come up with you."

Alfie shook his head. This man, this wonderful, protective man. He was everything Rutherford would never be, never even be able to understand. Dominick knew Alfie belonged to him, but he belonged to Alfie just as much. And it wasn't the sort of "belonging" that meant "owned". It was "belonging" like feeling that you were where you were meant to be. Like home.

Alfie smiled sadly at his Dominick, his home. "You need to stay down here, Nick. If something happens, I need you here. Not for me, but for James. The ledge isn't very wide, watch your footing. If Rutherford throws or pushes, there's nothing to be done. But if it's just a fall, the ledge is still wide enough that... *whatever* goes off will land there. If this all goes wrong, if I'm the one who falls, stay out of my way. You won't be able to do anything but risk losing your own life too. But if it's James, I need you to catch."

Under the best circumstances—if there was such a thing in this case—it would be difficult for Dominick to pluck a falling infant out of the air safely. With his bandages, it would be nearly impossible. But some hope was better than none and if there was any man Alfie trusted to do it, it was him.

Dominick winced, but to his credit, he didn't try to stop him. He only reached down and touched Alfie's hand, the one that wore Dominick's ring, as if he'd be able to feel the engraved bird through the layers of bandages.

Swallowing thickly, Alfie turned to the folly and faced what needed to be done.

CHAPTER 25

The climb up the spiral staircase inside the folly was tortuous on his overworked leg, each step sending a bolt of agony from ankle to hip. But slowly and surely, Alfie climbed.

When he reached the top, he gingerly poked his head through, afraid Rutherford would be waiting to attack the moment he came through the trap door. But Rutherford was still standing at the edge of the folly looking down at Dominick below, no doubt watching for some sort of trick.

As Alfie staggered onto the platform, Rutherford turned towards him, one of his heels now over the edge. James had ceased his struggles and slumped in Rutherford's grip, eyelids heavy with exhaustion.

"Drop the stick," Rutherford said.

Alfie froze. He'd sparred with Dominick in the gymnasium occasionally, but he was no brawler. In a fair fight, he'd almost certainly lose. If he was going to get any sort of upper hand over Rutherford, he'd need his sword.

He licked his dry lips. This high, the wind cut through his coat like a knife. James was wrapped in only a small blanket. Even if Rutherford didn't kill him, the cold might if Alfie didn't act quickly.

Up here, the folly looked even taller than it had from below, the ground an impossible distance away. He felt a rush of light-headedness at the height, but used it to his advantage, catching himself on his cane.

"I have a leg injury," he said evenly. "If you've been watching Balcarres, you've seen that I need it to walk."

"Nowhere to go up here," Rutherford replied. "Drop the stick or I drop him."

Cursing internally, Alfie did as he was told, not willing to take the chance with James' life.

"All right," he said, setting the stick down and rolling it away from him for good measure. Not so far it went over the edge, not if there was a chance Alfie would need it later, but far enough that Rutherford hopefully wouldn't see it as a threat.

"Let's talk this through, Rutherford. You want your wife back. You want the law to leave you alone. Both those things I can do. What else do you want? I can make it happen, but only if no harm comes to the infant. Even an earl's power has its limits when it comes to child killers."

Rutherford hummed in thought and to Alfie's relief, took a few steps closer. Still far too close to the edge, but at least both his feet were firmly on stone, not air.

"What I want," Rutherford said slowly, "Is to know if the whispers are true, my lord. Did you cuckold that bastard McConnell and get a child on my wife?"

Time slowed to a perfect moment of terrible understanding.

Dominick had warned him about the rumours of James being Alfie's child. Hell, they'd discussed that very thing the night of their walk in the garden with James. Depending on what parts of their conversation Rutherford had heard, or what parts he *wanted* to hear, of course he'd believe it.

"I suppose I can see the resemblance. Natural sense of command, stunning eyes, flawless skin, entire household at his beck and call, yes, he most definitely takes after me..."

"...It's a shame his mother isn't of noble blood. Now he'll never be allowed to inherit."

They'd been joking, but to a madman listening in the shadows, their words would be damning. And Alfie had talked about Mrs. McConnell that night as well.

"I'd like to remain in her good graces, considering the circumstances. I certainly don't want to risk my chance of having 'the most beautiful in the county if not nation' now that the opportunity has presented itself."

The "circumstances" had been the work being done and the gardens were "the most beautiful", but Rutherford had been cuckolded by his wife already, was it so surprising he'd think she'd do the same to her current husband? He might have thought Alfie was talking about not risking losing Mrs. McConnell now they had a secret child together. And the more he'd eavesdropped on the servants and workers gossiping about James' paternity, the more certain he would've become.

All this time, he and Dominick had been so worried someone was trying to kill them because of their relationship and it hadn't been about them at all. In all their worry about being discreet, they'd led Rutherford to believe just the opposite. If they hadn't been so focused on themselves, perhaps they would've given more consideration to the other rumours going around and James wouldn't be in danger now.

"Well?" Rutherford asked, the gleam in his eyes shining with the light of madness. "Is the bastard yours or not? I told McConnell it was when I strangled him. Made sure the last thing he knew was how that woman betrayed him just as she betrayed me.

"I was too quick about it though. I should have made it last longer. As justice, you see? The coward got behind me with that rope then left me for dead in the wood pile. Only fair I do the same. Although I was smart enough to be sure he was dead before I left him."

Rutherford grinned then, a horribly wide showing of teeth.

"I'm sure he thought it was the end of me when he left me there. But I awoke. He was a weak man, too weak to do the job properly, but me? I'm strong. I had to be strong with all the wrongs done me. Back in Australia, the bush nearly killed him, but I learned from it. Learned how to track, how to stay hidden. I knew he was in these woods, hiding here in the folly at night, but he never knew about me. Not until it was too late.

"I had my justice in the end, when I put him in the same wood pile as he left me. I only wish I'd been closer when you set it alight so I could see her face better when he was pulled out. Still, the mask let me get closer than I expected, and I could hear her. Do you think she would've cried the same if my body had still been the one in there when you lit it?"

Rutherford stopped and Alfie realised he was actually waiting for an answer.

"I don't know," he said, barely able to croak out the words. "You can ask her as soon as we all climb down from here."

Rutherford ignored him. "I don't think so. I think she only makes that sound for her bastard lovers. And maybe her bastard child."

At that, Rutherford cocked his head to the side, the movement unnaturally precise.

"And now I have both."

Alfie froze. This man had brutally killed his wife's new husband and now he not only believed he had his wife's child within reach, but her lover too.

In that moment, he wished Dominick was there with him. The height and angle of the folly stopped him from being able to even see Dominick below. He wanted nothing more than to lean back into his warmth, to feel the steady reassurance that meant Alfie wasn't confronting a madman alone. But Dominick needed to be where he was and Alfie had to stop Rutherford, whatever the cost.

"You called me 'reasonable' before," Rutherford said. "I am. Very reasonable. And I'm not cruel, no matter what a magistrate, or a jury, or that liar of a wife says. I know it was never really your fault, she seduced you with more of her lies. That's why I tried to give you a quick death with those rocks. I'm a reasonable man.

"So I won't take both her remaining lover and her child away. I'll even be *reasonable* enough to let you choose. Jump and I'll let him live, you have my word. Refuse…"

Rutherford shrugged. Then he pulled James away from him and held him over the edge, one arm outstretched over the drop and a single hand knotted in James' blanket. The blanket was wrapped around James, but not tightly. Sensing some change, James started to fuss, wriggling and sinking lower and lower in the tangle of cloth.

"No!" Alfie cried. "Please, stop!"

Rutherford shrugged again, his grin filled with malice. "You know how to make me stop. Jump. I want to hear if my wife cries for her second lover the way she did for her first."

Alfie's mind whirled. He had to think of some way out of this, some way to save himself and James both. But all he could think about was Dominick. Dominick, who'd looked so peaceful as they'd lain in bed just a few hours before, tucked together warm and safe, their feet tangled under the blankets cocooning them. Dominick had trusted Alfie to climb up here alone and to climb back down to him. He couldn't let Dominick see what happened next. See him fall.

And Alfie didn't want to die. He wanted to wake up in bed with Dominick thousands more times, wanted to climb to the top of this folly with him, to put this horror behind them and watch the sunset together. And he wanted to see Gil again over a chessboard, and see Janie come into her own confidence, and Mrs. Hirkins finally listen to reason and properly retire. He wanted all that, but not at the cost of James' life.

"You're taking too long," Rutherford grumbled, then he cocked his arm back again to throw.

James began to cry in exhausted half-sobs that broke Alfie's heart.

"Wait!" he shouted. Then with a deep breath, Alfie stepped to the edge.

His gait was uneven from pain, so he took each step slowly, ensuring he was stable before taking the next. He got as close as he dared, his toes just barely hovering over empty space. He could feel the slide of grit under his feet and heard the delicate plink of the small rocks he'd knocked over as they tumbled down the tower.

"Alfie!" Dominick's voice drifted up from below. "Alfie, no! Please!"

"Stay there!" Alfie shouted without looking down. He was at the side of the tower above the clearing. The wall with their window jutted out from somewhere along this side; he'd have to watch for that. The fall might be survivable here, unlike a leap from the front with the crag below. Although Dominick would be sure to try and catch him, the damned fool.

Dominick's voice was full of panic and Alfie wanted to reassure him, to find some way to make this all right, but if he looked down, he wouldn't be able to do it. He looked out to sea instead, watching the sunlight dancing on the waves.

He teetered on the edge, then stepped back onto solid stone.

"Can I at least kiss my son goodbye?"

Rutherford's face twisted from an expression of sick anticipation into a furious scowl.

"What kind of fool do you take me for?" he snarled.

"No fool at all. I know there's nothing I can do to stop this. I'm an injured man and as you said, all those hard years have made you strong. If I try to fight you, you'll easily toss me over and I imagine James as well. But since I have your word he'll be spared if I make the choice myself, I might as well face my end with dignity. But first, one kiss. That's all I ask."

Rutherford's scowl deepened. Alfie's heart was pounding in his chest, a rapid tattoo counting the long seconds until he finally answered.

"One kiss," Rutherford said at last. "Any tricks and you both go over."

Alfie nodded and walked towards the front of the folly, approaching Rutherford the way he would any snarling beast. Rutherford pulled his arm back in and gripped James to his chest with both hands, squeezing him so tightly that James let out a shriek of pain, his wet eyes wide with fear.

Alfie got as close as he dared, which was far closer than he was comfortable with. He kept his eyes on Rutherford's until the last minute. That mad light in them was a bonfire now.

Then Alfie leaned down and pressed a kiss to the top of James' head. The soft baby scent of him filled Alfie's nose, a single moment of pleasure in the horror around them. James' scalp was far too cold, but the tiny wisps of hair were soft against Alfie's lips, like threads of silk. They were too fine yet to have a real colour, but Alfie expected that they'd grow into a thick head of brown hair like his mother's when James grew older.

However, regardless of the promise he'd made, Alfie knew that Rutherford had no intention of letting either of them come back down alive.

"I'm sorry, James," Alfie whispered.

Then he flung his arms around Rutherford, pinning James' small body between them. Rutherford twisted and thrashed, his greater strength tossing them about so that Alfie lost track of who was closer to the edge, but he held on.

In a fair fight, he'd almost certainly lose.

Alfie dropped to his knees, the hard stone sending a shock of pain through him. The soft mats in the gymnasium hadn't hurt when Dominick had taught him this manoeuvre. It wasn't the sort that belonged in any gentleman's boxing ring, but in dirty underground fights like the one Dominick had been in the night they met.

So don't make it a fair fight.

As he fell, Alfie leaned back, using his full weight to pull Rutherford off balance.

For a moment, all three of them teetered on the edge, Dominick's shouts of panic drowned out by James' shrill cries of terror.

Instinctively, Rutherford dropped James, his arms cartwheeling wildly for balance. Alfie felt James begin to slip away and released Rutherford to grab him.

A sickening moment passed where his hands clutched nothing but empty blanket, then he felt the squirming weight of James in his hands. He pulled James to his chest, tucking the baby's head under his chin as if he could protect James from what was about to happen. Releasing Rutherford had caused Alfie to lose his balance and they were falling backwards, no way for Alfie to stop his own descent without dropping James.

Alfie closed his eyes. *I love you, Nick.*

Cold stone slammed into his back, knocking the wind from him. He gasped up at the sky above, before turning his head the barest fraction to the side. A few inches more and they would have gone over the side of the folly, tumbling to the ground. His knees were screaming and his injured leg felt as if someone had rammed a hot poker into it, but he was alive.

Something wriggled against his chest. James got his breath back before Alfie did and released it in another terrible wail.

At Alfie's feet, Rutherford was rocking back and forth, his arms spinning violently as he pitched between safety and death. One moment, his back arched and it seemed inevitable he would fall straight down, landing on that narrow ledge in front of the folly. The next moment, he yawed forward on his toes towards safety, before his own momentum drew him back again.

There was an even chance Rutherford would fall or steady himself. Alfie risked a glance backwards, but his sword cane was at the back of the tower near the trapdoor and far out of reach.

If Rutherford regained his balance, Alfie was in no shape to fight him off, or even just chase him if he decided to cut his losses and run. Rutherford was a cruel, vengeful, dangerous man. He'd hunted a woman across the seas, killed a good man, and nearly thrown an infant to his death. He'd escaped before, and if he didn't fall now, he'd likely escape again.

He'd come for James again. Alfie was sure of it. And himself and Mrs. McConnell too. Rutherford had stalked her for weeks with none of them the wiser. His obsession wasn't the only thing that made him dangerous. He also had his skills and his patience. They would have to constantly be on alert, watching for any movement in the dark and listening for any sound in the night until he inevitably struck again.

But he was at Alfie's feet. He was unarmed, vulnerable, off-balance, and incapable of fighting back. One kick and James would be safe from him forever.

Then Rutherford was vanishing over the edge, howling with rage as he disappeared from sight.

Alfie covered James' ears so he wouldn't hear what came next.

After, everything went quiet. James stopped crying. The wind dropped to a dreadful stillness. Even the distant waves seemed to cease their crashing against the cliffs. Alfie lay staring up at the sky, wondering how it could be so blue on such a black day.

At last, he noticed Dominick shouting his name. He sounded very far away and it took Alfie a moment before he could answer.

"I'm safe! *We're* safe!" he called out. Tucking James more securely into his blanket, Alfie tried to sit up and hissed as his leg throbbed. "But we'll need some help getting down."

Epilogue

One Month Later

From the top of the folly, Dominick could see the entire countryside stretching out before them. In the far distance, the sea was a heavy grey under heavier skies that threatened rain. Too hazy to make out the waves themselves, the salt tang on the air warned of the danger for the fishermen as they finished hauling in their nets and turned their boats to the harbour.

Coming in from the sea, the land was spotted with patches of bare rock that showed through the heath like an old coat worn out in the elbows. Here and there he could make out patches of darker green spotted with yellow. The gorse plants seemed to always be in bloom, the flowers kept safe by the sharp thorns surrounding them.

Directly below them, the forest spread out from the crag to meet the gorse. This late in the year, most of the trees were bare, save for a few proud pines that stuck up here and there. In the midst of the tangle, he could just make out the ruins of the chapel. The small glade it stood in was a welcome sanctuary from the forest around it.

Looking down on that forest from above, the twisted branches were an impenetrable thicket. It seemed impossible to believe that there was a way down from their tower or a path through those woods that led them home.

Home.

And there it stood, imposing yet welcoming—Balcarres House. Most of the windows were dark, the rooms within too numerous to all be in use, but a few glowed with light. Dominick wondered who each light could be. Was that the glow of a lamp illuminating the cramped numbers in a ledger as Gil poured over them or was it Mrs. Finley sweeping dust into a burning fireplace when no one was looking? Perhaps it was a candle carried by Mr. Howe as he went about his duties or Jarrett as he got up to mischief.

As Dominick watched, a carriage rolled away from the manor, making its way down the long drive before disappearing into the gradual curve of the trees. There was only one person who could be inside.

"Poor woman," Alfie murmured beside him.

"Good riddance," Dominick spat.

"Nick." But Alfie's tone held more agreement than rebuke.

Alfie hadn't told Carnbee she was an escaped convict as he'd threatened. In fact, he'd let Mrs. McConnell stay on to finish the folly, let her be the one to complete her husband's final work. The last stone had been set in place yesterday. She would never see his gardens in bloom, but it had still been a kindness Dominick wouldn't have granted after everything her lies had caused, and the worse things that had come so close to happening.

He shuddered just remembering it, the way his heart had stopped as he watched Alfie and Rutherford struggle at the edge of the tower and the deadly drop below. He could almost hear James' plaintive cries on the wind now, so much fear in such a tiny voice.

He'd run to the base of the tower directly below them, head craned upwards to catch two of the three people above—Alfie's orders be damned. From where he'd stood, he hadn't seen the moment Rutherford had stumbled backwards off the edge, a single misplaced step ending a man gone mad with years of obsession and hate.

That was what they'd said had happened when they limped their way back to Balcarres, James tucked inside Dominick's coat to keep him warm.

There was another story that might have happened.

A story about a choice being made. Not by Rutherford, but by the long line of heat that was now using the privacy of the folly to press up close beside him, letting Dominick's bulk shield him from the worst of the wind.

Dominick turned his head just enough so that his view was of Alfie, not the far less interesting landscape. His auburn curls had returned to their former glory and, as Alfie had given up on making any attempt to tame them with either hair oil or pomade, the wind was making them dance in celebration of their newfound freedom. Alfie was still looking at where the carriage had disappeared. He absently tucked one of the curls behind his ear, only to have it escape again immediately.

If it had been a choice, it was one Dominick understood. Rutherford was a danger to them all, a rabid animal with thoughts of nothing but revenge against the woman who'd spurned him.

No, he was worse than an animal. An animal only struck mindlessly. Rutherford had planned, calculating his moves to bring terror, his violence targeting not his wife, but those she loved—or those he thought she loved—his blows aimed to cause the greatest pain.

He'd killed Captain McConnell, left his body in the unlit bonfire knowing the chaos and fear it would cause when discovered, not just to his wife but to the entire village. He'd mutilated livestock, spied from the shadows, sent rocks crashing down towards them, and finally snatched an innocent child, prepared to do the unspeakable just because he could.

If it had been Dominick on top of the folly, the choice would have been an easy one.

But it wasn't. It was Alfie. Alfie, the boy who'd cried when he tripped on workhouse steps, the man who let kittens play with his pocket watch, and the earl who was responsible not only for his lands, but the people within them.

Time and again, Dominick had seen how fiercely Alfie protected those he felt responsible for. If this had been one of those times, if Alfie had made the choice to guarantee the safety of those under his protection rather than risk letting a dangerous man escape punishment once again...

Well. Dominick didn't see what happened. He couldn't say which story was true. But he wasn't an earl. He didn't have scores of people to protect—only one.

So he'd do just that. Rutherford had fallen of his own accord. James was safe. Alfie was safe. And if the servants now gossiped about working not in the cursed manor, but the one with the heroic earl, and the villagers in the inn told stories of Alfie's courage instead of his family's long absence, then all the better. Dominick certainly hadn't dropped choice tales of Alfie's previous brave deeds in the ears of some of the new gardeners, knowing they would spread.

Of course, after James' dramatic rescue, there was no stopping the rumour about him being Alfie's son, but at least now the villagers seemed pleased that out of all the lying, cheating toffs, theirs was honourable enough to protect his by-blow. Besides, as long as they were all giving wary glances towards their wives when Alfie walked by, they weren't raising their eyebrows at Dominick walking right beside him.

Or right behind him—the view was better there.

"What are you grinning about?" Alfie asked.

"Nothing, just thinking we should test out that little room again. I'm not sure it was thoroughly christened."

"Baboon. It's as christened as it's going to be until you find an inconspicuous way to drag a mattress up here." Alfie rubbed his leg. "Or at the very least, a good stockpile of blankets. Bare stone is hell on bare knees—bare knees whose bruises have only finally faded, I remind you."

Dominick snorted but decided against offering any alternate suggestions. Better to remind Alfie of his words that night when they had the use of both a mattress and blankets.

Instead, he caught Alfie's hand in his and held it between them, rubbing his thumb over his ring on Alfie's finger. His own hands had mostly healed in the month since the Samhain fire. There were a few new scars, but if Alfie hadn't minded the way Dominick looked when he'd first found him bleeding and beaten after losing a boxing match, Dominick doubted he would now.

They stood like that in silence, just enjoying the countryside and each other's company. Far below, through a thinning of the trees, Dominick caught another glimpse of the carriage carrying Mrs. McConnell away.

"I do pity her, you know," said Alfie. "I can't forgive her, knowing what her lies and lies by omission nearly caused, but I do pity her. She had a hard life with few options. With a little less luck, either of us could have found ourselves in similar straits."

Dominick couldn't argue with that. He'd certainly done things in his short career as a housebreaker to earn himself transportation if he'd ever been caught. If he and Alfie hadn't met again when they did, or if Alfie had never been adopted by the previous earl at all...

"You didn't tell the magistrate who she really was when Rutherford's body was being carted off," Dominick said. "Most wouldn't be that kind."

"You didn't say anything either," Alfie pointed out. "Besides, I didn't want any more bad memories associated with this place now that I'm going to be forced to look at it every day for the rest of my life."

"You love it as much as I do, admit it. You always wanted to hear stories of knights and castles. Now you have your very own."

Alfie laughed and waved his free hand towards Balcarres House. "Nick, I'm an earl. That's far above a knight. And I already own a castle."

Dominick squinted as if only just noticing the massive stone building below. "That's not a proper castle. It doesn't have any towers or... What are these called on top?"

"Crenelations," Alfie supplied, his eyes bright with mirth. "You're absolutely right. My life was sorely incomplete until this point. Thank you."

"You're welcome."

The wind chose that moment to pick up, a sharp blast that snuck down Dominick's collar with the chill of the coming winter. Alfie shivered against him and without needing to say any more, they turned and headed back down the tower stairs and towards the trail home.

As they passed the window in the folly wall, Dominick fondly patted the stone he'd laid and looked up at Alfie's keystone above it.

"Hold on just a second."

"What is it?" asked Alfie, but he didn't resist when Dominick pressed him back against the wall, taking his mouth in a deep kiss.

"Nothing," Dominick said when they'd finally broken apart. Alfie's curls were even wilder than they'd been before. "We're going to have to go back to being discreet again in a minute, so I wanted something to tide me over until tonight."

Alfie rolled his eyes, but he didn't call Dominick a baboon again, which was a promising sign.

They didn't talk as they walked down the crag, the fading sunlight meaning they had to give all their attention to the steep path. Dominick purposefully avoided looking at the pile of rocks that had nearly crushed them, already half-buried in underbrush.

The place near the bottom of the crag where Rutherford had landed was impossible to spot unless you knew to look for the broken branches and churned earth, both of which would be unrecognisable by spring. It wasn't until after they passed it that Alfie broke the silence.

"What do you think it's like, Australia? I suppose it must be a dreadful place if they both worked so hard to escape it."

Dominick shrugged. "I imagine being a convict is dreadful enough wherever you are. Why? Do you want to visit?"

Alfie paused to knock a bit of rotted wood from the path with his cane. "Hardly. I imagine a voyage of nearly a year is unbearable even with the most lavish passenger accommodations. And then you have to make the same trip back. I see why so many choose to stay. And the poor souls who make the journey in chains? I can't even imagine what kind of horror that is."

The discussion was becoming a bit too maudlin for Dominick's tastes.

"No," he said. "You're right. Short cruises only. Perhaps between the Greek isles. Or the islands of the West Indies, although we'd still have to cross an ocean first to reach them."

The path widened there and Alfie took advantage of the privacy to link his arm through Dominick's. Dominick hesitated, remembering how Rutherford had been spying through the trees. But Rutherford was dead, and he was damned if he was going to let the man's ghost keep him from such a simple pleasure as his lover's arm in his.

"It sounds like you're planning on running off to sea," Alfie said.

"Only if you are," replied Dominick. "Now that you've gotten your wish of being a knight with a castle, the next childhood dream to fulfil is becoming a pirate. Or would it be better to start at highwayman and work your way up?"

Alfie laughed. "You were the one telling me all those stories! And the castle—*folly* was your idea!"

"I think you'd make a very dashing pirate," Dominick offered. "Not as dashing as me, of course, but still. Shall we run away to sea and find out?"

Alfie shook his head but his voice was fond. "I'd ask why I put up with you, but I know all your reasons would be filthy. Yes, I would like to see a bit more of the world someday, but I will do it by entirely legal means and funded by my own purse, thank you."

When they reached the edge of the garden, they disentangled their arms, but it was hard to feel the lack when Dominick still had the man he loved beside him. Whether it was in a castle, on the deck of a pirate ship, or just with their feet stretched out before the fire, Dominick would be happy as long as he could share the adventure with Alfie.

The garden was still mostly bare earth and chalked out lines from what Dominick could see, but now that the piles of trees had been cleared, he could just about make out what it could be in future. With another year to get things planted and five years to let them grow, there would be something truly beautiful on this stripped ground. In another few decades, no one would even be able to remember this bare earth or the impenetrable tangle that had come before it, just the loveliness that had taken its place.

And Dominick would get to see that. It was strange to have a future to look forward to in his home, or to even have a home at all, but he found he quite liked the feeling. Balcarres would change. He would change. Alfie would change. But change could be for the better.

The gardeners were gathering up their tools as they passed and one of them, a local man Dominick had seen before but whose name he didn't yet know, paused to tip his cap at Alfie respectfully.

A change for the better already. Alfie nodded back, but just then, the sky delivered what it had been threatening and fat drops of rain began to fall.

A sharp whistle pierced the air, causing Dominick to jump, and Janie came tearing around the corner, two more gardeners with wheelbarrows following behind her, struggling to keep up. She rolled a large piece of paper as she walked—either the McConnells' original plans or one marked with her own revisions—and tucked it into an oiled leather tube under her arm to keep it safe from the rain.

"Step lively now," she called out to the men behind her. "One last load and we'll all be done for the day. Tomorrow though, I'll want all those roots gone from the north corner. Oh! Your Lordship, I didn't see you!"

"I won't stay to chat," Alfie said to their new head gardener, turning up the collar of his coat as the rain began to fall more heavily. "But things are progressing well?"

"Very well, sir. Better than I'd hoped, considering. And thank you again for this chance. I promise I won't disappoint."

"I'm sure you won't."

Janie smiled at Alfie's kind words. A real smile, not the nervous, half-embarrassed one Dominick had seen from her before. She stood straighter now too, more confident amongst the mud and weeds than she'd ever been in her maid's cap, or even worse, the kitchen. Another change and another good one.

He followed Alfie into the house, handing their damp coats off to one of the new footmen as Mr. Howe supervised. The soberness of his gaunt face couldn't mask the pleased look in his eyes of a job well done when a spot of mud was noticed on Dominick's coat and a brush produced without the butler having to direct his new charge to do so.

"A whisky before supper?" Dominick suggested.

But Alfie didn't get a chance to respond before a subtle throat clearing caught his attention. Mrs. Finley had appeared as if from nowhere.

"I beg your pardon, sir," the housekeeper said. "But if you could spare just a moment, I wanted to ask what your plans were for some of the newly opened rooms. Some of the furniture is in dire need of repair and I have a list of a few other items to bring to your attention."

Alfie opened his mouth to speak.

"There you are!" Gil's voice boomed as he descended the stairs. Jarrett followed along behind him, a few shirts draped over his arm as if he'd actually been working and not just distracting Gil all afternoon.

"Alfie, I heard back from that mining operation I told you about," Gil continued. "It's a good investment, but time sensitive. So if you're going to act, we should discuss it now so I can write them immediately."

"Not *now* now," Jarrett sniffed. "He's got to dress for supper. I've perfected the waterfall knot for his cravat and won't let my work go to waste."

Dominick grinned. "Find someone to practise on?"

Jarrett gave him a wink that just tipped the edge into saucy. "Wouldn't you like to know?"

Gil's much more subtle elbow to the gut stopped Jarrett from saying more.

"Oh, you think there's going to be a supper, do you?"

Dominick barely kept in a sigh at the sound of Mrs. Hirkins' voice. Had he known they were going to be ambushed, he'd have asked the men with the wheelbarrows to deposit them in some out-of-the-way toolshed for the night. At least then they'd have a little peace and quiet.

Mrs. Hirkins had a hand on one hip and James propped on the other. The child was sucking one tiny fist and looking around at the assembled crowd in wonder. His ordeal didn't seem to have affected him at all, but he hadn't been out of the arms of either his mother or great-grandmother since.

Dominick didn't blame them. James wasn't even his child and seeing him in danger had made want to swaddle him up and put an armed guard on him day and night. By contrast, the Hirkins women were being very reasonable.

Mrs. Hirkins didn't sound quite so reasonable when she said, "You think there's going to be supper set out any time soon, when the butcher had the gall to show up two hours late! Master Alfie, this is the third time this month. I won't have Agnes be made to look a fool because of some other soul's laziness. I have half a mind—"

"Enough!" Alfie shouted.

The hall went silent. There was a command in Alfie's voice that hadn't been there before and Dominick waited as breathlessly as the rest of them to see what he'd say next.

"Mrs. Hirkins, this isn't London. If you threaten this butcher, there isn't another. You may, however, suggest it would be worth his while to deliver to the manor first. After all, an earl used to London prices certainly wouldn't notice if his beef cost a few pence more.

"Jarrett, we have no guests. I'm not dressing for supper. That said, I do need to go into the village tomorrow and you can bedeck me however you'd like for that, waterfalls and all. Gil, we've discussed it enough. 'Yes' to the mine. Bring what I need to sign, and *only* what I need to sign, to the dinner table and I'll take them to town with me tomorrow.

"Mrs. Finley, I have no current plans for those rooms. Send out anything worth repairing and have the rest broken up for firewood. There's more furniture stored in the attic. You're welcome to whatever you think would suit. That, and the rest of your list can be taken care of tomorrow. Mr. Howe?"

The butler had his hands clasped behind his back and gave the most professional of bows. "I have nothing presently that needs your attention, sir."

"Glad to hear it. Dominick, I'll join you for that whisky now."

The servants dispersed on their errands until only Mrs. Hirkins remained. Her eyes narrowed as she gave Alfie a long look, the seriousness of which was marred somewhat by James swinging his spittle-covered fist around as he babbled in delight.

Alfie looked wary as she stepped forward. Then to Dominick's surprise, she patted Alfie on the cheek and held her hand there.

"Look at you," she said quietly. Her hands were spotted with age and gnarled by a lifetime of work, but Alfie swayed on his feet as if even the gentle touch was too much.

"You were just a scrap of a thing in London. I don't mean when you first arrived, of course you were then. I mean after your parents died. You were just hiding in that empty house all alone. But look at you now, all these people you've brought together. And you take care of them. You're more an earl than the last one ever was. More than any of them nobles who had it all handed to them. You earned it. You're a good man, Master Alfie."

She patted his cheek again gently. *Motherly,* Dominick realised, although he had no experience of that himself. One of Alfie's hands drifted down, landing on James' head and stroking through his fine hair.

Mrs. Hirkins cleared her throat. "So I'm not letting some ha'penny Scotch butcher think he can take advantage of you. *A few pence more.* Ha! I'll show him a few pence and a good bit more than that if he's late again!"

With that, she hitched James higher on her hip and made her way back towards the kitchen, calling out as she left, "Supper will be ready in two hours!"

Alfie stood frozen on the spot, his eyes suspiciously bright. His throat worked several times before he finally croaked, "Nick?"

Dominick put a hand on his back and steered him towards the library. Whisky. That was what they needed. "Yes, love?"

It took a few pushes before Alfie jerked into motion. "Is it too late to run away to sea?"

Dominick chuckled as they climbed the stairs. Perhaps it wasn't that ridiculous an idea. Certainly no more ridiculous than Alfie building him a castle just because he wanted one. A *folly*. That was a good word for it. Such a silly thing was a folly to even think of building.

But it was a folly to be with another man, and a worse folly still to love him. A folly to want to spend a lifetime with him, to make a home together and build it into something greater than it was before.

He pushed Alfie down into his seat in front of the library's crackling fireplace and went to pour them each a drink. On second thought, he grabbed the whole bottle and set it between their chairs with a pair of glasses. Outside, the rain beat against the windows and a bolt of lightning streaked across the sky. For a split second, Dominick could make out their folly on the crag, then it was gone.

"We can run away to sea once the weather clears up. But Alfie, if you're going to be a sailor, you're going to need to work on your knot tying skills first. Perhaps tonight? After supper?"

Dominick crossed his wrists to illustrate his point and gave Alfie a wink so lewd it put Jarrett's to shame.

Alfie gasped, a look of half-arousal, half-astonishment on his face. Dominick laughed and poured them each a glass of whisky, passing one to the man—*the earl*—he loved. And if loving him was a folly, it was one made of something stronger than stone.

He clinked his glass to Alfie's in a toast. He'd drink to that.

The End

Alfie and Dominick Will Return

Author's Note

There actually is a folly at Balcarres House. It's exactly as described in the book and is featured on the cover as well. I was lucky enough to visit a few years back and not only is the view magnificent, but the landscaped gardens are lovely as well.

One of the things I enjoy most about researching for my books is that I'm constantly surprised by what new things I learn. This book, the most surprising was learning that Samhain is not exclusively Irish, but also Scottish in origin. It comes out of the Gaelic traditions of both countries and there's a bit of debate between scholars as to who started it first. However, regardless of where it originated, by 1819 it would have been firmly established in both countries, but not so widespread that London city boys like Alfie and Dominick would've been particularly familiar with it. The traditions associated with how Samhain is celebrated vary over both time period and location, so I've chosen some of my favorites for this novel.

As always, I'd like to thank Emily for making this book what it is today. I'd also like to thank my brother for his military history knowledge that I used for Captain McConnell's background. The amount of information he provided was far more than I ended up using. Thanks also to him for double checking all my Australian history.

On a final note, please don't try to feed babies syllabub like Alfie did. It's delicious, but that's because it's basically cream whipped with white wine.

By Samantha SoRelle

His Lordship's Mysteries
His Lordship's Secret
His Lordship's Master
His Lordship's Return
His Lordship's Blood
His Lordship's Folly
Lord Alfie of the Mud (Short Story)
His Lordship's Gift (Short Story)

His Lordship's Realm
The Gentleman's Gentleman

Other Works
Cairo Malachi and the Adventure of the Silver Whistle
Suspiciously Sweet
The Pantomime Prince
An Heiress for Christmas

About the
Author

SAMANTHA SORELLE

Samantha SoRelle grew up all over the world and finally settled in Georgia, USA where the humidity does all sorts of things to her hair.

When she's not writing, she's doing everything possible to keep from writing. This has led to some unusual pastimes including perfecting fake blood recipes, designing her own cross-stitch patterns, and wrapping presents for tigers.

She also enjoys collecting paintings of tall ships and has one pest of a cat who would love to sharpen his claws on them.

Join her newsletter at **www.samanthasorelle.com** *and receive a FREE short story in your inbox. Also be the first to know about new books, sales, freebies, and other goodies!*

The Gentleman's Gentleman

His Lordship's Realm

A life of idle indulgence as a baron's nephew has never suited Gil Charleton. Fortunately, he's much better at being the Earl of Crawford's estate manager. The role requires the same caution, care, and charm he already uses to hide his true desires. On a discreet visit to a pub catering to men who enjoy the company of other men, he's dismayed to see the earl's imprudent valet there. At least the reckless, flirtatious Jarrett doesn't see him in return.

Jarrett Welch happily takes any chance to have a little fun—or *a lot* of fun, especially the kind The Cross Keys pub has to offer. But when a man he flirted with earlier in the evening winds up dead, he can't give his alibi without risking his life.

Gil knows Jarrett is innocent. However, his own secrets will come to light if he reveals the truth. The only other way to save Jarrett is to find the real killer, so they join forces to clear his name and keep their common secret just that—secret. As as they investigate, the attraction between them becomes impossible to fight. But the more the mystery unravels, the more it becomes clear that one of them will have to choose which is more important: his love... or his life.

The Gentleman's Gentleman is the first novel in the His Lordship's Realm series. While this series features characters first introduced in His Lordship's Mysteries, each His Lordship's Realm novel is a standalone and can be read in any order.

www.ingramcontent.com/pod-product-compliance
Lightning Source LLC
Chambersburg PA
CBHW061810190726
48289CB00007B/2140